CONQUERESS

BOOK 3

C.K. FRANZISKA

MORE FROM C.K. Franziska

A Speck of Darkness
A Speck of Dawn

Monsteress
Hunteress
Otyx

TRIGGERS/CONTENT WARNING

The Crymzon Chronicles series is a dark high fantasy with gothic vibes and dark world-building. The female leads in this series are cruel, domineering, and manipulative. They go beyond my typical morally gray antihero and are, in my opinion, actual villains who have a very disturbing past.

Triggers include:

- graphic violence

- rough and explicit sexual content

- forced proximity

- brutal injures

- betrayal

- graphic language

- trauma

- death

- murder

- intense violence

- graphic depiction of blood

- physical harm inflicted upon the main characters

- & more

Readers who may be sensitive to these elements, please take note, and prepare to enter Monsteress' world...

OCERIS
STARSTRAND
CRYMZON

TERMINUS
ESCELA
ETERNITIE
MYRE
TENACORO
NFINES

Even the strongest woman needs someone in her corner...

It takes a village to survive this rollercoaster we call life. I can't thank the members of the Conqueress Unleashed chat and Crymzon Baddies Discord enough for supporting me on this journey.

GUIDE

<u>Gods</u>

Zorus

King of the Gods

Lunra

Goddess of the Moon and Love

Otyx

God of the Underworld

Aqion

God of the Ocean and Strength

Emara

Goddess of Vitality

Nelion

God of Destiny

Odione

Goddess of Wonders

<u>Places</u>

Crymzon

Queen Soulin SinClaret/Lunra

Terminus

King Keres/Otyx

Oceris

King Usiel/Aqion

Tenacoro

Queen Synadena/Emara

Starstrand

Queen Caecilia/Nelion
Eternitie
King Citeus/Odione
The Confines
Godless
Shadowmyre
Underworld
Darklands
Caves beneath the Underworld for souls without chance of redemption

Names
Soulin SinClaret
Queen of Crymzon
Father: King <u>Obsidian</u> (†)
Mother: Queen <u>Ria</u> (†)
Brother: Crown Prince <u>Felix</u> (†)
Moths: <u>Adira, Velda, Storm, Barin</u>
King Keres
King of Terminus
King Citeus Matrus
King of Eternitie
Sons: Prince <u>Cyrus</u> and Prince <u>Cyprian</u>
Daughter: Crown Princess <u>Catalina</u>
Queen Synadena Roja
Queen of Tenacoro
Daughter: Crown Princess <u>Opaline</u>
<u>Verdant</u> (Opaline's Glimmarum)
Son: Prince <u>Crystol</u>
King Usiel Oarus
King of Oceris

CONQUERESS

Queen: <u>Cleolia</u>

Queen Caecilia

Queen of Starstrand

King Kieran Vale

King of Starstrand

Myra Eslene

Adviser of Queen Soulin

Wife: <u>Elia</u> (†)

Khaos Zedohr

Grand General of Crymzonian Army

Aemilius Vosdon

Outlaw

Liza

Outlaw

Devana

Outlaw

Father: <u>Wayne</u> (Blacksmith)

Mother: Liora

Jeremia

Trusted soldier of Crymzonian Army

Remy Cengor

Trusted soldier of Crymzonian Army

Conrad

King Obsidian's former trustee

Lady of Fate

Destiny Forgeress. Oracle.

Blake, Kasen, Charli, Rene

Soldiers of Crymzonian Army

Netherius

Prince of the Underworld

Mordecai
Beaked Dragon
Emberix
Fallen Dragon
Maeve
Healer
Malian
Keeper
The Seven
Heads of Sins
The Silent Sisters
Guards in Tenacoro

<u>Houses of Sins</u>
House of Lust
Avira/Temptress
Isabella Sternling/Mother of Lust
Lysander
House of Gluttony
Oliver Voracious/Feast Beast
Olive
House of Greed
Madison Avarice/Gold Gobbler
Ruby
Gavin
House of Sloth
Ethan Lethargy/Lazybones
Desiree
Sawyer
House of Wrath

CONQUERESS

Victoria Fury/Fury

Ryder

House of Envy

Lucas Green/Green-eyes Monster

Ava

House of Pride

Sophia Hubris/Ego Titan

Leo

ONE

Queen Soulin

My knees hit the ground hard as I land beside Khaos, pressing my trembling hands against his chest wound.

This can't be happening again. I've been here; I've done this before.

My mind catapults me back to the battle in Terminus when I found him in the same position on the ground. But this time, it's different. There's no blood, only black ooze seeping through his shirt, staining it.

I whisper words of disbelief as though by uttering them, I might reverse the cruel verdict of fate.

"No, no, please, no," I plead, my voice cracking and fragile, barely more than a whisper in the room's void.

"Breathe!" I scream, pressing my right hand tightly on his chest while moving his face in my direction with the other. His eyes are open and dilated, yet they don't react when our gaze meets.

My fingers trace the contours of his face, now colder and distant. I can still feel the warmth that was there only moments before, but it's subsiding fast.

How can this vibrant life, so full of dreams and aspirations, be reduced to this motionless, vacant form?

My fingers move lower, navigating the creases and curves of the body I know intimately, seeking that elusive thump. But the silence persists, a haunting reminder of the finality of the moment.

My sobs grow more pronounced, wracking my body with each heartbeat I cannot find.

"Breathe, Khaos! Please!" I'm not begging. I'm demanding him to give me a sign that I can fix him. But the longer I look at him, the more I realize his chest isn't moving under my pressure. The black liquid is cold against his still-warm body as it covers my skin.

"No!" I whisper, my throat closing with every heartbeat. "Please. Wake up!"

I know he won't. It's too late. But my heart doesn't understand what my mind already knows.

The room itself seems to mourn with me as the curtains sway gently with a breeze, a melancholy dance as if the Crymzon Palace itself is trying to offer solace. The soft glow of a nearby candle flickers, casting dancing shadows across the bookshelves of Librascendia, and the scent of wax lingers in the air, an incongruous reminder of the persistence of life even in the face of death.

"What happened?" a female voice shouts from the corridor, and when I see the familiar long, gray hair and the emerald-colored gown, I can't hold the tears back any longer.

Khaos is dead. How am I supposed to explain this to Myra? She was like a mother to us, raising us after ours passed away. I know she would never say it aloud, but he was her favorite. I always knew that, and I understood why.

"Stay back," I say, holding onto Khaos' lifeless body.

This wasn't supposed to happen. Nothing makes sense. Is this Otyx doing? Is this his way of punishing me because I used a shard of the Nullstone on him?

Myra comes to a screeching halt before us, and when I look up, I see the horror in her aged face. Her mouth stands wide open, her eyes frantically searching Khaos' lifeless form.

"Go away," I scream, trying to cover as much of his body with mine as possible, but it's not enough.

The confusion on Myra's face breaks into heart-wrenching sadness. Tears stream down her face as she jolts forward, grabbing his face while brushing his dark curls aside.

"Help him!" she whispers, and a tear drops onto the warm sandstone beside Khaos' face. "For Gods' sake, do something!"

The anger in her voice flows through my body and cuts my air supply off.

"I can't," I croak out, my voice breaking. "He's gone."

"No." Myra shakes her head over and over again. Sparks of magic sizzle out of her palms, radiating into Khaos' skin. I have to close my eyes to shield myself from the intensity of her power blasting into his body.

He doesn't move.

Slowly, I lean down and press my ear against his chest. I don't know what I'm searching for. A heartbeat? The slightest movement? Anything that tells me he'll be alright.

I strain to hear the sound I yearn for—the rhythmic thumping that has always been a source of comfort, a reminder of life's enduring pulse.

Nothing but an eerie silence mirrors the emptiness now settled within me.

"What did you do?" Myra asks, releasing Khaos.

"I didn't know," I whisper, tears running uncontrollably over my cheeks, soaking his shirt.

I still don't understand what happened. One moment, I'm standing before Otyx, and the next, he vanishes, and Khaos crumbles to the floor. He wasn't supposed to be there. So why was he?

Beneath my touch, I can feel his heat fading. Just a few hours ago, he carried me into our bed. Just a few hours ago, he held me tight and asked me to stay so he could wake up beside me. Everything was perfect—not outside the Crymzon Palace, but in that tiny bubble we created for ourselves. It was supposed to be him and me against whatever fate had in store for us.

"Fix him," Myra demands again from above, and I don't have the strength to look up at her. My body shakes violently as I fight the nausea creeping up my throat. My vision blurs as my tears flow freely, drenching my cheeks. I push my face into his chest, an act of utter surrender to the reality that has enveloped me. It's a final, desperate plea for the world to return to how it was just moments before when Khaos was alive and vibrant.

As I kneel there, the minutes slip away, and I cling to the brief hope that his heartbeat might miraculously return. But in the room, there's only silence, save for the muffled sobs that escape my throat.

I don't know how long I lay there, my forehead pressed against him. Maybe minutes, perhaps hours. Just like me, Myra can't move. She stands there, staring at us, unable to rip her gaze off us.

He was like a son to her. To make matters even worse, I took the only two people from her she loved—her Soulmate and now Khaos.

"We were supposed to fulfill our Soulmate Connection," I mumble to myself.

Today was supposed to be the happiest day of my life. Yes, I fought every moment against Khaos to get there, but when I finally let in the feelings I've buried for so long, I couldn't imagine anything better than being bound to him for the rest of our time.

"I know," Myra whispers, and I hear her knee pop when she kneels beside me. I cringe under her touch as her hand drives over my shoulder. "You need to let him go."

Let him go? Is she insane?

"Soulin. There's nothing we can do for him," she whispers, pulling my arm gently. "Everyone in Crymzon knows by now that he got severely injured in Terminus. Even I heard of it, and I was hiding in the tunnels. There's nothing you could have done to save him."

"You're wrong," I growl, sniffing. Myra is so wrong. I know it's my fault. Somehow, Khaos and Otyx were connected. By injuring the God, I killed him. I don't know how, but it was me.

"I need you to step away from him so I can arrange his departure," she says, her voice filled with motherly strength.

"How are you so fucking calm? He's dead, Myra. Dead!"

Until my last breath, I will fight for him. No one is going to take him from me. Not Myra, no God, and for sure not fate!

Myra should understand that. So how does she move on from this heartbreak in mere minutes?

"You know how I survived all those years without Elia?" Myra asks as I tighten my grip around Khaos' chest. "I let her go. And I'm not speaking of the memories we shared, nor the joy she brought me. I let go of the ache I felt every time I thought of her. I know she's with Zorus and looking down on me, guiding me."

I shake my head slightly. "I'm not as strong as you are."

Myra clicks her tongue. "You're right. You're stronger. At thirteen, you climbed a throne you never wanted. You know how many people can claim to lead an entire kingdom before they even meet their Soulmate?"

"I had to. Because of me, my brother and father are dead," I press out through clenched teeth. "And Elia."

Myra stiffens for a moment. There's nothing she can say to turn this conversation around. She knows as well as I do that everything is linked to me. Every horrible event in Escela's history is connected to one person—Queen Soulin SinClaret.

"You saved so many Crymzonians yesterday," she whispers, her voice thick.

"And doomed thousands more when King Citeus marched against me."

For every good deed she points out, I have at least two to debunk her statement. I know it's me; I'm not a fool.

A palpable heaviness fills the air, suffocating all my emotions. I inhale, taking Khaos' scent in once more before I rise to my feet. "I'm not willing to let him go," I say, wiping my tears. "That's why I'm going to bargain with the Gods."

"You can't," Myra replies, grabbing my shoulder.

I shrug her off. "I can't live without him," I bark, watching as she steps back. With a solemn expression etched across my face, I extend my right hand, my fingers elegantly outstretched, each one adorned with rings that bore the symbols of my lineage and the power I possess.

With a subtle yet powerful gesture of my hand, I summon my magic—a force as ancient as Crymzon itself. The room's temperature shifts as if the air responds to my will. A faint, ethereal glow emanates from my fingertips, illuminating the space with more power than a person should ever harbor.

Khaos' body, seemingly weightless now, levitates from the floor, suspended mid-air. My eyes, a deep, relentless shade of emerald, remain fixed on him, unwavering in my determination to restore him to life.

I walk with measured purpose, my hand still guiding his levitating form. The soft echo of my jeweled sandals against the polished sandstone floors marks our journey through the palace's corridors. Khaos follows me, his body floating behind me in chilling silence.

The palace's inhabitants, who witnessed the tragic event that unfolded in Terminus and outside the Crymzon Wall just a day ago, now peer from the shadows drawn by my procession. Some whisper prayers to Lunra while others bow their heads in our direction, unable to move another muscle.

My heart aches, knowing how fast his death will spread through the kingdom. Besides me, no one knows what really happened. Correction: I don't even know what happened.

What I *do* know is: whatever Otyx did, he must reverse it. If he wants my soul, he can have it if that means Khaos will live.

TWO

DEVANA

My legs tremble as I step over a bridge made of clouds. It's my second day in Starstrand, and I still haven't gotten used to being thousands of feet above the ground, my life depending on a cloud-like substance to keep me afloat.

"How's your neck?" Cyrus asks beside me, eyeing the metal collar my father forged for me before I sent him on Erinna's back to Tenacoro.

I press my finger between the thin metal to scratch my new souvenir from the Crymzon Queen. "It's itchy," I answer, finally reaching the spot that bothers me the most.

"Same," Cyrus says, rubbing his palm over the crescent moon imprinted on the back of his hand. "Something seems off."

I stop in my tracks to look at him. "Why do you say that?"

He looks down at me, his brown hair falling into his face. "Because I've been carrying this mark for a few days now, and it's the first time it bothers me."

Thinking of Monsteress' hand enclosing my throat, cutting off my air supply, sends another shiver down my spine. I don't want to think of her. Not now, not here. We're safe and far away from Crymzon.

But what if all of this is just an illusion? What if the feeling of safety is misleading me?

I bite my lip. "Maybe it's a warning. What if she knows we're here? She warned us. She told me to get as far away from other people as possible. Perhaps she can feel where we are."

Cyrus presses his lips into a thin line and shrugs his shoulders. "What if it was a fluke? I don't think she can track us with those marks. It wouldn't be the first lie crossing her lips."

I smirk. "I won't test your theory. Besides, I don't belong here. We should really get going."

My gaze wanders over the bright sunrays dancing over the clouds before us. Everything is white, bright, and creepily sterile. It's like someone took a bucket of water and washed all the colors away.

Cyrus steps into my view and grabs me by the shoulders, forcing me to look at him. "No one is going to figure out who we are."

I pull my chin in and glare at him. "Are you serious? Half of the battlefield watched you kill your father. Besides that, look at them." My eyes land on the bustling streets, filled with blond-haired, fair-skinned, winged Starstrandians. "No, of course, they won't notice me here."

I watch as Cyrus takes in my dark coils and golden-brown skin. There's no hiding my differences.

"Aren't you sick of hiding?" he asks, grabbing my hand.

"I'm sick of feeling I don't belong," I answer truthfully. "That's why I need to seek the Silent Sisters."

Cyrus cocks his head. "The what?"

I shouldn't be embarrassed talking about my past—no, it's not embarrassment I feel, it's shame. "When my mother learned about my muscle weakness, she thought I could never become a warrior."

Cyrus huffs. "Yeah, right. Look at you now."

The way he confirms I beat the odds and became a warrior without my mother's help warms my heart for a split second. "She wanted to send me to the Silent Sisters," I continue.

"Are they healers?"

A huff escapes my throat. "I wish. No. They are guards. They guard all the Tenacorians too weak for battle."

Cyrus swallows. "Like prison guards?"

I nod, looking at the ground.

No Tenacorian would ever admit that the Silent Sisters are anything less than saviors. Because of their help, Tenacoro keeps producing powerful warriors while weeding out the imperfections.

All those years in hiding, I could have helped the poor children and adults guarded by the Silent Sisters. Instead, I hid with my father in plain sight to wait for a moment to attack Monsteress again. I've wasted so many years training for the Queen's assassination while my father knew I would probably die if I killed her. Knowing I could have made a difference for those boys and girls feels like a blade being held to my throat.

"That's where you want to go?" Cyrus asks, squeezing my hand to pull me in.

"That's what I must do," I confirm, leaning into him. "But I can't go without checking on Liza first. I need to know she's okay."

Liza. The woman I thought Cyrus had a relationship with. The woman who shared her hut with him. Also, the woman who turned out to be exiled from Starstrand after her wings were clipped.

"I don't think we should linger much longer if you want to keep a low profile," Cyrus says, guiding me towards the street that leads to the Cloud Palace. "She's fine. But if you don't trust my word, we can tell her our goodbyes before we leave."

He's funny. Even if I want to leave, I can't. Erinna, my Glimmarum, a beautiful brown griffin, isn't here. I'm stuck in this floating kingdom above the ocean without her wings.

"In and out," I answer, lowering my head to avoid any more attention than we've already gotten since returning the Lady of Fate to the Queen. Maybe by the time we're done visiting Liza, Erinna will be back to carry me away.

The palace is filled with light, clouds, and white marble. I have to squint my eyes to make out the carvings depicting battles on the ceiling.

I guess I get why everything up here seems so pure and brilliant. It starkly contrasts the brown and green huts suspended on massive trees in Tenacoro, where I was born. Or the Vine Palace, filled with candlelight, animals, and plants. I wouldn't say Tenacoro is dirty, but it's dark and cozy compared to this place.

Crystal chandeliers refract the soft, iridescent, glow-like celestial bodies when we enter. As I admire the beauty, a serene breeze rustles my shirt and carries with it the gentle hum of the cosmos. At this moment, I feel a deep sense of tranquility that I haven't experienced in years. It feels like all my worries are taken from my shoulders and hung on a hook far away from me.

Cyrus leads me through the corridors, following the guard who intercepted us at the gate. His grip is firm, as if he's scared I could vanish if he lets go.

My heart pounds as I follow them deeper into the palace, my eyes gazing out of the windows enclosing us. From here, I can see Crymzon. The red sandstone the kingdom is carved of is vibrant, like fresh blood. I still feel the beaming heat of the sun as my eyes scan the houses and the Crymzon Palace.

I never have to set foot in that hellhole again. After freeing my people from the Silent Sisters, I will make it impossible for the Crymzon Queen to find me. Her wish to never see me again is something I intend to keep.

A stabbing pain curses through my cheek as I ram into Cyrus' shoulder. Rubbing my hurting jaw, I pinch him. "Ouch. Why are we stopping?"

Too distracted by the pain that usually wouldn't bother me, I didn't notice the Starstrandian soldiers looking out the window ahead of us.

"Go back to your posts," the guard leading us barks, but his comrades don't move. "Are you deaf? I said *get back to your posts*!"

Curiously, I step closer to the nearest window, and my stomach bottoms.

"What is that?" a soldier asks from afar, and I open and close my mouth, not understanding what I'm seeing.

Right outside the Crymzon Wall is a black line that leads through the desert like a vein of death.

"Catalina," Cyrus whispers behind me, pressing his face against the glass.

My heartbeat quickens when I follow the line that seems to stretch all the way to Eternitie. "We have to go," Cyrus says, tugging my arm.

Panic surges through me. "We can't. I can't fly."

He strengthens his grip. "I need to go to my sister. Whatever this line is, it leads home."

Home. I'm still struggling to accept that Cyrus, who I met as Aemilius Vosdon over a year ago, is the Prince of Eternitie.

"We don't even know what the line means," I answer, my eyes zigzagging from one kingdom to the other.

"Nothing good," the soldier beside us says, and my eyes practically throw daggers at him for cutting into our conversation.

I get it. Cyrus wants to check on his sister, just like I wanted to ensure Liza is safe before freeing my people. But he can't go to Eternitie. Not even a day ago, he killed his father and watched as his brother got dragged away by some of Soulin's creatures. If someone saw him and he returns home now, he's a dead man. And for all the Eternians know, he's dead. His father made sure to fake his funeral after he fled.

"There's nothing to see here," the soldier beside us says, stepping closer to his comrades to shoo them away.

That's when an ear-splitting noise erupts below us. The glass just inches away from my face vibrates before it explodes. If it weren't for Cyrus, who tackled me to the ground, forcing all the air out of my lungs, my face would be unrecognizable from the thousand splintering crystalline shards. I gasp, grateful for Cyrus' timely intervention.

The rumbling below us intensifies, and even though every fiber of my body tells me to keep my head low, I'm already on my feet, looking out the shattered window. What I see below is nothing short of catastrophic.

My heart pounds in my ears, and my eyes are glued to the river separating Eternitie from Crymzon—at least where the river used to be. Gigantic rocks are being flung into the air by an immense and terrifying force originating from a colossal opening in the earth. The ground churns and trembles as if the planet is in turmoil. My chest tightens as the ground beneath the river caves in, and the water drops into the depths of the world below Escela.

My gaze is drawn toward the source of this calamity, and there, before my disbelieving eyes, a rift, like a monstrous maw, tears open the planet's crust. It's a seven-pointed star platform, radiating an ominous glow that seems to draw energy from the very essence of this world. Palaces, like mirages from a forgotten age, are poised to burst forth from the depths of the planet, each placed on a star's point.

But those palaces are nothing compared to the one towering in the very center of the platform.

My heart sinks as I recognize the symbolism of the seven-pointed star; it's a sign of impending catastrophe, a precursor of ancient prophecies.

My father told me the stories of the seven sins that lead to the center—Otyx.

As the palaces emerge from the breach, they appear as though they're of a different world, their architecture bearing testament to an era long past, lost to the annals of history.

The Cloud Palace was supposed to be our place of refuge, far removed from the other kingdom's tumultuous events. But now, even here, the disturbance of the world below has reached us.

I watch in stunned silence as the palaces ascend from the newly formed chasm, their presence casting darkness over the land. My gaze locks on Cyrus, who, with a resolute expression, understands the gravity of the situation. With a solemn nod, he takes my hand and tries to drag me away from the window, but I hold my ground.

"There's no hiding," I whisper, my voice shaking.

I know we're doomed as the ancient palaces continue to emerge and the explosive force below churns with unfathomable power. No one can hide from Death.

No one.

THREE

Queen Soulin

The throne room, the heart of the Crymzon Palace, is a grand chamber resplendent with red sandstone columns, regal tapestries, and a magnificent throne carved to look like moths.

To this day, my heart aches every time I step over the threshold, knowing how many innocent souls took their last breaths before my uncontrolled magic erupted and killed them all. But it's also the only room I feel close to my brother Felix, beside the East Tower, where he used to spend most of his time.

As I approach the throne, my gaze is fixed upon the new one beside it, a duplicate of my Crymzon Throne. It was supposed to be a present to Khaos after our Connection Ceremony. He was destined to reign over Crymzon alongside me.

I carefully lower his lifeless form, now at my side, with the same reverence one might show to a cherished relic. My magic gently releases its hold on him, allowing him to rest on the polished floor.

I take my place on the Crymzon Throne, my expression unwavering as I ignore the nosy people streaming into the room. With another graceful hand motion, my magic extends outward, encircling his body. It's a delicate dance of energy, a manifestation of the deep love that binds us.

Death won't stop me from being close to him. I will move heaven and the Underworld to get to him, and if I'm not able to bring him back to the living, I'll have to go to the Underworld to be with him.

But for now, I have to keep him safe until I can find a way to join him again.

With regal composure and a mind sharpened by anger and pain, I extend my hands toward my lifeless King. My fingers dance with a subtle grace, each movement infused with the ancient magic that courses through my veins.

The atmosphere surrounding me shifts once more as my magical energy swirls and envelops Khaos' fragile form. From the very essence of my magic, I conjure a protective barrier, a delicate yet impenetrable cocoon. It shimmers with a translucent sheen, like a ripple on the surface of a tranquil pond, and then solidifies into a glass-like substance. This protective casing cradles every inch of him.

Nausea washes over me again when my eyes land on Khaos' face. He looks peaceful, as if he's just resting, ready to wake up any moment. But I know it's not true. I know it's a cruel trick my heart plays on me.

I continue to weave my magic, enhancing the protective layers with intricate runes and sigils to strengthen the protection. As the last incantation leaves my lips, the protective glass cocoon fully encases my King, encircling him in a translucent chamber. The sight is both haunting and beautiful.

My next step is equally deliberate. I rise off the throne, descend the steps, and gently touch my fingertips to the surface of the protective barrier, infusing it with the essence of my own life force. My love and devotion flow into the cocoon, creating an unbreakable bond between us.

I will know if someone tries to break through the glass to get to him. While he's held in this state, it will give me the time I need to search for a way to bring him back to me.

With Khaos' body protected, I straighten my shoulders, my eyes still locked on the glass-like cocoon that contains him. I can feel the eyes of my subjects on me. They're burning into my skin like a million candlelights.

Shoving my nausea down, I lift my head. "A part of me died today," I say as anger grabs hold of me. "But I will do everything—*everything*—in my power to bring him back."

A gasp rumbles through the throne room as more soldiers and servants stream in. I spot Myra standing amidst the onlookers and see the deep frown line between her eyebrows. She disapproves. Good, because this is my fight, and I don't want her anywhere near Otyx.

This is the moment to hold a speech to demand my citizens to join me, but the ground beneath my feet trembles, almost throwing me off balance. My eyes dart to Khaos, checking if the glass surrounding him keeps him safe, and my panic eases when I see it unscathed.

"Clear out!" Myra yells, her eyes fixed on me as she searches my fingers for any signs of magic.

Confused, I shake my head when I realize she thinks it's me causing the earthquake. She thinks I'm losing control over my magic again, like I did as a child. But it's not me. At least, I don't think so.

Nevertheless, soldiers and servants stream out of the room in panic, their footsteps frantic and loud.

It's not me. I'm not causing this quake. Or am I?

The walls shake again, and the floor cracks. What the fuck is going on now?

As Myra helps the rest of my subjects to flee, I march behind the thrones. Approaching the tapestry, I extend my hand, fingers brushing gently against the ancient fabric. To my amazement, a flicker of heat passes from my fingertips to the tapestry, and suddenly, it ignites with an azure flame. The fire dances across the delicate fabric, revealing a hidden stone door concealed behind the threads of history.

My heart pounds as I push it open, revealing a pitch-black chamber beyond. A rush of cool air greets me, and I step to the side to make way.

As my eyes adjust to the darkness, I discern a subtle humming sound growing in intensity. It's a sound my heart can't get enough of—a beautiful resonance that sends shivers down my spine.

Out of the darkness emerges a swarm of colossal, horse-sized moths, their crimson wings shimmering like molten rubies, followed by smaller moths. They swirl around me, their movements as graceful as a dance, though the effect is far from tranquil. The moths transform the throne room into a living, fiery symphony.

The magnificent creatures spiral, leaving ephemeral trails of scarlet luminescence in their wake. Each wingbeat is a thunderous note, and their collective hum reverberates like a divine orchestra.

My heartbeat quickens when I look at the last moth stepping over the threshold—Storm. I wait for a few more moments, hoping to see my first Fighter Moth, but my throat swells when the door stays empty and Adira doesn't appear.

Please, no.

No.

I don't have the strength to go into the Silk Keep just to see what I already know. I don't have the strength to lose Khaos and my oldest moth in one day.

Storm seems to sense my distress and comes closer to press her furry head against my chest. I want to cry. I want to scream and burn this place to the ground, but the earthquake strengthens, leaving no room for any sentimental moments.

I've lost everything. Khaos. Adira. My family. Myra's trust. I even let the Lady of Fate go, who could really help me right now.

I planned to skim through Librascendia, hoping to find anything about resurrection. I already dabbled with Blood Magic, summoning the God of the Underworld, and he warned me. I made a mistake, but what stands now in my way to use it again? If Blood Magic is stronger than the power I receive from Lunra, there's a chance it's enough to bring Khaos ba ck.

There's a reason this kind of magic is forbidden. Because of you, I can unleash Hell on Escela.

I stiffen, recalling Otyx's words.

What if this earthquake has nothing to do with me but with what I've done?

I planned to release the moths to let them guard Khaos' body while I searched Librascendia, but now, I have to find out what's causing my palace to shake.

What if Otyx makes it to the surface? Hasn't he done enough? Haven't I paid enough souls already?

"I need you," I whisper to Storm, who still has her head pressed tightly against me.

My heart longs for Adira. She was mine. I nurtured her. She was my first. But Storm, Barin, and Velda followed in her footsteps just weeks later. If I don't take the chance now to fly them, I might never get to.

Storm steps back, pressing her wings to the ground to give me access to her back. If my instincts wouldn't confirm my suspicion about Adira's death, Storm's reaction does.

She's my stubborn one. Her track record of throwing people off is high, and listening to commands is something she struggles with. Seeing her offering her back forces tears into my eyes, but also warms my heart. Storm is the new alpha, and she knows it.

When I climb onto her back, I see Myra standing in the doorway through the fluttering moths. But her eyes are not directed at me. She looks beside me, and when I hear the grunting noise of an older man, all the emotions I'm trying to keep down almost burst out.

"What are you doing? Get off!" I bark at Conrad.

"I'm going with you," he says, climbing Barin.

I haven't seen him in days. A part of me thought he might never return because of his old age. He should be beneath the prison with his family, far away from me.

"You're not. I'm going alone," I say through clenched teeth.

"You shouldn't be alone," he answers, and I'm surprised he makes it onto Barin without my help.

My eyes wander to Khaos' cooling body. I'm not alone. I will bring Khaos and Adira back, and I will find a way to resurrect them.

Plus, I have Storm.

As much as I want to retaliate, I'm relieved to see him though. Knowing he would leave his family voluntarily to be by my side fixes something in my heart I didn't know needed mending.

But I can't go soft on him now. "If you just say one word, I will push you off," I warn as I inspect him closer. His hair is messy, and he looks even older than I remember. His usually bright smile is missing, and my eyebrows furrow when I see his jawline tick.

Something has changed in his demeanor.

He doesn't even reply to me, which is a good sign because if he says one word, the barrier I'm trying to build around my heart will shatter.

My eyes land on Myra again. She looks fragile and scared. As Barin lifts off the ground with Conrad on his back, I give my moth a hand movement, and as expected, Barin bucks him off.

"She needs you more than I do," I say, looking at Conrad's bewildered facial expression as he lies on the ground. "Guard her and ensure that every Crymzonian able to walk collects the Nullstones outside the Wall. We'll need them once I return."

FOUR

Avira

Watching someone's past fade away shouldn't feel this good, mainly since I finally retained my memories after searching for them for ninety-seven years. I know how it feels to feel empty. Even though I knew those memories were there, I couldn't grasp them.

But the knowledge of hurting the Crymzon Queen feels good—too good. She tried to take my most valuable possession from me—Otyx.

I didn't survive Nekrojudex and regain my past just to have everything stripped from me because she declared war on the Underworld for something *she* did. Allowing her people to use their magic to cheat death comes at a price. And even though the scales are now even, she went too far.

I must admit, though, that she has good taste. The man she picked as her Soulmate has muscular shoulders, long dark hair, and a beard. His face is marked with a scar on the left cheek, but besides that, he's purely breathtaking. Perhaps not more handsome than my God, but for a mortal...

Since I offered my blood to bind my devotion to Otyx, I feel differently. I can sense the Underworld as if my being is tight to it. I can feel the souls roaming Shadowmyre and even the Darklands. Every single soul seems to intertwine with mine, and it's ecstatic. Besides my new built-in soul counter, I can tap into the God's emotions.

He's livid.

This should be when Otyx steps before the new arrival to let him pick his sin, because that's not my responsibility. I might have some of his powers, but there are things I don't want to meddle with. Even though I know I could offer Khaos the orbs to see which sin resonates with his soul, I've done enough. I'm also afraid if I use the orbs to show the sins, I will take them all.

Before I became the last contestant, I never had the longing for a sin. But now that I can feel the Underworld, Otyx's power, and my memories, I'm consumed by the thought of using them as they brush against me like docile cats.

"There's someone who would like to meet you," I say to Khaos, who's inspecting the wings protruding from my shoulder blades.

Khaos looks confused. He keeps shaking his head as if he could clear his mind and break through to his past.

I know better.

It doesn't matter how hard he tries to access his memories; he won't get there. Eventually, he will find it out the hard way, like I did, and it will either make or break him. Only time will tell.

Maybe my former self, without my memories, would feel pity for him. But I'm not that person anymore. Now, there's envy and wrath that keep me moving through the ballroom.

Envy because his memories showed me how happy he was when he swept the Crymzon Queen into his arms. They shared something so deeply that I want to have with Otyx, something so profound and un-explainable that it seems unimaginable to others.

Wrath because I want to make her pay for injuring my God. How fucking dare she lay a finger on him!

Khaos follows me silently as I make my way through the winding, black stone corridors.

When I reach my room, I see Ruby standing in the hallway inspecting the chandeliers and just as I step beside her, she notices me.

"Sorry, I had to step away for a second," she says, her white hair falling into her face. "I watched Maeve remove as many rock fragments as possible, and then it got weird. Without warning, the shards seeped out of him on their own accord like worms before the wound closed itself."

Her eyes fall on my lips. I know what she wants...she wants me to ask more questions to keep talking. When I don't react, Ruby looks surprised.

His speedy recovery is news to me, but somehow, I know that offering my blood to him plays a significant role in his healing. I felt, the moment we connected through my blood, that his heartbeat got stronger.

"You already know, don't you?" Ruby asks, her eyes narrowing to slits.

"You told me yourself: he's in expert hands," I say, repeating the words she used as she pulled me away from Maeve to let her pull the fragments out of his chest.

Ruby steps to the side and peeks behind me. "Who's that?"

I shrug nonchalantly. "Just a new soul I need to bring to the God," I say, looking at the door I know too well.

When I tried to flee on the back of a dragon during the first Nekro-judex trial, Otyx thought it would be wise to lock me away in his palace. He's in the room I stayed in during the following trials until I tried to escape on the same dragon again. But that time, my mother...no...the Mother of Lust—the woman I was assigned to after Otyx stuffed me into the House of Lust—she put me into a gold cage to force me to finish Nekrojudex.

I wonder how she is doing. Did she survive the fall after our altercation? I better hope so, not because I want to see her again, but I don't want to become one of the Seven before I can kick the Crymzon Queen's ass.

"So, what are you waiting for?" Ruby asks, shuffling her feet.

That's the real question. *What* am I waiting for?

I approach the door, and it jumps open just as I reach for the handle, revealing Maeve. Her hands are covered in black, her eyes are glassy, and her dark curls dull.

"Thank you," I whisper, because she can only read my lips. I still feel stupid for not realizing sooner that Maeve can't hear.

Maeve nods before she marches past me, ignoring Khaos.

"Did someone die?" Khaos whispers into my ear, and I almost jump at how close he is.

"Ever heard of personal space?" I snarl back, pushing him with my shoulder away.

I should remind myself that this isn't his fault, yet it feels like it. He doesn't know how he got here or who is missing him. For all I know, the Queen might be the only person noticing his death because most of his memories included her.

That thought sends another wave of anger through me. This thing between Otyx and me is fresh, not like their connection. I've seen the Queen through the years through his eyes. He was always watching her, always in the background, focusing solely on her.

How does it feel to have someone's full attention at all times? Did she know? Did she know how much she meant to him?

The light falling through the door darkens, and I see Otyx standing before me when I look up.

"You're back," he says, grabbing me by the shoulders to pull me in. I'm about to hit his chest with my cheek and snuggle up when he stops mid-motion. "Why did you bring him here?"

I shudder when his hands release me, leaving me cold and unloved. I take a moment to realize that he's talking about Khaos.

"He hasn't picked a sin yet," I say, my heart pounding.

See, Khaos deserves to be here. Without him, the God would have showered me with his attention instead of the Queen's play toy.

My nostrils flare. "And because I want to use him against the Queen."

Otyx's eyes turn unusually dark as he takes me in. "This is not you. We can just reach the surface and create disorder. Be patient. Her time will come."

"Patient? She almost ended you," I growl, digging my hands into Khaos' shirt to pull him forward.

Otyx laughs and shakes his head. "She injured me, nothing more. I'm a God. She'll need more than a crystal to get rid of me."

"We have the perfect leverage," I answer, yanking on him so hard that I hear his shirt rip.

"You're beside yourself," Otyx replies, grabbing my hand to force me to let Khaos go. "Let's move on."

Slowly, I take my hand back. "Fine. If you won't go up against her, that's your choice. But I will," I growl through clenched teeth, storming off before he can call me back.

As I march toward the outskirts of Shadowmyre, the world around me transforms. The familiar sounds of civilization fade into the distance, replaced by the whispering winds that carry secrets of the obsidian mountains. Ominous peaks loom high above, casting long shadows that stretch endlessly across the rugged terrain. My steps echo through the silence, creating a haunting rhythm that resonates with the land.

Each footfall is deliberate and feels so familiar. I've done this walk a thousand times in search of more supplies in the Dreamlands to sew clothes.

At last, I arrive at a clearing, a small oasis of relative serenity amidst the foreboding landscape. In the center of this space, the opal ground shimmers, a peculiar and almost ethereal substance that marks the boundary of my destination.

I know, without a doubt, that beneath the surface, the skeletal remains of a dragon lie dormant, a creature of immense power that has long ago been laid to rest—no, not rest—the other Gods banned Emberix. She's a reminder that no one is allowed to leave the Underworld.

I kneel, remembering the exact spot where Netherius, the Prince of the Underworld—who turned out to be Otyx—placed his hands to show her to me.

I don't need Otyx's help anymore. The power coursing through my veins since I spilled a drop of blood feels enough to move mountains. Literally.

My hands tremble slightly as I lower them. I understand the magnitude of the task ahead, the resurrection of a creature whose death has darkened my God's spirit. The knowledge, the power to awaken this ancient being, is more than a sign of my love for him. If I bring her back, it may show him I haven't changed. I'm still the same Avira he led down into his domain when my mother betrayed me.

Closing my eyes, I delve deep within myself, seeking a connection to the primal forces that now flow through me. Otyx has passed down his wisdom, secrets, and magic through our new bond; now, it's my turn to call upon those ancient energies.

With my hands firmly planted on the surface, I channel my intent.

As my fingers press into the ground, a surge of energy courses through me, and the ground responds. Lines of iridescent light extend from my fingertips, tracing patterns across the surface like glowing veins.

Beneath my touch, the dragon's skeleton glows through the surface and stirs. The ground trembles and cracks and a brilliant light emanates from the earth. It radiates with cobalt blue and emerald hues, casting a breathtaking glow that illuminates the clearing.

My heart pounds with exhilaration and fear as I continue to pour my energy into the earth. The dragon's skeletal remains shift and assemble. Bones fuse, forming a sturdy framework. Muscles and tendons materialize, weaving themselves around the bone structure. Once dulled by centuries of slumber, scales regain their luster and color, shimmering in shades of deep sapphire and gold.

As the transformation continues, the air crackles with magic and the once-skeletal dragon takes on a lifelike appearance. It unfurls its majestic and colossal wings and lets out a thunderous roar that reverberates through my soul until the ground breaks open beneath me to let her out.

Emberix is reborn.

Her eyes, fierce and intelligent, lock onto mine as she climbs out of her grave. The ground shakes with every step she takes in my direction. She's way bigger than Mordecai, the beaked dragon I used as I tried to flee after the first trial.

With the resurrection complete, I know this is just the beginning. When I kneel before her to show her I'm no threat, I press my hands into the ground again, and this time, I force my energy into the land, lifting it mentally toward the surface.

Everything around me vibrates as my powers go to work.

Why hasn't Otyx done this earlier? If I can use his power to bring the Underworld to the surface, why hasn't he done it a long time ago?

Marveling at my new abilities, I don't realize how fast Shadowmyre moves towards the heavens. Nevertheless, once the Underworld breaches the crust, my eyes fall on the palace in the clouds, and I feel the smile tugging on the corner of my mouth.

My mother is probably up there with a grin on her face, and I can't wait to finally pay her a visit.

"This way," the soldier, who led us into the Cloud Palace, yells as we follow him frantically. "We need to warn the Queen."

Is he damn serious? Does he really think she didn't hear the commotion?

My eyes zigzag between the broken windows and Cyrus, who keeps pushing me to move faster as a wave of muscle pain hits me like a hungry lion sinking teeth into its prey. There it is again—the ache I haven't felt for an entire day.

"Something is wrong with Queen Soulin," I whisper, my eyes darting to the red kingdom in the distance.

"Don't worry about her," Cyrus presses out between ragged breaths and immediately regrets his words.

It's easy for him to say, as he's not the one connected to her. If she's in pain, so am I. If she dies, so do I.

"I didn't mean that," he says, grabbing my hand. "But we have to worry about ourselves first."

I want to. I really do. But if something happens to her, I will pay for it.

Yet, even if I want to aid her, I can't. Erinna is still gone, and without wings, it will take me days to reach Crymzon, and by the time I get there, it might be too late. I also can't convince Cyrus to bring me there. He's done enough for me.

He squeezes my hand. "Listen, Devana. She has magic. Whatever is brewing down there, she will manage."

"You know exactly what's happening. If this is the arrival of who I think it is, no one is prepared," I say, almost running into the soldier's wings as he stops before us.

"Do you see that?" a soldier close to us asks, pointing out a cracked window.

We're almost in the heart of the Cloud Palace as I scan the horizon.

"Commander!" another man calls out, his voice sharp and urgent.

The commander, the man before me, swiftly joins the soldier at the window. "What is it?" he inquires.

"Look there." The soldier points outside, his finger trembling, indicating a peculiar sight in the distant sky.

At first glance, it appears to be a winged creature soaring toward the Cloud Palace, casting a striking silhouette against the endless blue expanse. Upon closer inspection, the approaching figure is not a creature but a woman with magnificent wings that span like an angel's. Her presence is almost surreal.

The woman wears a flowing dress that appears to be woven from molten lava, its colors shifting from fiery reds to gold, as if she's a living embodiment of the earth's inner fire. Her hair cascades in golden waves, and her eyes shimmer with the same intensity as the magma that flows deep within the planet's core.

As the mysterious winged woman draws nearer, it becomes apparent that she's not alone. Behind her, a colossal dragon trails in her wake, its scales glinting with the reflection of the sunlight.

"She's coming here," I whisper, digging my nails into Cyrus' hand. "She's aiming straight for us."

"Guard the Queen. Now!" the commander yells, bolting for the massive doors at the end of our room.

I can't think straight. What are we supposed to do? We're no match for a dragon. A real, fire-breathing dragon!

As the winged woman and her companion draw closer, the clouds beneath the palace tremble in response. It's as if Starstrand's foundation acknowledges her presence, the air humming with the energy of her arrival.

And then, in a breathtaking display of power and grace, the winged woman bursts into the Cloud Palace right into the throne room before us. I watch in horror as she passes through the grand wall, her wings brushing the edges of the structure. The clouds within the palace swirl in her wake, almost throwing me off balance.

The woman lands gently, her molten dress flickering with every step. Her dragon settles beside her, its massive talons digging into the cloud beneath it.

"I'm home," she yells, and I dig my feet into the fluffy ground to stop myself from sliding over the threshold into the same room as her.

She's for sure a Starstrandian with her blond hair, blue eyes, and white wings. She even said it: home.

So why is everyone acting so strange? Why are the guards trying to protect the Queen from her if this is where she belongs? Perhaps it's just a coincidence that she returns at the same time as the Underworld pushes its way upwards, and we're all overreacting.

"Back away, slowly," Cyrus whispers behind me, grabbing me by the waist.

So much to coincidence. He can feel the hostility in her stance, too.

Following his command, I take a step back, then another.

The atmosphere within the palace is charged as the woman surveys her surroundings. What brought her here, and what intentions does she have?

"We need to jump," Cyrus whispers, pulling me another step away from the throne room.

My heart hammers so loudly that I hope my voice is quiet enough so she doesn't hear me. "Are you mad?"

Another pull and another step. "If something happens to the Queen, we're stuck here until the next successor is elected."

"How do you—" I catch myself. Of course, he knows about the other kingdom's successions. He's a royal, after all.

He tugs on me again. "We need to get away from Starstrand if we don't want to get stranded here with her," he says, pulling me closer to the next window. "I got you. I just need you to trust me."

I haven't forgotten about the wings Queen Caecilia granted him. But do I trust him? I've never flown through the sky with anyone but Erinna.

Intrigue and tension have taken hold of the Cloud Palace as we move closer to a broken window. From my vantage point, I can see the grand throne room, a vast space with magnificent crystal chandeliers and a throne of shimmering light at its center.

"Oh, Queen. Where are you?" the woman sings, spinning around herself. Her dragon companion stands guard behind her with a watchful eye, its scales gleaming.

The Queen's voice resonates through the chamber like a melodious aria before I can spot her. As much as I strain my hearing, I can't make out her words because fear claws at my heart, forcing it to pump faster.

We inch closer to the broken window in the shadowed corner, now hidden from view. To my surprise, our presence goes unnoticed amid the grandeur of the unfolding scene as Starstrandians surround the woman.

No one dares to move as the woman clicks her tongue. "Is this how you greet your own?"

As the tension in the room reaches its zenith, the dragon behind her, seemingly provoked, releases a deafening roar and spews forth a torrent of searing flames that lick the air. The heat of the dragon's fire slams into me, and I'm not even close to it.

With the flames erupting and danger imminent, Cyrus acts swiftly and decisively.

I can see the fear on Cyrus' face as he grabs me by the shoulders and turns me around. Just as he pushes me out of the window, he follows, launching himself into the open sky, desperate for our survival.

The winds whip around me, and the clouds offer no purchase. I'm in freefall, descending from the Cloud Palace to the earth below.

As we plummet through the sky, hurtling toward a world of solid ground and mortal consequences, we cling to each other. That's when Cyrus opens his cloud-made wings and flaps them to catch us. His face contorts and the veins on his neck strain as he tries to slow us down, to no avail.

I know he wouldn't have pushed me, knowing that his wings can't carry two. But here we are, seconds away from our sealed fate.

Weightless, I move my legs around him to pull him closer, pressing my lips against his. We're together—one last time.

When I pull back to smile at him, I see the tears streaming from his eyes when he realizes he can't save me.

"I love you," I say, his eyes glued to my mouth to make out my words. That's when I pull my legs in and push him as far as possible away from me, knowing he can't reach me again.

Just because he can't save us both doesn't mean he has to shatter on the ground with me.

SIX

QUEEN SOULIN

High above Crymzon, I soar on Storm's back, her wings like fine silk gently swaying in the hot wind. My kingdom lies below, enclosed within the colossal wall of a circular barrier, shielding my realm from the harsh expanse of the red desert. From my elevated vantage point, I look down upon my beloved kingdom, a tapestry of thousands of sandstone architectures and cruel beauty.

But I seek more than just the comfort of Crymzon's embrace. I'm drawn to the mystery beyond the protective wall, an enigma that has intrigued me for as long as I can remember. The land outside the barrier is a vast desert, its sands as red as rubies, stretching out to the horizon in every direction. It's a harsh and unforgiving place, the evidence of the power and isolation of my territory.

As I guide Storm over the boundary, my gaze falls upon an unexpected sight. Like a vein of onyx running through the red sand, a black line catches my attention. It starkly contrasts the fiery landscape, a dark ribbon etched into the desert.

Curiosity and a deep sense of duty drive me to follow this mysterious trail. Storm descends gracefully, her wings fluttering with grace as we venture closer to the line. The desert stretches out on all sides, but the dark vein holds my focus.

Where did it come from? It wasn't here when I returned to my palace after battling my undead father again.

Minutes pass as I follow the straight path, and my surroundings remain silent and lonely. But then, on the horizon, I see a sight that makes my heart quicken. Black stone palaces emerge from the desert's depths, like obsidian monoliths reaching skyward. Unlike anything within my kingdom, these structures weren't there when I flew over Escela the last time. No, they never existed on this planet—I would know.

My mind floods with possibilities. These newfound palaces are a disturbing revelation, for I recognize them as the work of a being beyond the realm of mortals. Like the gates to the Underworld itself, these dark stones stand as proof of a power transcending my world's boundaries.

This is all my fault. I should have known better than to anger a God. But he started it. If Otyx had left me and my kingdom alone, I would've never considered summoning him.

I know that the God of the Underworld, a force ancient and formidable, breached through Escela's crust, bringing a presence that threatens the balance of what I know. The veins of darkness, like tendrils from a shadowy realm, now extend into my world, revealing that our two domains have become inextricably linked—all because of me.

I'm the one who opened the path to merge our worlds. Through my blood, he could bring Hell to Escela, just as he promised.

Dread and determination well within my heart as I approach the palaces. Seven. There are seven small palaces, each just a hair smaller than the Crymzon Palace. But my stomach turns when I see the eighth towering in the center. It's bigger, darker, and brutally breathtaking.

Storm circles above them, revealing their ominous and foreboding designs. The architecture is foreign and unsettling, a stark contrast to the elegance and beauty of Escela's kingdoms.

But it's empty. Shouldn't I be able to see the creatures who roam the Underworld? Where is everyone?

I inhale sharply. Are they invisible to my eyes? Can a mortal not see what's not living anymore? What if they're overrunning the land of the living, and I can't see them?

Clenching my teeth, I press down on Storm, signaling her to fly closer. My burgundy dress, vibrant as the desert's sands, flutters in the wind as I approach the closest palace, my heart heavy knowing that the fate of my kingdom rests on my shoulders.

I'm still determined to confront the God who has finally emerged from the Underworld. Yet, if I die, so will my kingdom. Without a vessel to distribute Crymzon's magic equally, it will consume itself, leaving only dust behind.

With every flap of her silk-like wings, Storm draws closer to the heart of the mysterious palace in the center. A sudden whistling sound pierces the air as I navigate the crimson skies searching for a soul. My keen senses alert me to the danger before I can see it. Still, I'm not fast enough because an arrow whizzes past me, mere inches from my face. My heart races as I scan the horizon, my eyes tracing the arrow's trajectory.

Following the path it came from, my gaze falls upon a sight that takes me aback. Beyond the threshold of the desert and the black star-shaped platform presenting the palaces, I spot another kingdom—Tenacoro.

While the Underworld claimed most of the desert separating me from Eternitie, it luckily wasn't quite large enough to reach Tenacoro. While the river still seeps through the cracks into the planet's center, the Underworld missed all the vital parts of the land for now.

Narrowing my eyes to get a better visual, I spot a woman stepping out of the thick bushes. Her black curly hair and ebony skin blend seamlessly with her kingdom's surroundings as she stands beneath the vibrant canopy of trees. My eyes are locked on her as I divert my path from the darkness and towards her.

Storm touches down gently upon the soft grass across the draining river, and Opaline and I stand face to face within seconds of our landing.

As I approach, there's a moment of recognition, a spark of memory from a time long past. We used to be friends back when my family was still alive. Whenever our parents were called to a Council meeting, we spent our time creeping through foreign kingdoms, exploring as much as possible before returning to our homes. I admired Princess Opaline's strength. Not only is she as jaw-dropping as her mother in her jade dress made of leaves, vines, and branches, but she also possesses a heart big enough to drown an entire kingdom with her love.

But I don't see her usually bright smile and warm eyes as I draw closer. Only a fool would think that a Tenacorian—no, not any Tenacorian—that the Princess of Tenacoro is weak. She comes from a long line of warriors, each generation earning more precision in hunting than the one before.

It's a voice tinged with nostalgia that breaks the silence. "Is it truly you?" Opaline asks, her voice both soothing and resonant, revealing an intimacy I haven't heard since storming out of Starstrand after leaving her in tears.

My eyes widen as I gaze into the face of my childhood friend, a companion I haven't seen in what feels like a lifetime, even though I saw her in Starstrand and Terminus. "Opaline," I whisper, disbelief and joy merging in my voice.

How can I tell her that Khaos still died after she saved him from my attempt to ease his pain by killing him, and after she nurtured him back to health? I wasn't her only friend; she knows Khaos as well as she knows me.

"Khaos—" my voice breaks.

She stiffens, and her fingers tremble as she searches my mouth for the words that won't come.

I can't tell her. She will think it's her fault.

Opaline's eyes wander to the new palaces behind me. "Did you bring Otyx here?"

Choking on my tears, I dig my fingernails into my palms to distract my emotions with a new pain. Maybe she didn't hear me. Perhaps by just saying his name, she doesn't understand what I'm referring to. "I fucked up."

There, I said it. I fucked up. Big time. Again.

My plan was to storm into the palace of the Underworld and bargain for Khaos' soul. Well, until I saw Opaline.

If I have learned something from the last few days, it is that no matter my choice; I destroy everything I try to fix. I know it's *me* who keeps making everything worse.

But maybe I can put a stop to it. Perhaps I could finally turn this around by asking the only other friend I had besides Khaos for help. That is, if she hasn't given up on me yet.

A tear rolls down Opaline's cheek as she understands all the words I can't say. If my unregal posture wasn't enough to give my heartache away, my unsteady voice might have been it.

"What do you need?" Opaline asks, carefully stepping in my direction as if she's scared to spook me away.

My body slumps at those words. How? How can someone be so forgiving? I've given her so many reasons to hate me, yet she stands before me, brushing off all the horrible things I've done.

"He's dead," I whisper, my body shaking uncontrollably.

Opaline rushes forward and embraces me with her strong, lean arms as tears fill my eyes. My first instinct is to pull away and hiss at her, but my heart can't take it anymore. Leaning into her, I close my eyes and let my feelings consume me.

"Where have you been all these years?" Opaline whispers into my ear. "I've missed you, Soulin."

For Lunra's sake, I've missed her, too. But I was so consumed by the loss of my mother and brother that I hid my emotions underneath a thick layer of magic to keep going.

Now that I have nothing left—no composure to keep the wall around my heart strong and no family or Khaos—I'm done pretending.

"I can't finish this alone," I say, wiping my tears away. "But I also don't want to drag you into this. I angered a God, and he took him from me. Khaos was everything I had left."

"That's not true," Opaline says, pushing me away to look into my face. "I'm here for you. You don't know how long I've waited to be with *my* Soulin again."

Her Soulin.

All these years, she held onto the young girl I once was. But there's nothing left of *her* anymore. Killing your family and climbing the Crymzon Throne will do that to you.

"I changed my mind. This is my mess, and I need to correct it," I say, straightening my shoulders when I realize how easy it is to lose Opaline, too.

I'm not talking about a war with another kingdom or Undead soldiers sent by Keres. I'm facing the God of the Underworld. A *God!* While Tenacoro produces exceptional warriors, their bows, arrows, and spears won't be able to harm Otyx.

"Don't shut me out again," Opaline says, looking past me at the darkness behind me. "This isn't just your fight. If Otyx thinks he can raise the Underworld and conquer Escela, he's wrong."

"You don't understand. He's not here for you or the other kingdoms. He's here because of me."

She crunches her face. "Oh, I understand. You might have summoned him, but this all started over a decade ago. For years, he's been building an army in the North, which had nothing to do with you."

She's right. When the word about the new King in the North went through Escela, I was as surprised as the other rulers. Yet, it feels personal when I recall my father's signature red hair and pale and hollow face when I faced Keres in Terminus. From all the deceased souls Otyx could have picked from, he chose my father.

Plus, I can't forget the war I saw through the vision of a book in Librascendia. The God of the Underworld fought my ancestor a long, long time ago.

Perhaps it's not a coincidence that he's back. Maybe I can stop him if I find out why he targets my family and kingdom.

"If you want to help me, I need you to alert the other kingdoms. Gather as many troops as you can," I say, looking at the breach from the Underworld, the obsidian palaces, and the encroaching darkness that threatens both our territories.

"What are you going to do?"

"I have to prepare my army," I say, snapping my fingers to call Storm. "Your strength and my magic won't be enough to threaten a God, but I have something even better."

SEVEN

Avira

My body floods with so many emotions that it's hard to concentrate.

How do people do it? How do they keep a straight head when more than one sin tucks at their being? After feeling none for almost a hundred years, it's overwhelming trying to pinpoint which one currently possesses me.

"Mother?" I scream, my eyes glued to the last flames extinguished by the clouds surrounding me.

I'm not sure how, but Emberix's fire left me unscathed. It should have burned me, charcoaled me, but I'm still here.

"You need to stop," Otyx says, stepping through a cloud wall in my direction. "Take my hand and let's go home."

My knees almost cave at his beauty. I thought the Underworld suited him and brought out his best features, but here, above the clouds, the stark contrast of the darkness enclosing him against the bright backdrop is just jaw-dropping.

Grinning at him, I wave my hand, taking in the fresh breeze that follows him through the opening before it closes on its own accord. "I am home. Actually, this could be ours. You don't have to live in darkness anymore."

Black smoke swirls around him as he extends his hand. "Avira. Please take my hand."

My eyes wander to his long fingers reaching for me. "No," I say, taking a step back. "I know what you're doing."

He cocks his head. "What would that be?"

"Once I take your hand, I'll surrender all my memories to you again."

As much as Otyx wants to deny my accusation, his hesitation shows me my instincts are correct. And from all people, he should know how deeply the loss of my memories affected me.

"A mortal body isn't designed to wield a God's power." His void eyes glide past me, and I don't need to turn to know he's looking at Emberix. "You're taking this too lightly. Just because you're now connected to my kingdom doesn't mean you can use that power to resurrect whomever you like. Don't you think I would have resurrected her if I could? Power comes at a steep price."

I laugh. "Now that's where you're wrong. Unused power does. If—"

I can't get any more words out because I recognize his absent facial expression when a soul reaches out to him. Someone is going to die soon, and I can bet my life on it I'm going to be the one delivering that soul to him.

EIGHT

DEVANA

As I plummet through the boundless expanse of the sky, a rush of wind roars in my ears. My heart pounds like a tribal drum, its rhythm synchronizing with the frantic flutter of my thoughts.

Why isn't he opening his wings to catch his fall?

"Live," I scream through the wind whipping past me. But Cyrus dives after me, his cloud-like wings pressed firmly against his body, his arms outstretched.

He won't make it; we both know it.

I imagine myself as a lone leaf spiraling from a magnificent tree for an endless moment. The world dissolves into a blur of colors and sensations. The air presses against my body, and the sensation of weightlessness envelops me, making me feel simultaneously fragile and invincible.

Fear courses through my veins when I open my eyes again, but I'm determined to face it. With every fiber of my being, I focus on my breath, slowing it down as if I can control the descent by sheer willpower. Seconds stretch into eons, and my mind races with memories, regrets, and moments I've yet to experience.

I know I don't have long, and when his eyes widen, and his arms and wings flare out to finally break his fall, I squeeze my eyes shut and inhale fresh air for the last time before my body shatters on the ground.

Then, when I expect the inevitable impact, the sensation of falling changes. The rushing wind and deafening din of my descent fade away.

Coldness surrounds me as I make contact.

The harsh, biting air is replaced by a strangely comforting chill, as if I've plunged into an abyss.

Instinctively, I open my eyes, only to be met with a surreal, dreamlike world. A mesmerizing spectacle of bubbles surrounds me, each shimmering with iridescent hues. Some are pearlescent, while others glow with the colors of a setting sun. These bubbles dance around me like playful spirits, defying gravity in their never-ending dance around me. They caress my skin and clothes, imparting an unknown sensation.

Is this what death feels like? Cold and weightless?

With every passing moment, the bubbles grow more vibrant and alive. They pulse with a rhythm that resonates with my soul, calming my nerves.

As the bubbles guide my descent, the colors shift and merge, creating a harmony of light and water. The coldness that first embraced me begins to feel invigorating and refreshing as the world around me becomes a surreal underwater dreamscape, with tendrils of seaweed and the silhouettes of marine creatures passing by in the distance.

That's when fear sets in.

The cold water closes in around me like a vise. Panic threatens to overwhelm me as I struggle to swim toward the surface, my lungs burning for air.

As the seconds tick by and my strength wanes, a profound sense of helplessness washes over me. The surface looks so close, yet every stroke seems to drag me further away from the sun filtering through it.

I can't stop fighting. I'm so close.

Just when the thin layer of water separating me from the air my lungs so desperately search for comes into reach, my body feels weightless, and my surroundings blur.

Something grabs my leg and pulls me away from the surface with an alarming urgency. Instinctively, I gasp for air, my lungs burning as I inhale water instead. Panic surges through me, and the world above, with its shimmering sunlight and breaking waves, seems impossibly distant as water rushes into my mouth. I brace for the choke of drowning. The sensation of water filling my lungs is excruciating, and I wait for the inevitable darkness.

It never comes.

As my body convulses, I realize I'm not drowning; I'm breathing. My gasps turn into slow, rhythmic breaths as if my body has undergone an unknown transformation.

Confusion sweeps over me as my body adapts to this surreal situation. My lungs no longer scream for oxygen, and my limbs move with an ease I've never experienced before.

My eyes, previously blinded by the chaotic underwater darkness, now adapt to the subdued aquatic light. I see with astonishing clarity as I descend deeper and deeper into the ocean's fathomless abyss. The world around me becomes a spectrum of blues and greens, the colors intensifying with each passing moment.

Sunlight filters through the surface in radiant beams when I look up, but I'm no longer sinking; instead, I'm being carried away by a surreal current, surrounded by a pair of figures unlike anything I've ever seen.

As I blink away the remnants of fear, my eyes widen in disbelief. A man and woman hold me tightly in their arms.

How? How are they moving so fast?

I look over my shoulder and see the beautiful, iridescent tails that glisten with color. Their scales are like precious gems, reflecting the entire rainbow spectrum.

The woman's hair flows behind her like a cascade of dark liquid silk, and the man's eyes burn with kindness and curiosity. In their presence, I feel a profound sense of serenity and safety when I shouldn't. I should fight them because I have to get back to the surface, back to Cyrus.

With a grace that speaks of years beneath the waves, the Ocerians pull me deeper into the ocean's depths. Schools of vibrant fish dart around us, and coral gardens sway in the gentle current. Strange, luminescent creatures glide past as they drag me through breathtaking underwater caves and shimmering kelp forests, introducing me to the diverse marine life that thrives in their domain.

Then there's darkness. Fear claws in my chest, not knowing how I will find my way back. This has to be a dream. I have to be dead. Otherwise, how can I explain that I'm breathing underwater while being carried far away from everything I know?

Suddenly, the water becomes crystal clear as bioluminescent creatures glow with gentle radiance, creating an enchanting and surreal world. Schools of silvery fish dash around me, leaving trails of shimmering light in their wake.

I blink as the world around me unveils its secrets. Beneath me, an entire kingdom materializes on the ocean's floor. Elaborate coral structures of every shape and size stretch out in all directions, adorned with vibrant anemones and swaying kelp forests.

As I continue to explore, I encounter a bustling city of Ocerians, their homes nestled among the coral formations. The streets of this underwater metropolis are alive with activity. Ocerians of all ages swim about, engaged in their daily lives, tending to gardens of bioluminescent plants, and interacting with curious marine creatures.

The two Ocerians lead me through the coral streets, their communication transcending words. While I notice their non-verbal exchanges, I can't decipher them.

"What is going on?" I say, surprised to hear my voice dampened but audible.

My captors pause for a moment, turning to me before they tighten their grip around my arms to keep going.

The initial fog that settled over my brain, pushing my fear of drowning and my longing for Cyrus aside, clears, and all I can think of is getting back to the surface.

But it's not just for Cyrus. A creature from the Underworld attacked Starstrand, and I'm not talking about the dragon. I mean the winged woman who looked like a fallen Starstrandian.

What if more angered souls have reached Escela, demanding revenge? What if Cyrus' father and brother are up there?

I fling my hands and feet around, trying to break loose, and when they finally release me, I fall to my knees as if the water's weightlessness has suddenly forsaken me. When I lift my head to reach for the sky, my eyes land on a man before me.

I've seen him before, but the last time, he was agitated, refusing to go to war against the Crymzon Queen.

Before me, on a throne made of corals, sits the ruler of Oceris, King Usiel, and he looks very displeased.

NINE

Queen Soulin

This time, I soar with Storm back to Crymzon, following the draining river. The sandbanks are still wet as the water level plummets drastically. If the leak doesn't stop soon, the ocean might be gone when I return to Tenacoro with my army.

The sun hangs low in the sky, casting a warm, golden hue over the vast expanse of the Crymzon Wall. When I reach the palace, I spot that my subjects have been hard at work during my absence, and now their efforts will come to fruition.

Storm lands at the grand archway to the palace that leads into the entrance hall. As I dismount and march through it, I immediately notice a flurry of activity. Soldiers and servants painstakingly carry in broken rock pieces, their faces covered with sweat.

I hesitate when I see the closed doors to the throne room in the distance. If I step over that threshold, I will see him. While I could push the thought of Khaos aside on the flight home and pretend this was all a horrible dream I would wake up from, I know that delusion will shatter when I see the glass coffin.

Conrad bows before me, and I cringe at his unnoticed approach. "Your Majesty. We're almost done with collecting all the Nullstones from the desert."

"Never creep up on me again," I whisper as I continue to make my way through the entrance hall, observing the precautions taken by my people. Everyone wears thick fabric gloves, careful not to touch the precious stones with bare hands as they stack the rock fragments into carefully arranged piles against the walls.

The entrance hall leads to a grand corridor, and my heart rate and pace quicken as I progress.

He's not dead. He will walk through those doors, pick me up, and carry me away from this nightmare.

"I locked the doors," Conrad says from a distance. He might be unable to keep up with me, but he knows exactly what I'm about to do.

My fingers curl around the warm doorknob, and that's when I feel the ancient spell hitting me like a brick. It courses through my body, boiling the blood in my veins. Summoning my power, I lean into the door and force my magic to counter his spell. When I realize I can't overthrow it, I release my grip and whirl around. "Unlock it," I bark as Conrad finally reaches me.

How is that possible? How can a normal Crymzonian cast a more powerful spell than the Queen, who's right beneath their Goddess?

"No," he answers, resting his hand on my shoulder. "I can't let you in there."

"I need to see him," I growl, reaching for the knob again, but Conrad grabs my hand with his other.

"No good comes from you seeing him in this state right now."

"Don't tell me what to do or feel," I spit out, my fingers curling around my whip's handle that tightly curls around my thigh.

Conrad follows my motion with his eyes. "Do it."

Do what? Kill him?

My nails dig into the clasp to release the whip, but I halt. I won't fight Conrad. Even though he's pissing me the fuck off, I need every ounce of my energy for Otyx.

But I also can't let him win in front of all my subjects. What if someone is watching us and sees my grief as a weakness?

"Your order was to protect my King," I say loud enough for the Crymzonians in earshot to hear. "Don't let anyone get to him."

What else was I supposed to say? If I can't get into my throne room, at least it has to look like it was my order to keep it sealed. No one can know that Conrad is overthrowing me right now.

"Thank you," he whispers, looking down at his hands. "There's one more thing."

My gaze falls onto his glove-covered hands. There, resting on his open palms, are a set of silken red gloves, a small dagger, and a long metallic whip. It looks just like the one I was about to pull and punish him with, but under closer inspection, I notice the sharp Nullstone fragments built into it.

Carefully I grab the gloves and I can't help but smile when I realize Conrad thought this through. As I slip the left glove over the faded scar my undead brother left on me, the fabric reaches up to my shoulder while the right stops above my wrist. After protecting my skin, I pick up the whip and curl it around my left arm, starting at my wrist and up to my biceps.

"I need my moths to transport the Nullstones to Tenacoro with as many soldiers as we can spare," I say, adding another task to his list.

The feel of the cold metal through the glove eases the stinging pain of betrayal just a little. As much as I want to make a scene to see Khaos, he's right. I need to keep my head leveled.

"Consider it done," Conrad says, bowing before me. "May I ask what we're up against and where you're going?"

One word is enough to answer both of his questions. "Otyx."

TEN

Avira

Amid the hushed whispers of the wind, I stand beside Emberix and Otyx, my senses captivated by the sound of wings beating in the distance. The even cadence grows louder, harmonizing with the thud of my heartbeat. As the anticipation escalates, the cloud-covered sky parts, revealing a celestial figure descending gracefully from the heavens.

Golden locks cascade like sunlight, framing the face of a woman whose ethereal beauty radiates a divine glow. White wings, pristine and expansive, unfurl majestically as she touches down upon the cloud-kissed ground.

Her eyes sparkle with tears of happiness as she opens her arms to embrace me. "You've come home," the Queen says, her voice thick with tears.

This isn't how I expected her to greet me. My mother looks relieved, as if she has been waiting for this moment for a long time without aging a day.

Yet, in my heart, a storm brews. This reunion wasn't supposed to be emotional and sweet. For years, I've been stuck in the Underworld because of her. She chose my father over me. I've weathered storms, both internal and external, while Queen Caecilia dwelled in celestial opulence, shielded from the harsh realities below the surface.

My response is veiled in a smile, concealing the turmoil within as she hugs me. My mother's embrace feels like chains, binding me to a world I've struggled to get back to.

"Mother," I reply coolly, my voice measured. I force a smile that doesn't reach my eyes, a mask worn to conceal my emotions. "It's been a while."

My mother steps back, wings folding gracefully behind her. "Oh, my dear," she sighs, touching my cheek. "You've grown into such a remarkable woman."

I cringe at the contact. "Remarkable, perhaps," I say, pulling away, "but not because of your influence."

Queen Caecilia's face falters as a flicker of sadness crosses her features. "Avira, please understand. I had to let you go to protect you."

"Protect me?" I scoff, my voice laced with bitterness. "You abandoned me. You left me to rot in the Underworld alone."

Tension hangs in the air, like the unspoken words that have festered over the years. The clouds above us mirror the turbulence within my heart as they turn darker.

"I had responsibilities," she explains, her eyes pleading for understanding. "But I never stopped thinking of you."

Her eyes fill with tears as she reaches out again, but I dodge her touch. "I can't just forgive and forget," I declare.

The clouds above release a soft rain that falls upon us. We stand, separated not only by physical distance but by the chasm of time.

"Thank you for bringing her back," Caecilia whispers over my shoulder, and I know it's directed at Otyx.

How dare she thank him? It was *me*. *I* brought the Underworld to the surface. It was *me* who won Nekrojudex, and with that, also my memories.

"It wasn't his doing," I say, hatred bubbling inside me. "For almost a century, I thought Mother of Lust was my actual mother. For almost one hundred years, I asked myself every single day how I had ended up in the Underworld. I imagined who was missing me and how my life might have been before I was tossed into the abyss, forgotten by my mother."

The Queen takes a step back, her head cocked. "If I had known that he would take you from me, I would have never agreed to it."

I huff. "Stop lying. The agreement was clear. One soul for another," I muse, stepping over to Emberix to touch her cold, sharp scales.

"It wasn't like that," Caecilia says, shaking her head. "He promised me I could get your father back. And I planned to free you."

"So why didn't you?"

The silence stretching out between us tells me everything I need to know.

"You're a coward," I say, cracking my neck. "You never planned on rescuing me."

Caecilia's hands tremble as she turns to Otyx. "That's not true. Tell her. Tell her I wanted her back."

I look over at Otyx, who ignores my mother, his eyes resting on me. "We need to go," he says, reaching for me again. "You'll never forgive yourself if you stay."

I smile at him. "No, I'll never forgive myself if I let her live believing in her own lie," I reply.

Clicking my tongue, Emberix responds to my subtle command and crouches down. With a gentle nudge of my elbow into the dragon's flank, flames erupt from the creature's maw at my mother.

Caecilia stands defiantly amidst the swirling flames. Her celestial wings glow against the inferno, and I see the flicker of vulnerability in her eyes she tries so hard to cover up as the fire encircles her.

"Avira, please!" my mother pleads, her voice drowned by the crackling fire. "I know I've made a mistake, but we can work through this."

My expression remains resolute as I maintain control over the dragon. Our bond resonates with a power that transcends mere commands—an unspoken understanding forged through shared memories of being wrongfully imprisoned.

As Emberix unleashes her fiery wrath, the sky itself trembles in acknowledgment. Flames dance like serpents, coiling and hissing before converging upon the Starstrandian Queen. The air becomes charged with the scent of burning embers and the palpable tension between my mother and me.

Amidst the chaos, a figure emerges from the fire—the God of the Underworld, draped in darkness. Like pools of endless nights, his eyes reflect a mixture of concern and regret. He moves to shield Caecilia from the impending inferno; however, his efforts are thwarted by the relentless advance of Emberix's flames.

"Enough, Avira!" he implores. "There are consequences to tampering with the balance of the divine."

My gaze briefly shifts to Otyx. "She left me alone and forced me to face the Underworld without guidance. This is the consequence she faces."

The dragon's fiery assault reaches its zenith, engulfing my mother. The once majestic figure now writhes within the inferno, her bright aura dimming as the flames consume her form.

Otyx, unable to intervene in time, watches in solemn silence. The air is thick with sorrow and the acrid scent of burning magic, as the irreversible choice made in the name of revenge claims its victim.

As the last embers flicker, the dragon's flames subside, leaving behind a scorched spot on the cloud. My lips curl into a smile as I approach the ashen ground where my mother once stood.

"You went too far," Otyx says, shaking his head.

"Don't play like this is all on me. You know what I was about to do. You could feel her death approaching before I even made that decision. I saw the expression in your eyes when you felt the next soul reaching out to you."

"No," he says, staring down at me, the darkness in his eyes reaching a coldness I haven't seen before. He points at my mother's leftovers. "It wasn't her timer that startled me when it began ticking. It was yours."

ELEVEN

DEVANA

My long hair floats around me like a shimmering veil in the current. Before me, King Usiel, decorated in majestic attire woven from kelp and adorned with pearls, surveys me with eyes as deep and mysterious as the ocean itself.

"I know you," he says, pointing at me. "You're the girl who tried to save the Crymzon prisoners."

I didn't expect him to recognize me, which makes my part even more manageable.

"I bring news from the surface," I begin, my voice harmonizing with the gentle lull of the underwater. "Starstrand is under attack."

Before I can divulge further, a surge of water disrupts my words. A man, disoriented and gasping for breath, is tossed beside me. Recognition flashes across his face when he looks at me.

"I told you to flee," I gasp, jolting forward to wrap my arms around him.

"There's no way I'm leaving you again," Cyrus replies, pressing me against him as if I'm his oxygen, and he has finally found me.

King Usiel claps his hands, and we break apart. "I don't want to ruin your reunion, but I need to know what's happening on the surface."

"King Usiel," I continue, composed despite the disturbance, "I'm sorry about our intrusion, but alarming changes are unfolding on the surface—the Underworld found a way to break through the crust."

The Ocean King's gaze remains steady, his expression unreadable as the weight of my words hangs around us.

Cyrus, having caught his breath, adds, "Otyx isn't only a threat to our kingdoms but yours as well."

The King raises an eyebrow, a subtle sign for us to elaborate. I take a deep breath; the currents responding to my unspoken request for clarity.

"It looks like Otyx is sending his souls to eliminate all the rulers. We were there when one of them attacked Starstrand, and we could flee before she could injure us."

"How come that every time I see you, there's something horrible conspiring?" King Usiel asks, his gaze fixed on me.

"What is he talking about?" Cyrus whispers.

"Not now," I answer, shaking my head before raising my voice again. "I understand you stay clear of the conflicts between the kingdoms, but this is more than a disagreement. The God of the Underworld brought his kingdom to the surface, and if we don't do something, what will stop him from attacking you next?"

The King remains contemplative, his gaze shifting between Cyrus and me. After a moment of silence that feels like an eternity, he speaks, "No one dares to attack Oceris. We—"

"You're wrong if you believe water can stop Otyx. His dragon might not breathe fire down here, but it won't shy away from using its talons and teeth to rip your kingdom apart," Cyrus cuts in, straightening his shoulders.

The King's lips lift as he smirks at Cyrus.

"It's no use," I say, shaking my head. "We're wasting our time. He won't help us."

That realization hurts, yet I know there's nothing we can say or do to win him over. I've seen him talk his way out of helping me free the prisoners. He's a fearful King hiding behind a heavy coral crown.

A woman with a shimmering green tail rushes past us and comes to a halt beside the King. My fury deepens when I watch her whisper something into his ear. He nods again and again; then his eyes widen in disbelief.

"We have to get out of here," I whisper, my eyes glued to the King.

"And go where?"

Right. Is there still a safe place anywhere on this planet?

"Obviously, we can't go back to Starstrand," I reply, remembering the fiery flames almost scorching my skin. "Eternitie is cut off from the land because of the Underworld, and I'm not setting foot into Crymzon again."

"So…Tenacoro?"

No, I don't want to go there either, but what other choice do we have? I know Queen Synadena will welcome us with open arms, but what if Tenacoro is the next kingdom on Otyx's list? Even if we magically grow a tail, it will take us hours, maybe days, to reach my former kingdom.

"My father," I whisper as goosebumps erupt on my skin. "I sent him back there along with Erinna."

Cyrus cups my face. "They're fine. Your father is smart."

"And your sister," I add, panic clawing at my throat.

"Look at me," Cyrus says, forcing my chin up. "We can't save them all. We're at war."

"But—"

"Please be selfish for once and try to stay alive," he says, his brows drawn together. "My priority is to protect you."

"No, we should help—"

"*You*. Our best bet is the Crymzon Queen. She has magic and the biggest army. If something happens to you, she will die with you. And then what?"

My muscles stiffen when I notice a movement in the corner of my eye. "You're connected to Queen Soulin?" King Usiel asks, who's swishing his tail just a few feet away from us to stand tall.

Even surrounded by water, I feel my mouth go dry. No one was supposed to find out. *No one!*

"Yes," Cyrus says, stepping between us.

"What are you doing?" I ask, grabbing him by the shoulder.

King Usiel turns to the woman who interrupted our conversation. "I need you to keep her as far away from the surface as possible," he says, pointing at me. "Tell our army the time has come to ready the beast."

The beast? What is he talking about?

Instantly, my muscles hurt as the soldiers grab me by the arms. "No," I say, shaking my head. "Please don't do this. My father needs my help."

"And we need you alive if we want to win this war," King Usiel answers, snapping his fingers. "Take that one as well."

The fear in my chest eases a little as another set of soldiers grabs Cyrus to drag him away.

When I look over my shoulder at the King, I watch him kneel before the woman, and when she turns to face him, my eyes land on her rounded belly. King Usiel presses his head gently against it, whispering something under his breath.

Immediately, my anger subsides. All those days I thought he's too scared to stand up against the Crymzon Queen or Otyx, but now I realize he has more to lose than any of us.

Oceris is about to welcome its first heir in centuries.

TWELVE

Queen Soulin

Storm waits impatiently for me outside when I enter the courtyard through the entrance hall. Retrieving the Nullstone was the simple part, but turning them into weapons without being able to use any magic or physical touch turns out to be a challenge.

Crymzon only has a small supply of swords, bows, and arrows because our fighting techniques rely primarily on our powers, even in the years when it was draining. We're wasting precious time with less than a handful of swordsmiths on hand.

"Load them up," I say, already mounting Storm. I can feel her eagerness to roam the skies when I hold on to the fine hair on her back.

For a moment, I watch my citizens use anything they can find to transport the Nullstones. Some use ripped fabric to wrap around, while others fill stone bowls and clothes to the rim. All they need to do is bring the fragments to Tenacoro safely. Crymzonians might be unable to touch the rocks, but all other inhabitants of Escela can.

My heart pounds faster when I see my fully grown and beautiful moths awaiting their orders. After Conrad turned me away from opening the throne room, he unsealed the doors for a few heartbeats to let as many moths through as possible before sealing it shut again.

When I used my magic to enlarge more of them, I barely noticed the strength needed for it. At this point, I expected my magic to wean again since my Soulmate's heart stopped beating, but perhaps I was wrong. Maybe once the heir to the Crymzon Throne accepts a Soulmate, it doesn't matter if they live or die.

"We're ready," Grand General Cengor says, looking at me from afar. "What are your orders?"

Seeing him sends a shiver down my spine. He's Khaos' replacement. He's the one Khaos picked from his soldiers to fill his footsteps when I banned him from Crymzon. Back then, I accepted his decision because I thought it was the only way to protect Khaos. Now, it feels like a betrayal. My King should be here, leading our army beside me.

"Flank to the right and follow the water all the way to Tenacoro. Once you get there, deliver the Nullstone and help Queen Synadena wherever possible. By the time I return, I need everyone ready for battle."

The Grand General looks at me, his eyes resting on mine. "I'm very sorry about your loss. I knew Khaos very well. If there's something—"

Within a heartbeat, I'm on the ground, my right hand pressed against his neck to pull him in, and my left forearm just inches away from his throat. "How dare you speak of him this way," I growl, my gaze fixed on the shimmering Nullstone shards so close to his skin. "If you suggest taking his place in my kingdom, you're wrong. I *will* bring him back."

Grand General Cengor swallows deeply as he nods carefully. "That wasn't my intention," he coughs out, his eyes widened with fear.

"Get my soldiers to Tenacoro safely. If I find out you failed me, better hope the enemy cuts you down before I do."

When I release him, I notice our surroundings stopped moving. Wings levitate in the air without sounds, and people are frozen in place.

As I mount Storm, the turmoil around me picks up again, as if nothing happened.

Storm's red wings cast a shimmering glow over the desolate Underworld. The largest palace, a shadowy structure of imposing black spires, looms ahead as I prepare to land. The eerie silence of the realm envelops me as the moth gently touches down on the cold, black rock ground.

Where is everyone?

A sense of foreboding creeps over me as I slide off Storm, my dress billowing in the unnatural breeze. Accustomed to the company of my subjects, I suddenly find myself surrounded only by the haunting echoes of my footsteps.

As I navigate the vast, cold halls of the palace, an unsettling sensation tugs at my being. The seven sins, embodiments of temptation and malevolence, seem to cast their insidious influence upon me. Pride whispers in my ear while envy claws at my heart. I thought I was resilient against such forces, but I feel the weight of their pull in this desolate emptiness.

My knees quiver as I run through the halls to get out of here. The weight of the sins is too much, with or without my magic, and when I burst through the doors, I inhale sharply.

Why did Otyx bring his kingdom to the surface if no one lives here?

That's a stupid question. I know why he's here. I provoked him; now it's my turn to pay for my mistake. He warned me, and I didn't listen.

Still, where is he? The God of the Underworld can't be in Crymzon. I would have noticed him, wouldn't I?

My gaze turns upward, seeking solace in the sunrays warming my skin, only to be met with a shocking sight. Starstrand, a kingdom of sterile beauty that usually floats above Oceris in the clouds, now blazes with ferocious flames. My eyes widen in disbelief.

How did I not notice? Otyx isn't here because he's busy attacking another kingdom. But why? This war is between him and me, or is it not?

Without hesitation, I sprint to Storm, her wings unfolding for me. In a swift motion, we soar into the bright sky, leaving the empty Underworld behind.

My gaze is fixed on the distant horizon as I steer Storm north.

It's too late to warn Starstrand. As much as I want to help them, other kingdoms might still have time.

My army shouldn't take much longer to arrive in Tenacoro, strengthening their force. But what about Eternitie and Oceris? Are they under attack?

Oceris might be the only one safe from Otyx from all our kingdoms. That leaves me with the kingdom north of Crymzon.

Trying to tell myself that Eternitie isn't my responsibility is laughable. Has the new Queen been crowned already? Did Cyrus' sister descend the Brass Throne, knowing that her brother and father died at the hands of her brother in a war they brought to my kingdom? And then there's Cyrus himself. Don't get me started on how I treated him in captivity.

Catalina is a young Queen without experience or close family members to support her. She's alone because I did that to her.

My heart skips a beat when I open my connection to feel for my Soulmate. It's quiet and cold. I bite my lip as I let my emotional guard down and concentrate on Devana and Cyrus next. Before I let them leave Crymzon, I marked both of them. Instantly, my emotions try to drown me, but I push them aside to find any clue as to where they could be.

I hear water splashing, and the surrounding air becomes heavy and pressing. Are they...underwater? Devana has to be uninjured; otherwise, I would feel it right now. As much as I concentrate, I can't feel what Cyrus is experiencing, but I know he's with her because every time he's around her, the connection is silent and content.

If they are where I think they are, they are safe—for now. But that means Eternitie isn't, and I need to get there before Otyx does.

I won't be responsible for another death, especially not for one that is preventable.

THIRTEEN

AVIRA

Otyx is wrong.

It can't be my time that started ticking. I know he wouldn't allow it; he would do everything in his power to stop it. I'm his—his alone.

"Nice attempt to get me to follow you," I say, watching Emberix smolder everything around us.

He still stares at me, his face not giving away any emotion. "You know what's the worst?" he asks, slowly shaking his head. "I can't intervene."

Rage sizzles through me, overpowering even the heat of the dragon's blazing fire. "You're full of shit. You did it before, I'm proof. I know you can do it, but you just don't want to."

His breath quickens. "I can't ignore the rules again."

"Because you can't or because you don't want to?"

He stares at me for so long I have to blink a couple of times to convince myself that time hasn't stopped.

"What do you want me to do? Just say it, and I'll do it."

"I thought you were a God," I snarl, "but you act even weaker than any mortal I've ever known. What good is your power if you don't use it?"

"Using and abusing are two different things."

"Don't lecture me. I know what you're capable of. I can feel it in my veins. And it's a waste. All this power and not enough guts to use it."

Otyx clenches his teeth. "That's not fair. I—"

"You know what's not fair? Everyone thinks I'm the damsel in distress who needs saving, that I'm too weak to stand up for myself. But this is me. It always has been. And honestly, who cares if I die? Apparently, you're not concerned in the least. So what's stopping me from making the Crymzon Queen pay for inflicting that wound on you?" I point at his chest.

Even though the gashing hole isn't there anymore, I can still see it before my eyes. The emotions I felt when I looked into his face rush through me again. I was horrified, scared, and helpless.

But not anymore.

Otyx opens his mouth, and I wave my hand. "You've said enough," I say, clicking my tongue, and before he can reach me, I feel Emberix beside me, her nostrils flaring as she stares down the God of the Underworld.

"I wouldn't do that if I were you," I snarl, and my anger turns into triumph when I see him retreat.

"Avira," he pleads, but I turn my back to him and start climbing on Emberix's back, using her leg and scales to pull myself up.

"I thought you would do anything for me, but I was wrong," I whisper as Emberix pushes us into the air, breaking through the flaming wall into the open.

FOURTEEN

DEVANA

I can't be responsible for a child losing their father before it's even born. That wasn't my intention when I was dragged down here.

Even worse, no one was supposed to find out about my connection to Soulin. I turned from a thorn under his skin to irreplaceable leverage within minutes.

"This isn't your fault," Cyrus says, coming up behind me.

Amidst the tranquil dance of bioluminescent sea life, we find ourselves confined in a prison, its walls woven from vibrant corals that shimmer with a bluish glow. The surrounding liquid darkness swallows my desperate gasps for air as panic settles in my bones. We need to get back to the surface.

"We will find a way out of here," Cyrus assures me, breaking off a piece of coral to use as a tool. But it pulverizes when he lifts his hand to hammer the piece against the coral bars.

As the realization of our predicament set in, my panic intensified. My chest tightens, and I frantically scan the surroundings, my eyes widening.

"We have to get out of here! We can't just stay underwater while people on the surface need our help!" I exclaim, my voice muffled by the water.

Cyrus, ever the calm presence, gently clasps my trembling hands. "Devana, we need to stay composed. Panicking won't help us or those above. There must be a way out of here. We just need to think."

Just as he attempts to calm me, a mysterious voice echoes through the watery enclosure. "I can release you," it resonates, causing us to turn our heads toward the source of the sound.

A silhouette emerges from the depths, revealing a majestic woman with flowing iridescent scales that mirror the colors of the surrounding corals. Her eyes hold both a regal grace and a hint of desperation. "I can free you," she repeats, her voice soft but commanding, "but only if you promise to help me protect my husband."

I know little about Oceris. The kingdom under the water's surface keeps to themselves, far away from outsiders. Yet, this offer sounds too good to be true, above or below the waves.

Cyrus and I exchange a puzzled glance before I turn my attention back to the mysterious woman. "Why would we help you?" I ask, my earlier panic giving way to mistrust.

That's when I follow her webbed hands, cradling her belly. It's her. I should have realized it when she approached us, but I never saw her entire face when she swam to King Usiel or when he held her belly, showing us only her profile.

"I know it's his duty to protect our kingdom, especially since the sea level is decreasing drastically because of the hole the Underworld created, but we're not made to fight above the water. Your skills and knowledge could make a difference," she implores.

I glance at Cyrus, silently communicating a shared understanding. "We'll help you," he declares, grabbing the bars.

"What's your name?" I ask, following Cyrus.

"Queen Cleolia," she answers, bowing her head.

Cyrus stretches his hand through an opening in her direction. "I'm—"

"I know who you are, Cyrus Matrus, Prince of Eternitie and son of Citeus Matrus. You look so much like your father, but you have the heart of your mother."

I feel Cyrus' body stiffen beside me, and I can't tell if it's the memory of his father or because she mentioned his mother that spooks him.

"I knew her well," Cleolia adds, pressing her lips into a thin line. "I miss her dearly."

No one ever mentions Eternitie's former Queen. Now, thinking about it, I'm not even sure I ever heard her name. Somehow, there is an unspoken rule every Escelian inhabitant follows: Never speak of a dead royal. I've seen it before in Starstrand. I've heard of the silence that followed the Starstrandian King and his daughter died. But my father never cared much for unspoken rules—or any rules, therefore.

"So do I," Cyrus says, lowering his gaze. "You're the first person ever to address her again."

My throat swells. What happened to her? While I told Cyrus what my mother had done and how much I loathe her for it, I never thought about asking about his mother. By the way he reacted, I know he loved her, and she left a gaping hole in his chest that I didn't see before.

"You did the right thing," Cleolia says, tilting her head to look at the surface. "Your sister will make a fine Queen."

Oh Gods, she knows what he has done. How is that possible? When Eternitie attacked Crymzon, only two more kingdoms were involved, and Oceris wasn't one of them.

"Blood is thicker than water; therefore, it can carry memories better than any other substance. A lot of blood and tears have seeped through the earth into the water stream below in the last couple of weeks," she explains, and the thought of someone retrieving information through a drop of blood seems uncomfortable to me. "I understand it sounds barbaric, but memory reading is an important skill down here if we want to stay in the loop with the world above."

"Do you know how Catalina is doing?" Cyrus asks as if he hasn't listened to anything she said since reflecting on his mother.

"She's safe for now. But we have to act quickly," she answers, her dark eyes resting on me.

That's my cue to jump in. "Okay. Let us help," I repeat, switching the subject to get us out of here finally. I want to ask her about *the beast,* how it's possible to extract memories from liquids, and about Cyrus' mother, but we must get going. If that winged woman already finished what she started in Starstrand, she might already be on her way to another kingdom and I try hard to keep calm because Tenacoro could be her next stop.

Cleolia nods appreciatively. "In return for your assistance, I shall release and guide you back to the surface. Together, we can bridge the worlds above and below."

With those words, the corals dissolve, freeing us from its grasp.

"Hold on to me," she says, stretching her arms.

I cling to her like a newborn to its mother. With a powerful stroke of her tail, Cleolia darts towards the sky as a surge of bubbles and currents washes past us. As we ascend toward the surface, I feel the grip of water releases its suffocating hold. Gasping for air, I breach the surface, my chest heaving as I gulp precious breaths. The taste of salt and freedom mingles in the surrounding air, but not for long.

As my head emerges into the world above, a sudden, ominous shift in the atmosphere catches my attention. From Starstrand high above, fire rains in a spectacular display of destructive beauty. Molten embers descend, casting an orange-red glow upon the ocean's surface.

Fear flashes in Cleolia's eyes as she senses the impending danger. With swift determination, she tugs at us, her voice a haunting melody in the chaos. "Dive!"

Understanding the urgency, I relinquish my fresh air gasps and descend again into the ocean's embrace. As we dive deeper, the fiery deluge continues, transforming the ocean's surface into a chaotic battleground between water and fire. Cleolia positions herself as a shield, her scales deflecting sizzling stray embers, protecting us.

This time, when I allow the water to fill my mouth and lungs, I'm not scared, and even though I'm prepared, it's still the same suffocating feeling that makes me want to change my mind.

Once the pain subsides, and we're safely submerged, Cleolia turns to face us. "We're safer beneath the waves, away from the Underworld's wrath." She gestured towards the mainland, away from the fiery storm above. "Eternitie or Crymzon?"

I want to answer Tenacoro, but I've seen what happened to the river leading to it. There's no way we can pass the Underworld unnoticed by water or foot.

"Eternitie," we answer in unison without looking at each other.

I remember Cyrus's words that he can never return to his home after what he has done, but we don't have another choice. This also allows him to check on Catalina to ease his mind. Besides, the Crymzon Queen will lose her mind if we show up at her doorstep again, and it's too dangerous to be that close to her again.

Yet, choosing Eternitie is equally hard. If Catalina isn't the person everyone thinks she is, Cyrus' life might be on the line. Would the new Queen punish her brother for their family members' deaths despite everything that's going on?

I guess we're about to find out.

FIFTEEN

DEVANA

As we ascend towards the surface again, guided by an unseen force and propelled by Cleolia's tail, my eyes widen when I notice it's almost nighttime. How long were we underwater?

My lungs hurt for a heartbeat as I take the cooler air in and then seize as I see the flames. Before us, nestled deep in the craggy mountains, the once majestic Eternitie is ablaze. Flames leap skyward, casting a red glow against the darkening sky.

A guttural scream tears from Cyrus' throat, his voice echoing over the waves. Cleolia, her eyes reflecting the flickering flames, turns to him with concern.

"No!" he screams, and I swiftly cover his mouth, my eyes pleading for silence as his muffled cry presses against my skin.

In the eerie half-light, we float on the surface, Cleolia's fin gently breaking the water. Cyrus' eyes remain fixed on the distant inferno, shock etched across his face. My fingers still pressed against his lips, I share a solemn gaze with Cleolia.

As night tightens its grip, the flames continue their destructive dance. We bob in the water, suspended between the depths below and the chaos above.

"There's nothing we can do," I whisper, my words lost in the gentle lapping of the waves as I release his mouth. "Listen, Cyrus, we can't help your sister."

Silence envelopes us for a moment, broken only by the crackling of distant flames. With a subtle nod, Cleolia swims towards the distant shore, her tail creating a rhythmic pulse in the water. Our gazes linger on the burning kingdom as she pulls us.

"I-I need to—" Cyrus stutters, and my heart breaks watching him sort his thoughts.

He knows. He absolutely knows that we're not strong enough against the winged woman and her dragon. If this was her doing, and by the fire it looks like it, we're no match.

"There are only two more kingdoms left on the surface," Cleolia points out as we reach the shore, and my stomach bottoms.

My heart hurts for Cyrus—it does so freaking much—but my instincts tell me to find a way home. My actual home. I never thought I would say that again.

Starstrand and Eternitie have fallen. It's easy to figure out which kingdom comes next. But everything I love besides Cyrus is in Tenacoro. My father, Erinna, and all those children I never met who are being held by the Silent Sisters.

When I look over at Cyrus, I see his red eyes. "I hate to ask this of you right now, but I need you to come with me to Tenacoro," I say carefully, pulling myself to my wobbly feet.

Cyrus faces me, but his gaze looks right through me as if I'm not there. "I can use my wings to check on her," he says, unfurling them behind him.

Cleolia studies his wings, and I can tell this is something she couldn't learn through water and blood. Cyrus' wings were a gift from the Starstrandian Queen—I wonder if she made it out of Starstrand alive.

I grab his hands, squeezing him tightly until his eyes focus on me. "We have two options," I drawl. "We can make our way to Tenacoro and hope it's still intact, or we can head to Crymzon."

I don't have to explain why I added Crymzon as an option. If we want to survive, the Crymzon Queen is our safest bet.

SIXTEEN

Queen Soulin

As I head towards the distant, cold gray mountains, the sun dips lower, casting long shadows across the red sand dunes. The wind whispers tales of the impending turmoil, and my steely gaze focuses on the ominous horizon.

With every wingbeat, my heart sinks lower. While I tell myself that the Underworld emerged with no inhabitants, my mind knows better. They have to be somewhere.

As Storm and I approach, the once-imposing gates of Eternitie come into view, now breached and battered. Smoke billows into the sky, blending with the ever-shifting hues of the setting sun. The air carries an echo of screams, the crackling of flames, and a symphony of chaos that reaches my ears even from afar.

Descending closer, my keen eyes behold the devastation below. Houses lay in ruins, their splintered remains pointing to the brutality that has swept through the once vibrant kingdom. Panic ripples through the fleeing inhabitants, their colorful attire contrasting with the gray and lifeless figures pursuing them.

I was right; they are here. Otyx sent his souls to destroy Starstrand and now Eternitie.

Guiding Storm with practiced ease, I survey the destruction from above. The kingdom's heart reveals itself as the Brass Palace, a structure made of gears and cogs, now under siege—the rhythmic clanking of machinery clashes with the dissonant sounds of battle.

Without a moment's hesitation, I direct Storm to land on the palace's rooftop. She settles, her wings folding in a display of elegance amidst the chaos. With a determined stride, I walk to the edge of the palace roof, peering through the smoke-obscured air.

The window beneath my boots offers a glimpse into the chaos that unfolds within. Gray and colorless assailants swarm the once-gilded halls, their relentless advance leaving destruction wherever they go. My jaw tightens as I witness the struggle of the palace guards valiantly defending against the dead invaders.

With a swift motion, I unclasp my whip—the cold metal reflects the fiery glow of the besieged palace. Gathering my emotions, I shatter the window with a single, resounding strike, shards of glass cascading into the tumult below.

I need to find Catalina before those souls do. Even though I don't know the God's command, whether he wants the new Queen alive or dead, I don't care. While I use my magic to dampen some emotions to keep me going, it's also working hard to keep my broken heart somehow stitched together, but it's doing a horrible job of keeping my conscience clear.

Entering the fray, I move with purpose through the labyrinthine corridors. The clash of metal against metal and the hiss of steam fill the air. Storm, stationed above, stands vigilant, ready to take flight at my command.

As I delve deeper into the palace, I encounter survivors seeking refuge. With a glance, I reassure them I'm here to help. Nevertheless, I see the fear on their faces. They know who I am and what I'm capable of.

I press forward, determined to reach the heart of the conflict—the Brass Palace's throne room.

My walk turns into a run when I realize I haven't encountered a single Underworldler. So far, I've only seen wounded servants, scared maids, and lifeless soldiers. But if they are not here to fight against the Eternians left in the halls, they've already reached their destination—*my* destination.

The destruction intensifies with every corridor. Ornate chambers lie in ruins, metallic machinery shattered, and the once-grand tapestries now fumed in the aftermath of relentless onslaught.

I burst through the open doors of the throne room, a once-majestic chamber now lying in disarray. The attackers, devoid of color and life, face off against a woman. She, undeterred, steps into the circle of gray-skinned souls, her blade dancing before her face. Each stroke is powerful and precise.

That can't be her. This woman can't be Cyrus' sister. She is gorgeous and tall; her short brown hair flies with her motions. If it weren't for the crown on her head and the royal attire covered in brass, I would have thought she was one of Eternitie's well-trained soldiers.

"Are you going to help or just stand there?" she barks at me, looking me up and down before returning to the attackers.

Excuse me?

Her ignorance and tone slap me square in the face. She must know who I am. Everyone does! Fuck, for the way she addressed me, I should just let her handle those souls by herself.

That's when a stabbing pain in my heart reminds me that the Underworld targets her because of me. She lost her brother and father because of me.

I should change my name to Male-Succession-Killer after this.

No, stay on track. I can beat her ass later, but right now, I need to get her out of here.

The attackers slowly but deliberately step forward to shrink the circle around her. I really want to see what she can do, yet I think I'll have plenty of time to watch her in action and compare her to her weak brother.

Cracking my neck, I lift my hand, the Nullstone shards of my whip sparkling in the light, right before I throw my arm back and lash it forward. I could have used my magic to free her, but I want to see if those souls react to the Nullstone like I do.

It's satisfying to feel the resistance of my whip after it ankers itself into flesh. That's why I chose this weapon. It gives me a sense of power and control no other does. And even though I can end a life in seconds by pulling it hard, snapping a neck, it also allows me to change my mind if needed. Only a little magic is required to close the wounds my sharp edges inflect.

But I'm not here today to show mercy.

The man who currently wears my whip like sparkling jewels around his neck lets out a gut-wrenching scream. I wait a second to determine if his reaction is surprise or pain. That's when I hear the sizzling sound the Nullstone makes at skin contact. Before he can reach the whip with his hands, I jolt the handle back, and a grin forms on my lips when I hear the snap and the attacker crumbles to the ground.

One down, five more to go.

As the attacker hits the ground, the others jump into action. Within a blink of an eye, my whip finds a new target while I use my other hand to blast magic at the remaining four.

I already gathered what I needed to know. Not only does Otyx react to the Nullstone, but so do his creations. That will make things easier.

"What is that?" Catalina asks, her chest heaving as she points at my weapon.

"You must have the biggest balls in the Matrus family if you think addressing a Queen like that is acceptable," I answer, studying my whip. Small pieces of dried skin cling to it like dead leaves to a tree.

"The same goes to you. By the way, I know who you are, but that doesn't mean I respect you," Catalina snarls, squaring her shoulders.

"That goes both ways," I smile, curling my whip carefully around the long glove.

"Then what are you doing here?"

"Let's say I owe someone a favor," I say, turning to the doors. Outside, I can hear footsteps—a lot of them.

She shakes her head. "Who has so much power over you?"

That's the same damn question I've been asking myself. Am I doing this for Cyrus or because I want to do the right thing for once?

"Can you just come with me?" I ask, throwing my hands in the air.

"And go where?"

"Enough with the questions," I snap, unfurling my hand to redirect my magic at her. Instantly, Catalina goes stiff. "I didn't want to do this, but you're not giving me another choice."

I feel her strength as she tries to break through my magic, but when I tighten my grip around the invisible hold I have on her, she finally caves.

My eyes dart to the corridor I used to enter the throne room. I see the billows of smoke rising through a broken window and the unsettling dance of flames against the darkening sky. Houses lay in ruins, their former inhabitants fleeing from figures draped in gray.

As I walk to the door, Catalina trails me unwillingly. My exit gets cut off by more incoming Underworldlers as they stream into the room like roaches, finding a crack in a foundation. Handling six wasn't a problem, but as the number rises to over three dozen, my heart hammers in my chest.

There's no way I can secure Catalina and fight my way out of here simultaneously. I need to let her go.

Catalina gasps as I release her, channeling all my magic into holding the souls back.

"Is there another way out of here?" I ask, holding both arms out.

Her eyes flicker. "Of course not."

I know she's lying, but I don't have the time to force the truth out of her. If she doesn't want to tell me, well, then we will do this my way.

"I can't hold them any longer," I say through clenched teeth, my arms shaking.

"I'm not leaving," she says, widening her stance to take on the new wave of Underworldlers.

"For fuck's sake. You're even prouder than your brother," I groan, inhaling sharply to dip into more magic.

Catalina lowers her swords and stares at me, and her reaction relieves me. She's not only beautiful and deadly, she's also intelligent.

"You know Cyrus? Is he really alive?"

Ah, there it is. It didn't take her long to realize that I didn't mean Cyprian. How could I? If she's this smart to put one and one together, it must be because, just like me, she had been lurking in the shadows long enough to know exactly what her father and Cyprian were up to.

"Yes. But I would appreciate it if we could have this conversation elsewhere."

"Please don't tell me you bonded with my baby brother," Catalina says, making a gagging noise.

What is it with this family? That's where her head goes. Not how he's doing or why he pretended to be dead?

Well, under deeper consideration, she isn't wrong. If Cyrus chooses Devana, and Devana is connected to me, isn't that a connection?

I need to stop drifting away from what's important.

Slowly, I take a step back, then another, without breaking the barrier between the Underworldlers and us. With every retreating footfall, I back Catalina closer to a window behind us.

She's going to really hate me after this one.

"Cover your face," I say the moment I drop the barrier, grab my whip, and aim for the glass behind her. The window explodes, sending glass in every direction right before I ram my shoulder into Catalina to push her out the window.

She's surprisingly calm for being shoved out a window. I expected a scream or erratic hand movements, but nothing seems to break her iron will. I whistle as I dive after her, my eyes solely on the falling Queen. With the twist of my finger, I force air to rise from the ground, slowing our fall until I hear Storm's familiar wing flaps.

SEVENTEEN

Avira

My wings are outstretched as I soar through the sky astride Emberix. Our trip takes us over undulating dunes until the distinct circular silhouette of the walled kingdom emerges on the horizon.

I chuckle when I see the Crymzon Wall come into view. While living in Starstrand, I always wondered what the purpose of enclosing Crymzon was supposed to accomplish. Every Starstrandian can easily fly over the barrier, most animals from Tenacoro can climb it, and I'm sure there are enough devices Eternitie can use to get through it.

They have magic. Isn't that enough to keep them safe? Why rely on something so colossal and ugly?

Emberix's scales shimmer in the starlight as we approach Crymzon, its walls carved meticulously from red sandstone, forming an absurd panorama in the desert. Another question I asked myself: why red? Why does everything have to be red in this part of Escela? The houses, the streets, the palace, even their uniforms.

It reminds me of the drop of blood I used to strengthen Otyx and the color of the sin I thought I belonged to—lust.

Together, we circle the kingdom. As far as I remember, Crymzon comes alive at night. They feast, run their errands, and pleasure themselves all night until the sky changes its colors.

Yet below me, there's no one. There is no market, no lights, and not a single soul.

Good, they know I'm coming; I think to myself as I sign my dragon to bring us down.

As we near the Crymzon Palace, Emberix dives, her wings creating a gust of wind that stirs the fine red sand below until her talons drill into the soft sandstone steps. My red golden gown billows as I land and stride confidently towards the entrance door, the echo of my footsteps blending with the distant howl of the wind. Emberix, having completed her task, rumbles contentedly, standing guard near the entrance.

The doors are wide open, inviting, and mysterious.

I was surprised to find my mother, Queen Caecilia, alone. None of her soldiers came to intercept me after I burned the initial wave. I thought they were afraid because they'd never seen a dragon, but now, I'm unsure. Letting me arrive in an empty kingdom seems to be a drill I didn't know about. Is this their way of protecting their subjects, or are they just cowards?

It doesn't matter. Their subjects mean nothing to me besides if they step in my way.

Grinning, I stroll to the entrance door. As I prepare to cross the threshold, an invisible barrier halts me. It's like an invisible force field has materialized, preventing me from entering.

Anger forces its way through my body as I reach out tentatively, my hand encountering an unseen resistance. A ripple of energy emanates from the barrier, and I withdraw, pondering the nature of this unyielding obstruction.

It's obviously magic, yet it feels more potent than anything I've felt when I visited Crymzon in my former life. Whatever this is, it feels ancient and warm.

Undeterred, I take a step back, assessing the situation. The palace, with its red sandstone, looms before me, a silent sentinel guarding its secrets.

As I stand there, a figure emerges from the shadows within the palace—a guardian adorned in regal red attire with eyes that hold the wisdom of ages. The guardian's voice echoes through the air.

"The threshold is a boundary between worlds, woven with the threads of time and magic," he intones. "Only those who prove their worth may cross into the heart of Crymzon."

Determination ignites in my muscles as I accept the challenge presented by him.

"So you're telling me I'm not worthy?" I say, clicking my tongue. "Do you know who I am?"

The man finally steps into the starlight just inches away from me. "I know exactly who you are, Avira. That's why I'm telling you to turn around, climb that dragon, and take the God's hand."

The wrinkles on his forehead, around his eyes, and mouth are deep. Is he one of the souls that forced Otyx to even the scales? He looks like he's supposed to be dead already, yet he stands here, crossing his arms.

"And who are you?" I ask, trying to mask the confusion clouding my mind. I've never seen this man before. Or maybe I did, and I don't remember.

"A friend who's trying to help you," he says, pressing his hand against the barrier. "You've made your mark. What your mother did to you was beyond malicious, but she paid for her actions. You've accomplished what you came for, and now it's time to turn your back on everyone who wronged you and start a new life. Because that's what you have: a second chance to live. Don't take it lightly."

With every sentence, my heart hardens. He's right, I accomplished that. I got rid of my mother. But now what? He wants me to ignore the fact that his Queen tried to kill my God? He expects me to turn around and pretend like it never happened? Where are the consequences of her actions?

"I can't do that," I grin, hammering my fist against the barrier that sends magical sparks through it. "Break the barrier," I say to Emberix, stepping aside.

The man doesn't flinch when Emberix releases a hot tornado of flames right at him. He just stands there, watching me through the fire hitting the magical wall, flames bouncing off it like rain rolling over a feather.

"You can end this," he says as Emberix lowers her head when she realizes she won't be able to break through. "Leave while you can."

Who is he? How is he strong enough to shield the entire palace from a dragon's flame?

"That's not possible. A passant shouldn't be strong enough to withstand a God's power."

Perhaps I'm reading too much into it. This is probably the Queen's doing. Only she can be powerful enough as she's directly linked to her Goddess, Lunra.

"I don't see no God," Conrad says, looking over my shoulder. "I only see a woman and her pet. So, take this as my last warning: Please do us all a favor and leave."

And go where? There's still Tenacoro, Eternitie, and Oceris, but they did nothing to deserve my wrath—no, this is between the Crymzon Queen and me.

"I'll go because, eventually, she *will* seek me out. I have something that belongs to her," I smile, waving my hand to tell him I won't listen to whatever he plans to say next.

Fine. If she's playing hard to get, I have to bring her to me. And what better leverage could I use than her recently deceased lover?

EIGHTEEN

Queen Soulin

"Put me down," Catalina yells into my ear as Storm carries us away from Eternitie. "I need to help my people!"

I knew this wouldn't be a fun ride. After all, I pushed her out a window without including her in my plan. I thought the free fall would lure any emotions out of her—it didn't—so it surprised me when her eyes widened when Storm appeared beneath her. Can people fear moths? It could have been Storm's size, but everyone in Escela should know about my Fighter Moths by now.

"And what are you going to do? Slice their throats one soul at a time? You know they're already dead, right?" I snarl, turning around to pull her closer, but she scooches even further away, her hands death-gripping Storm's fine hair. "It would be easier if you held onto me."

She flashes her teeth. "I would rather—"

With the click of my heels, Storm flips to the side, and a broad grin forms on my face when Catalina slips off her back.

I shouldn't be messing with her, but I need her to trust me. Maybe this isn't the best approach to get her to like me, but at least it will ensure

90

she'll hold on to me during the flight in case we're attacked, and I need to rely on Storm's maneuvers to get us to safety.

Storm immediately dives after her, and when Catalina's nails dig into my shoulders as she lands behind me again, I feel better.

"I fucking hate you," Catalina mutters, wrapping her arms around my waist to hold on.

I shrug. "I get that a lot."

"That's nothing to be proud of."

"On the contrary. Hate gives you power. Every emotion you have towards another person gives them power over you."

Silence. Good.

"We got off on the wrong foot," Catalina says after a few seconds, as if she had to digest my words first. "I appreciate you coming to my help, but I can't abandon my people. They need me."

"Alive."

"What?"

"They need *you* alive. Your brother is a horrible candidate for the throne."

"Don't talk about him like you know him."

"I wish I didn't," I answer, shrugging.

That's not true. Because of him, I learned what my biggest weakness is—Devana. Correction: Devana isn't my biggest weakness; I know it's Khaos, but she's the key to my ruin. There's still a chance that if she dies, so will I, which reminds me...

Closing my eyes, I reach out to her through my mind. The oppressing weight around her has lifted, and I can smell salty air and hear the crackling noise of fire.

For Lunra's sake. Is she in Starstrand? I told her to get as far away from people as possible, and she ventured to Starstrand?

My eyes dart to the kingdom in the sky, which usually shines like a second moon under the starlight. But tonight, it's different. The typically bright white clouds are dull—luckily not on fire anymore—but so dull they look almost gray.

Catalina must have followed my gaze. "What happened to Starstrand?"

"All I know is that it's not burning anymore," I answer, my eyes fixated on it.

"Burning?"

"You think you're the only one under attack?"

Another few seconds of silence follow.

If Starstrand isn't in flames, that can only mean that Devana is close to…Eternitie.

Did I just leave her behind? Is she safe?

"Where are you taking me?" Catalina asks, looking over her shoulder back at her home.

I should turn around and find out where Devana is instead of risking my life for someone who isn't even important to me.

That's until I feel Cyrus is still close to her. He might not know it, but I know he would protect Devana with his life, so I will do the same—well, kind of; I wouldn't die for Catalina—nevertheless, I will keep his sister safe.

"Once we reach Tenacoro, I will send as many of my moths to retrieve your subjects as possible," I say, finally breaking my gaze away from Starstrand.

I guess my second attempt to win her over is better than my first. Yet, I leave the part out that this is more a calculated move than generosity.

From what I saw, Otyx has gathered enough souls to overrun an entire kingdom—two kingdoms—within the same day. Currently, I only have Tenacoro and my army at my disposal. Hopefully, Opaline could reach

Oceris and maybe even Starstrand before the attack to convince them to join us.

Yet, I can't rely on her. This leads me to believe I must recruit more able bodies for what's coming.

Catalina shifts behind me. "What's in it for you?"

Instinctively, I want to use my darkest humor again to ruffle her feathers, but when I think about the war ahead of us and the pain throbbing in my heart, I can't pretend any longer.

"He took my King from me," I say through the ache pulsating through my chest.

Catalina's speechlessness makes it easier to shed a silent tear before biting my lip and using my magic to dull the pain. It's not enough to make it disappear yet, just enough to fade it into the background.

She probably didn't know I'd chosen my Soulmate, but now she does.

Under the moonlit canopy of Tenacoro's forest, Storm's wings cast dark shadows on the dense foliage below. The night air hums with the ominous stillness of the unknown, broken only by the rustle of leaves and the soft fluttering of her wings.

As we land, a sea of wary eyes glow in the darkness, spears, and arrows pointed menacingly in our direction. Tension hangs in the air like a thick mist as I dismount gracefully, my eyes keenly scanning the surroundings as I hear Catalina dropping to the ground behind me.

Just when the tension reaches its zenith, a figure emerges from the shadows—a regal ebony woman adorned in woven vines and leaves. Her eyes are as deep and mysterious as the night itself bore into us. With a commanding presence, she steps forward, parting the foliage like a queen approaching her throne.

"Hold!" she exclaims in a voice that vibrates through the stillness, and the warriors reluctantly lower their weapons.

The woman, radiant against the moonlight, regards us with her warm voice. "I have been expecting you," she declares, her words carrying a weight reverberating through the jungle.

"We come in peace," Catalina says beside me, lowering her head.

Is she kidding me? She bows before Tenacoro's Queen but not before me?

Queen Synadena studies her momentarily before she signals her warriors with a subtle nod to stand down. The rhythmic sounds of retracting arrows and sheathed spears fill my ears, and an uneasy calm settles over the clearing.

"This one never comes in peace," Queen Synadena says, walking in my direction. I see Catalina strengthen the grip of the hilts of her swords. "Especially after she ordered my daughter to do her dirty work."

It's good to know that the new Queen hasn't yet met the oldest royal ruling over a kingdom in Escela. If Catalina had known her, she would have known that Queen Synadena is the lowest threat of all rulers.

"That makes us even considering you raided my prison during the last war," I say, watching a smile form on her lips. "I hope you found what you were looking for."

Tenacoro's Queen stops right before me. "More than that. I always suspected, but now I know." Her words are neither a threat nor enough to let Catalina know my secret.

While Queen Synadena could free some of my prisoners, she must have noticed that more than half of the cells were empty. Every other person would think the worst, but she knows me too well. She might not be aware of the tunnels beneath the prison to keep my people safe and the Ordinaries I captured before King Keres could reach them, but she must suspect I didn't kill them.

Queen Synadena's face crumbles as she leans in to press her forehead against mine. "I'm sorry for your loss."

My heart tears apart again as her words remind me of what I've lost. For brief moments in between, I forget what happened. Now that the memory comes back, I feel like a traitor. There's no way he's already in the back of my mind when he should be my only thought.

Catalina moves nervously beside us. "I don't think we have been introduced," she says, breaking our moment. "I'm Catalina Matrus, Queen of Eternitie."

Or at least what's left of it, I think to myself, not finding the strength to word it aloud.

"I know who you are, my child," Synadena says, releasing me to turn to her. "You're the shadow of Eternitie, the rightful heir your people have been waiting for."

"Shadow of Eternitie?" she asks, drawing her brows together.

"While King Citeus favored his boy and spent every breathing second teaching him to run a kingdom, you were quietly watching in the background," she answers, and Catalina stiffens. "I noticed your presence during our last meeting in Eternitie. Always there, but never seen. You're smart, and you'll make a fine Queen."

I don't know how she does it. Not only is Synadena aware of everything that's going on, but she also delivers vital information so subtle, as if it's common knowledge.

"How bad is it?" Queen Synadena asks, looking toward the kingdom we just came from.

"Terrible," I say, watching Catalina's facial expression harden. "From what I've gathered, Starstrand has fallen, and I arrived just in time to retrieve her before Eternitie did the same," I say, nodding at Catalina. "Any news about Oceris?"

She shakes her head. "Opaline should be back soon. But your army arrived not too long ago. You want to let us know what your plan is?"

"I'd rather show you," I answer, gesturing to Synadena with my hand that I will follow her if she leads the way.

NINETEEN

DEVANA

Cyrus is beside himself, his body sluggish as I try to lift him to his feet. Finding purchase in the wet sand doesn't help my effort to get him away from seeing his home in flames. Occasionally, the wind carries screams from the mountain range, and I'm trying not to think those are the last sounds of his people being burned alive.

There has to be something I can do to help. But whom am I kidding? I don't have magic, and I don't have any other abilities that could grant me the power to extinguish the inferno.

"Please help me," I beg Cleolia, but when I glimpse at her rounded belly again, I shake my head. "You've done enough. Thank you for bringing us here."

But now what? Eternitie isn't an option anymore, and it's ludicrous to think we can make our way to Tenacoro on foot, passing between the fallen kingdom and the Underworld. First, we don't have any supplies to support us on the journey; second, I don't know where Otyx's souls are.

If they're on their way back to the Underworld, we could end up crossing their path.

And worst-case scenario—I look at the fire erupting in the mountains—Cyrus isn't just a runaway anymore. If his sister didn't get out of Eternitie in time, I'm holding onto the heir of the Brass Throne. If Catalina is dead, he's the last remaining Matrus to carry Eternitie's crown.

"Are you sure you're fine?" Cleolia asks, her tail splashing in the waves. "I can help you. It just takes me a little longer to transform."

And there's that. Transforming from tail to legs isn't as easy as most people believe. It takes quite some energy to change half of their shape. And in her condition, it requires way more of her power to keep her unborn safe.

"I'll find a way to help King Usiel. You kept your promise, and I'll do anything to keep mine," I answer, kneeling beside Cyrus, whose muffled cries escape through his fingers.

What am I supposed to do? Cleolia must know I'm lying, yet she closes her eyes and includes us in her prayer to Aqion, God of Strength and Oceris. I should join her and raise my voice to Emara, Goddess of Vitality and Tenacoro, but I haven't addressed her in years because when my father left our kingdom behind, we became godless—or at least that's what it felt like.

Before I can thank Queen Cleolia again, she's already gone.

"Cyrus, I need you to pull yourself together and listen," I say, grabbing his cheeks to lift his face. "Your sister could still be alive. She's smart, right? Until we have proof, I need you to push those feelings down."

His eyes are blotchy. "I can't lose her."

"Gods be damned. I don't want to lie to you, making you believe everything is fine, but even if she's dead, it won't change our situation." My words are way harsher than I intended, but I had to say them. "Look at me. Deep down, I pray that she's alive and well, but if she's not, your entire kingdom needs *you.*"

I watch the wheels turn in his head, and they eventually click into place. He knows what I'm referring to.

"It's too much," he whispers, wiggling out of my grip.

Anger slowly rises inside me. I've tried it the nice and understanding way, but we're at war, and if he doesn't get to his feet soon, we could lose everything.

"Pull your head out of your ass and be a leader," I bark, grabbing him by his shoulders to pull him up. "Until we don't know for certain, I need you to think of our future to push the pain down."

Cyrus' eyes widen as he levels up to me and straightens his shoulders. His facial expression sends a stabbing pain into my heart, but he had to hear it. This isn't about just us anymore.

"I can't carry us both," he says, looking over his shoulders as if his cloud wings are visible just to his eyes. "So, our safest bet is Tenacoro."

The pressure on my chest eases when he makes the decision I've been dreading. We both know returning to Crymzon would be the wisest choice, but my heart longs to check on my father and Erinna.

Still, on foot, we might not reach either kingdom in time, and both ways lead past the Underworld.

"I'm scared," I admit. "I don't want to die."

Years and years of training through pain finally take its toll. I've always had a goal. I was trained as an assassin. Every day I woke up imagining piercing the Crymzon Queen's brain with an arrow. But now, knowing if she dies, I might do the same, and with everything we know being ripped from us, I have nothing to concentrate on.

I know I told Cyrus to think of our future, but what does it look like? How can we survive a God?

Cyrus closes the distance between us, hugging me tightly. "I won't let anything happen to you," he says, brushing a strain of hair from my face. "You know what I imagined when you said *our future*? You. It wasn't a throne, a crown, or a place. It's you. Wherever you are, I want to be. And if this is our last day, we'll go together."

As corny as it sounds, I believe him. It's also all I needed to hear to regain my inner strength.

Under the moonlit canvas of the night sky, the sandy beach stretches out like a silver ribbon kissed by the gentle lapping of the tide. My clothes cling to me like a second skin as we stand at the water's edge. My lungs fill with the tang of salt and smoke, and the air is charged with the distant murmur of the waves. The night seems to grow darker, amplifying the red and orange flickers in the mountain.

Now that we have picked our destination, how are we supposed to get there?

Just as uncertainty casts its shadow upon my face, a subtle sound of rustling feathers graces the air. I turn my gaze upward. The night sky, adorned with shimmering stars, holds a secret Cyrus must not have heard yet—my Glimmarum spiraling down towards us.

His eyes widen as my griffin, her majestic wings slicing through the air, descends. Moonlight dances upon her feathers, and with a soft thud, Erinna lands before us.

My heart pounds with relief and gratitude as I approach the magnificent creature. I gently run my fingers through her feathers, a silent exchange of understanding passing between us.

Cyrus exhales. "How did she find us?"

With my eyes fixed on Erinna, I reply, "Our bond transcends the physical. She heard my silent call through the night."

As if affirming my words, my griffin nuzzles against me, and a glimmer of hope rekindles inside me.

With determination, I turn to Cyrus, "She can carry both of us."

"I can fly, remember?"

Right. It was never about how Cyrus would get to another kingdom. This entire time, he held back because of me. He could have already been halfway to Eternitie to check on his sister if it hadn't been for me.

As if he can read my mind, his eyes wander to his home, the crease between his eyebrows deepening. "If we want to take the night to our advantage, we need to go now," he says, swallowing a lump in his throat before turning back to me.

"Are you sure?"

"As you said, my sister is smart."

Wings unfold behind him, and I take his action as a sign that he's ready. Effortlessly, I climb onto Erinna's back and grab a fistful of hair and feathers to lock me in place. The beach below fades into obscurity as she catapults us into the night sky.

"Can you fly above the clouds?" I ask, watching Cyrus keep up with us.

"We're about to find out," he answers, ascending even higher.

I know the darkness surrounding us should be sufficient to keep us safe from prying eyes, but staying above the clouds is safer until Eternitie and the Underworld lay behind us, not only because of Otyx but also because of how Cyrus keeps looking at his kingdom. Just one millisecond will be enough to make him change his mind, and I can't have him enter a blazing graveyard.

TWENTY

Avira

I ride with flowing hair atop Emberix, her scales reflecting the muted glow of distant stars. The night envelopes us as we soar through the obsidian sky, the beating of her wings resonating in the quiet emptiness as I guide her toward the heart of Shadowmyre.

As we approach, the silhouettes of the palaces emerge, their walls crafted from black rock that absorbs the scant moonlight. I steer Emberix towards the biggest palace in the center.

The ground trembles slightly as the dragon lands, her colossal wings folding against her powerful form.

Silhouetted against the palace walls, a smaller dragon, also dark as the abyss, awaits our arrival. His eyes widen in disbelief at the sight of us, and he bows deeply, acknowledging the formidable creature in submission.

I dismount, letting my fingers run over her scales before she moves away without even batting an eye at Mordecai, who's still frozen. After Emberix is out of reach, he raises his head, his eyes meeting mine with a mix of anger and surprise.

"What have you done?" Mordecai asks, jumping down the palace's steps.

"You're free. That's what you wanted."

"It was, but not like this," he says, looking around.

I roll my eyes as I push past him. "I'm sorry my fulfilled promise doesn't meet your standards."

"Did *you* bring her back?" Mordecai asks, looking after Emberix disappearing behind the palace's wall.

"A simple *thank you* would be enough."

His head whips back to me. "I don't know what's going on anymore. What happened to you after the Nekro-Ball? You were so eager to leave, and then suddenly, I was sent back to the Darklands right before the ground started shaking."

I'm not here for small-talk. I've fulfilled my bargain and released him and his family by bringing the Underworld to the surface. They're free to go wherever they please, and he has the guts to question me.

"Stop when I'm talking to you, mortal," he snarls, and when I turn around, he takes a step back. "Your eyes—they are black. You—"

"I pledged my soul to Otyx," I say, and the feeling of his power surges through me. "The Avira you know doesn't exist anymore."

He studies me momentarily before scratching his talons over the stones beneath him. "We'll see about that," he murmurs, his eyes resting on me patiently.

I clench my teeth. "You're free. Just go."

"I don't even know what freedom is anymore," he says, his nostrils flaring.

That's when I put it all together. "You can't leave, can you?" I ask.

A smoke cloud escapes his nostril. "I could, but why should I? You're back, and you're mine."

My heart gets overrun by emotions as the realization hits me. I might have set his family free, but as long as I live, he'll be bonded to me—Otyx made sure of that.

While I dearly enjoyed Mordecai's company during Nekrojudex, his demeanor is too mellow for what I've planned. Emberix doesn't care if I live or die. She only cares about repaying the debt she owes me for resurrecting her.

Mordecai, on the other hand, will do everything possible to protect me.

"Your services are no longer needed," I say, walking toward the entrance. "I'll speak to Otyx to release you from our bond."

"That's impossible," he snarls, coming up beside me.

If I know something for sure, it's that nothing is impossible. I'm a mortal who lived in a kingdom filled with immortal, doomed souls. I regained my wings and am now tied to a God's powers. And there's the time I resurrected a dragon with my bare hands. Yes, *my* hands.

Keeping my head high, I keep marching. The palace looms before me, a reminder of the God's power. Yet, as I stride towards the stairs, I notice the eerily quiet streets, an unsettling emptiness permeating the air. Curious, I turn fully around. The usually bustling kingdom lacks life, and an ominous stillness hangs like a shroud over Shadowmyre.

Something isn't right. I haven't seen another soul or Otyx since I got here.

My steps echo through the deserted streets as I climb the steps. The glow of torches flickers, casting elongated shadows on the empty buildings in the distance.

I know he's here. I can feel him. But somehow, the soul count has decreased.

Inside, the throne room awaits me, its towering pillars and darkened tapestries creating an aura of solemnity. I ascend the dais, Mordecai following in silence. Seated upon the dark throne, I survey the vast hall that holds so many memories. My first dance with Netherius; Otyx warning just before my last trial; me reaching out my hand to request a dance with the God; the offering of my blood; Khaos.

He's the real reason I came back.

"Where is everyone?" I whisper, my voice carrying through the emptiness.

Mordecai, now perched beside me, growls as his eyes scan the vacant hall.

"Once they realized they were free to leave Shadowmyre, they spread out like roaches. Some fueled by the sins, others out of sheer desire to create havoc," he says, blowing out small smoke clouds.

"And my prisoner?"

"He's right where you left him, yet I'm not sure if he's your captive, or rather a prisoner inside his own head."

I rise off the throne. "What is *that* supposed to mean?"

"See for yourself," Mordecai huffs, curling into a ball. "He must be the most tortured soul I've ever encountered."

Alarmed, I break through the doors, my feet hitting the ground so hard that my teeth click with each step.

He's all I have to lure the Crymzon Queen out of her palace. If something is wrong with him, my plan won't work.

TWENTY-ONE

DEVANA

Above the clouds, I watch the sun slowly touch the horizon before us, guiding me home—a home I haven't set foot in since I was a little child.

The air is thick with the heady fragrance of exotic blossoms and the distant hum of unseen creatures as we break through the tree line. In the heart of the dense jungle, sunlight filters through the thick canopy, casting dappled patterns on us.

Erinna's talons find purchase in the lush clearing, where memories of my childhood stir like leaves in the wind. As I slide off her back, my eyes widen as memories flood my consciousness. My stomach tightens as my feet touch the soft ground. I walk over and trace the contours of a towering tree that might have witnessed my childhood escapades, and the earth beneath my feet seems to echo the laughter of my youth.

I remember little of my time here, but I can feel it.

Cyrus must sense the weight of my emotions because he comes over and lightly touches my shoulder. It's an insignificant gesture, but feeling his warmth through my clothes helps reel my mind back in.

If it weren't for him, I would go down the memory path—hard. But instead of teasing myself with how I would have turned out if I had stayed in Tenacoro, I retract my hand and turn to him.

That's when I notice the crowd of warriors materializing from the surrounding greenery, their eyes sharp and vigilant. Markings adorn their bodies, and my heart sinks even further when I realize I don't know what they mean. I should; this is my kingdom, but my father never mentioned them.

Exhaling, I survey the faces before me. There's a mix of surprise and curiosity in the warriors' eyes, as if they recognize me and yet can't pinpoint who I am. Cyrus stands by my side, his presence adding an air of the path I chose instead of the one chosen for me.

Amidst the warriors, the vibrant hues of the jungle come alive as various creatures, known and unknown to me, emerge from the shadows of the leaves. Green parrots with iridescent feathers observe from above, and mischievous monkeys swing from branch to branch above with glowing eyeballs that track us in the shadows. I feel a surge of connection with the surrounding wild, as if the very essence of Tenacoro recognizes m e.

Amid the bustling scene, I raise my hand, and the warriors fall into a respectful hush. I turn to Erinna. "I'll let you know when I need you," I say to her, lifting my head to signal her to give us some space, not because I don't want her here, but in case I need an escape plan.

"I'm here to speak to Queen Synadena," I say, my voice cutting through the air. The request lingers, carried by the wind through the ancient trees.

As anticipation settles in the clearing, a path forms through the crowd, and a regal figure emerges—a woman clad in vines and leaves, a living embodiment of the jungle's grace.

She aims straight for me.

"I was wondering when you would arrive," Queen Synadena says, a warm smile curving her lips. "But I wish it was under different circumstances."

"We didn't know where else to go," I say, looking over my shoulder to ensure Cyrus is still behind me.

"You've come to the right place," she says, slowly spinning on her heels. "Come, come. Your father will be delighted to see you."

I knew he was alive the second Erinna found me at the beach. Yet, hearing it from someone else's lips is freeing.

"We have much to discuss," Queen Synadena says, waving one hand, and the warriors encircling us scatter.

I almost trip over my own feet as I hurry after her. "Can I see him first?" I ask, stopping to grab Cyrus' hand to drag him after me.

"After the meeting," she says as we pass a blue lagoon to our right. Without even setting foot into the water, I can feel the warmth on my skin as if the liquid is enclosing me.

"What meeting?" Cyrus asks, speaking up for the first time. "Your Majesty," he adds quickly, lowering his head.

"There's no need for formalities," the Queen says, looking over her shoulder at us. "We're all equals in this war."

War.

That's exactly what's happening, but I haven't had the guts to say it. The Underworld declared war on the living. But why? Why now?

"I've seen nothing like this in my lifetime, which means a lot if you consider my age. Two kingdoms cannot aid our counterattack against Otyx. We're still waiting to hear from King Usiel while Crymzon sets up camp around the Vine Palace."

My mouth goes dry. Soulin is here?

"We have word from Oceris," Cyrus cuts in when I open my mouth to ask about the Crymzon Queen.

If she's here and she finds out that we've ignored her warning to stay away from other individuals, she's going to be pissed. But what did she expect us to do? When she announced her conditions in return for my father, we weren't under attack. And isn't it safer for me to be close to her? With her magic, she can protect me and, with that, herself.

"Excellent," Queen Synadena says, coming to an abrupt halt. "But before we get to that, there's one more thing."

"Cyrus?" Jealousy instantly bubbles inside me when I hear the strong female voice saying his name. Who dares to address him by his first name?

Cyrus drops my hand and steps beside me, his eyes wide and chest heaving. "Yes?"

Oh Gods. It can't be.

Before I can see the woman who addressed him, I jump to the side as a long arm swings in my direction, almost hitting me square in the face. The loud thud of a body meeting another echoes in my ears as my feet struggle to find purchase.

I'm not fast enough to lift my gaze to see her, but without looking, I know that the next noise is her flat hand connecting with Cyrus' face. "How fucking dare you pretend to be dead? You left me to the wolves," she barks before jumping forward again to wrap him in her arms. "I can't believe you're alive."

Damn. That was one powerful smack.

Cyrus rubs his cheek with his left hand over her shoulder as he slumps down to embrace her. "And I thought I would never see you again. I saw Eternitie. How did you get out?"

Catalina pulls away to study him. "The wretched Queen kidnapped me."

That's rude. Why would she insult Tenacoro's Queen like that?

My eyes wander to Synadena, who presses her lips together and shakes her head.

If it wasn't her, who—

"Queen Soulin," Catalina adds as if it were obvious.

An uncontrollable laugh escapes my throat, and that's when her eyes dart at me. "Who are *you*?"

Instantly, my laughter dies as Cyrus quickly walks over, grabbing my hand again. "This is Devana."

Catalina's eyes move over my face and dirty clothes to our intertwined fingers. "Why is she laughing?"

Ok, that's rude. Why is she addressing him and not me?

"I'm right here," I say, holding her gaze. "I'm laughing because you must be mistaken. There's no way *she* saved you."

"Why's that?" another voice asks, and when I hear the biting undertone, sweat immediately forms on my skin. Her red wavy hair bounces with each step as Queen Soulin steps beside Catalina.

Cyrus' nails bite into my skin when he sees her. This isn't a dream or a mirage. There, right in front of us in a red dress—no, that isn't one of her signature thin and flowy dresses—in a red one piece with a long sleeve shirt attached to pants, is the woman I shouldn't be anywhere near.

"Cut her some slack, Soulin," another female chimes in, and my muscles tense even further when I see a junior version of Tenacoro's Queen step through bushes in our direction, "you can be a real pain in the ass."

Oh, fuck. What have we gotten ourselves into? It's not surprising that the royals know each other, but the way Tenacoro's Princess roasted Queen Soulin on such a personal level shows me they're more familiar with each other than I thought.

"What are you doing here?" Queen Soulin hisses, ignoring the Princess. "What part of *stay away from other people* didn't you understand?"

I feel her eyes drill into me like arrows. "I didn't know where else to go. If you haven't noticed, there isn't much hiding ground out there anymore."

She clicks her tongue as she contemplates my words. Oh, she knows; she has seen what's going on out there.

The Princess shoots forward, stepping between us. "I don't think we have been introduced yet. I'm Opaline Roja, Princess of Tenacoro."

I bow before her, thankful for her intervention. "I know who you are. It's a pleasure to meet you."

"I'm glad you finally came home," she says, and I freeze mid-motion. "We can use a capable warrior like you."

Come home? Is that what she thinks? I mean, it's probably easy to guess that I'm a Tenacorian. Still, does she know my story? Did Queen Synadena tell her I'm a runaway?

"Let's talk inside," Queen Synadena says, breaking the unbearable silence that followed her daughter's words. "They're waiting for us."

"Who are *they*?" Cyrus asks, breathless as if he just ran.

Queen Synadena smiles at him, Catalina, and then me. "The emergency council. We need all hands on deck."

What does she mean by *all hands*?

This isn't good. Being invited to the emergency council is the opposite of keeping a low profile. Queen Soulin must think the same because she stares at me, shakes her head, and presses her lips together.

Queen Synadena might not know it yet, but the Crymzon Queen will do anything to get me out of the meeting before it starts. I can feel it by the way she looks at me.

TWENTY-TWO

QUEEN SOULIN

I should have imprisoned her when I had the chance. There's no way
I wasn't clear with my instructions when I pressed my fingers against
her throat, marking her with my magic. When I squeezed, I could feel
invisible fingers around my throat as well, but my magic was more potent
than any pain.

That's a lie...magic is stronger than *most* pain. The stabbing in my
heart and the nausea that rolls over me every time I think of Khaos
reminds me that magic is strong but not all-powerful.

The air is thick with the scent of damp earth as she falls into step beside
me. Vines hang like nature's tapestries, intertwining with colossal trees
that reach toward the sky, creating a natural sun shade. I push through
the underbrush, my steps accompanied by the rustling of leaves and the
crunching of fallen twigs beneath my feet.

"Nice collar," I say, bumping my shoulder into Devana as we fall in
line behind Queen Synadena.

While Cyrus wears his crescent moon on the back of his hand without concealing it, I couldn't help but notice the thick metal around her neck to cover my fingerprints up.

"Leave her alone," Cyrus presses out through clenched teeth, looking past her at me. "You've done enough."

"That's a very interesting way of thanking me for saving your sister," I reply, smiling back at him.

"What was in it for you?" Devana asks, staring me down.

A clean conscience? Returning a favor for keeping Devana safe? Maybe even trying to convince myself that I'm not a bad person after all?

All those are true, but I still can't say it out loud. Being the bad guy—or rather girl—has kept me alive. No one fucks with a narcissistic, magic-wielding, cruel tyrant.

"I couldn't stand the thought of *you* leading an entire kingdom," I say, looking at Cyrus. "Let's be real. You're not made for a throne."

After meeting his sister, I know it's the truth. She's swift with a blade, and quite clever. Those are characteristics and nothing she could have picked up within the year he was gone, so he must know precisely what I'm referring to.

"You're unbelievable," Devana snarls back, patting Cyrus on his shoulder.

Maybe I am, but it doesn't change the fact that I've done something out of my character, and they know it.

Our group trudges through the thick, humid air, following Opaline, who hacks her way through tangled vines and foliage. The vibrant hues of the exotic flora create a lush and mysterious canopy overhead, dappling the sunlight that filters through. The atmosphere buzzes with the symphony of unseen creatures, their calls echoing through the labyrinthine greenery.

As we press on, the distant murmur of flowing water reaches my ears. I know that sound.

My anticipation heightens with every step until we emerge into a clearing, where the jungle abruptly gives way to the banks of a broad river. The water, crystal clear and reflecting the emerald green of the surrounding leaves, flows gracefully towards a set of ancient stone steps.

The staircase, weathered by centuries, bore the marks of countless journeys. Moss clings to the surface, giving it an ancient quality. The river, seemingly inviting in this heat, laps gently against the worn stones.

What would I give to jump into it to replace the sweat coating my skin with fresh, cool water. My gaze zooms in on the ripples forming on the water's surface, and my heart races when a memory of Khaos flashes before my eyes.

He looked so handsome, gliding through the water in my water chamber. Broad shoulders, toned muscles, and dark hair falling into his face.

I pinch myself to regain focus, inhale, and exhale quietly to slow my heart rate. Everything reminds me of him. Everything!

Ascending the steps, I hear the gasps as the colossal palace carved into the living rock appears before us. Stone towers rise majestically around us, each telling its own silent story. The detailed domes and intricate facades speak of a civilization that has mastered art and architecture. Though time has taken its toll, the essence of grandeur lingers, giving the impression that every stone holds a secret that just waits to be unveiled.

Below the palace, the river snakes its way through the landscape, adding a tranquil melody. In its ceaseless journey, the water has sculpted the stone steps over centuries, creating a harmonious union of nature and human creation.

Before the palace, a central courtyard opens up, revealing a breathtaking panorama of the jungle below. From this vantage point, I can see the vastness of Tenacoro as it thrives in harmony with the wilderness. I also see the huts scattered through the scenery before us, which I haven't noticed before. Some are hidden between the trees on the ground, while others hang suspended atop trees.

For a fleeting moment, my mind wanders to Devana. Does she recognize the hut she used to live in? Can I see it from here?

This shouldn't be my concern right now, but we are connected. The more I know about her, the easier it will be to understand her. Or perhaps it's pity or envy that force me to gather more information about her.

All I know is my royal life. Everything I ever wanted was brought to me by servants and subjects before I even knew I needed it.

Those huts look like a home so foreign to mine—a life I wish I could experience like my brother always wanted—a simple but happy life without the responsibility of an entire kingdom on my shoulders.

Catalina and Cyrus whisper excitedly as my eyes scan my surroundings, and my heart takes another hit as I watch them smile at each other.

I know the feeling of being overwhelmed with joy. Khaos was one of the few people who constantly stirred up warmth in my heart, even when he wasn't around. But the first person who ever gave me that feeling was my brother. Felix didn't even have to say anything to make my heart feel full and to make me feel loved. Not a day goes by when I remember his dimples when he smiled genuinely, how the freckles danced across his face when he was rushing through one of his stories, or how warm and comforting his embrace felt when he hugged me.

The pain intensifies as I watch them, and I rip my eyes off them just seconds before my heart breaks in half.

When I lift my eyes, I see Devana holding her chest, her mouth open as she stares at me, her eyebrows drawn together in pain.

She feels it.

I didn't shield myself enough, and she can feel my pain as if it's her own. Her eyes fill with tears as she watches me, her fingers massaging her chest.

She either thinks I caught feelings for Cyrus and my heart is breaking because of him or...

The real reason I saved Catalina.

I couldn't save my brother from myself, but that doesn't mean that I have to witness another person losing their sibling because of me. I might not have been able to help Felix, and rescuing Catalina doesn't make up for the loss I still feel daily, but it eases the pain a little.

My shoulders strain as I whirl around to stop her from seeing any more of my emotions. It's already bad enough that she saw this vulnerable moment.

"Any news?" Myra asks as she steps through the open palace doors. The sadness in her old eyes is gut-wrenching. Without having to ask her, I know she thinks of him every time she sees me; I do the same. When I see Myra, all I can think of is Khaos.

That reminds me: Why am I wasting time trying to merge our armies? I should be out there strolling into the Underworld and demanding the God to face me. After all, that's what he wants, isn't it?

"Oceris was a dead end," Opaline says, shaking her head as she steps over the threshold. I pursue her. "There's no way of reaching them. I've spent all day hovering over the water."

When I instructed her to gather the other kingdoms, I didn't include Oceris because I knew better. King Usiel doesn't like to be disturbed.

"I guess this is where we come in," Devana says behind me. "King Usiel will fight with us."

Everyone halts.

"You spoke to him?" Myra asks, the wrinkles on her forehead deepening as she studies Devana.

"Involuntarily, but yes. When the winged woman attacked Starstrand with her dragon, we ended up in Oceris."

This makes little sense. Otyx has wings, but he's certainly not a woman. "A woman?"

"Let her speak," Queen Synadena says, grabbing my shoulder.

What the fuck? Not only did she enter Tenacoro after I clearly told her to stay clear of other people, but she also waltzed through Starstrand and ended up in Oceris. What was she thinking?

Devana continues, eyeing me carefully. "When we fled Starstrand, we stumbled into Oceris. At first, the King didn't seem eager to join, but he changed his mind."

"How exactly does someone *stumble* into a kingdom?" I mock, trying to imagine how all of this unfolded. "And what changed his mind?"

King Usiel never interferes with the affairs of the surface. He's highly protected by waves and no oxygen. So, what made him decide to aid Devana? What isn't she telling us?

Instead of letting the two answer my questions, Catalina cuts in as Opaline leads us through the damp halls into a massive room. "What about Queen Caecilia?"

Silence hangs in the air like a deadly veil until Opaline breaks it. "I was too late."

I don't know what to feel anymore. I know I should feel relieved to know that the woman who's partially responsible for my mother's death is dead. Because of her ignorance, my mother died during the childbirth of a winged baby. But somehow, the anger and resentment I've bottled up inside me against the Starstrandian Queen for years doesn't appreciate her death as much as I expected. This should feel like a victory, and yet it feels like another useless loss.

"Has a new King or Queen been appointed?" Queen Synadena asks, biting her lip. "I'm aware it can take weeks, but we need someone right now to lead Starstrand."

And there's that.

Besides Crymzon, every other kingdom's succession is optional. Without an heir, I'm the last of my bloodline, the only person strong enough to wield the magic surging through my kingdom. If I die, so does my kingdom.

The other kingdoms are easier to maintain. An heir is optional but not necessary. Anyone can be appointed King or Queen with or without royal blood.

Starstrand doesn't have an heir. The only descendant—their Princess—died within days of her father. I always wondered what happened, and no one seemed to know the answer.

"As of now, no," Opaline answers, wiggling her mouth from one corner to the other. "But I told every Starstrandian I came across to head to us."

"So what you're saying, it's just us and Oceris," I clarify, roughly counting our probability of defeating the Underworld. "It took those souls less than a day to destroy two kingdoms. No, let me correct that. A woman and a dragon flattened Starstrand while the God's souls overran Eternitie."

"That's not helpful," Myra replies from the corner of the room.

I snicker. "But it is. We know at least one dragon is involved," I say calmly. "And a *winged* woman. Who could she be? Otyx's evil bride?"

"From what we saw, she looked like a Starstrandian," Devana says, rubbing her chest again as if she can still feel my discomfort. "Her wings were identical to the ones of the guards that led us through the palace. And her hair was golden."

Interesting.

"What else can you tell us?" I ask, stretching my fingers.

"Her attack seemed…personal," Cyrus adds.

Queen Synadena tilts her head. "In what way?"

"She didn't go immediately after the guards, and she also left the building outside the palace alone. She went straight for the throne room as if she knew exactly where it was located from the outside," Cyrus answers.

Pinching my eyes together, I watch all of their reactions. Everyone is as confused as I am. Who is she?

The only person not showing any emotions is Queen Synadena, and I'm not surprised. I had a gut feeling that one of them knew more partially because the people surrounding me were as good at putting their noses into everyone's business to keep their kingdoms thriving as I was. And because most of them are older than me, some even experienced centuries before I was even born.

However, I twist and turn it, it doesn't make sense. If Otyx was the reason the Underworld breached the surface, why send a woman and not attack me immediately?

"Are we sure we're dealing with the God of the Underworld?" Opaline asks, voicing the same question I just asked myself.

"I'm sure," I say, recalling Otyx's warning.

"Ok, then. How much do we know about the Underworld? Not the stories people tell on the streets, but Otyx's actual domain?" Queen Catalina asks, her hands playing with the handles of her swords. "Maybe this isn't connected at all to him. What if those souls have their own agendas? What if this isn't his doing, and it's nothing personal against u s?"

"It seems fucking personal to me," I reply, my nostrils flaring.

Myra steps in as I hold my breath before I can say anything else. "He killed Khaos."

It feels like my intestines are being pulled out of my abdomen as everyone turns to face me. Breathing was hard enough when none of the other kingdoms knew about his departure, and by the reaction Devana gives me, no one shared my secret with her.

"Is that true?" she asks, her eyes filling with tears. "Is that why he isn't with you?"

I want to scream, to scratch, to roll into a ball and make everything stop. But I can't. The burden of carrying an entire kingdom on my shoulders stops me from doing anything irrational.

"Until I can get him back," I say, straightening my shoulders. "I promised you my army, but I never said I would fight beside you. This is something between Otyx and I."

"Are you insane? You plan to resurrect Khaos?" Cyrus squeaks, shaking his head. "What about Devana? What if you die during your attempt? This isn't just about you anymore."

I glare at him, signaling him to shut up, but it's too late.

"What is he talking about?" Myra asks, her eyes wandering from the silver freckles on my face to the ones sparkling on Devana's. Her mouth slowly opens as she takes us in, over and over again. "She's blessed by Lunra, just like you," she says, pointing at her.

"It's a coincidence," I reply, shrugging my shoulders. I look at Devana and her markings—so much for keeping a low profile.

I feel like a caged animal. Not only is everyone aware that my Soulmate is dead, but they're about to find another weakness I wasn't prepared to share with anyone.

Queen Catalina tilts her head to the side. "You have two Soulmates?"

Oh gosh, is she serious?

"No, I only have one, and it's time to bring him back," I reply, clenching my teeth. "Take my army and the Nullstones. Those stones are strong enough to weaken Otyx's souls to have a fighting chance."

"I won't let you go," Cyrus says, reaching for my arm. He gives me just enough time to release the handle of my whip and let it loose.

"I dare you," I hiss, circling the whip over the stone ground. "If you touch me, you will lose your head."

"Everyone, calm down," Opaline cuts in, tapping her boot on the ground to get everyone's attention. "This is what he wants. We'll all die if we don't work as a team."

"Team," I huff, scraping my whip over the ground. "Maybe that's what his plan is: getting us all into one spot so he can eliminate us all at once. We ran here like scared mice trying to escape a cat. Let's be real—we're currently sitting ducks."

Cyrus exhales loudly, "We can play this game all day long. There's no way of knowing what his next move is. All I know is that wherever you're going, I'm going."

Even though I understand where he's coming from and why he doesn't want to leave me out of his sight, I'm suffocating. It's too much all at once, and all I want is to have Khaos back, no matter the cost.

Instead of ignoring him, I do the only thing I'm known for to get him off my back, hopefully. "Did you finally find your balls? Let me guess, you found them in your father's grip right after you killed him?"

Cyrus grinds his teeth, and I laugh as his sister steps between us. "That's enough," she says, her knuckles turning white as she grips her swords.

"I guess your new owner has arrived," I say, winking at him. "Let's hope she survives you." Catalina pounces at me, and my smile widens when she hits the barrier I put up between us.

And this is my cue to take my exit. I've given them everything at my disposal to have a fighting chance against Otyx. They either take it or leave it, but if I were them, I wouldn't waste any more time to prepare for the inevitable.

I turn my wrist to call Storm with my magic, but something unexpected happens.

TWENTY-THREE

DEVANA

One moment, I'm staring at Soulin; the next, she is gone as if her body is dematerialized into thin air.

Where did she go?

"What's her problem?" Catalina asks, relaxing her shoulders while her eyes still focus on the spot the Crymzon Queen stood just seconds ago.

"She's lost more than all of us combined," Queen Synadena says, lowering her gaze. "I don't expect you to understand, but no one was there when she ascended the throne and needed our help. After leaving her to fight for herself for over a decade, you can't possibly think she knows how to work with others. We failed her."

Catalina clicks her tongue. "She did this to herself."

Queen Synadena throws a stern look in the new Queen's direction. "And this is where you are wrong. She was a child without guidance, without her parents, and with more power than all of us combined. She did her best while we all turned our backs to her." She lifts her head to look at Myra. "The only person in this room who can judge her is the woman who stepped up, who took the role as her mother when no one else wanted to."

My throat closes thinking about that part of the Crymzon Queen's history I never wasted a single breath over. We all know loss—in different ways and forms—but I wasn't left alone to fend for myself. While I might not have had my mother by my side or lived in Tenacoro, I was drowning in my tough father's love.

I can't imagine how my life would have played out if he wasn't in it and I had a crown and kingdom to carry.

"That doesn't change the fact that we need her," Opaline says. "Soulin is the strongest person in Escela. We can't do this without her."

"Maybe we don't have to," I say, rubbing my temples. "She said her army and those shards will be at our disposal. I've seen what they can do. If we use them wisely and hurry, we could make it to the Underworld in time to support her."

"And how do you expect us to do that? We can't just fly there."

The grin on Queen Synadena's face is haunting. "Technically, we could."

My heart pounds when I realize what she is referring to. While every Tenacorian has a Glimmarum like I have Erinna, this kingdom has many unclaimed animals with wings.

Catalina crosses her arms. "I think we should wait it out. If she really is as strong as everyone claims, she won't need us."

"We can't let her do this by herself. If she dies, so does Devana. I won't stand around and wait for that to happen," Cyrus says, and everyone's attention focuses on me.

Myra steps closer. "It's true then? You two are connected?"

Does it matter if they know my secret? We're about to go up against the deadliest God, knowing he's far superior.

I nod slowly, contemplating how to word it. "We were born on the same day, at the same time, and took our first breath together," I answer, eyeing the woman who's supposed to be Soulin's caretaker after her mother died. She's old yet beautiful in her emerald gown. Dark gray strands speckled her long, silvery mane, and her green eyes study me wearily in return.

"I've never heard of anything like it," Queen Synadena says, standing up from her chair. "Are you certain?"

"Not about the dying part, but yes, I'm certain about our connection," I say truthfully. "But that isn't important right now. We need to focus on preparing for war. Where are the shards?"

And just like that, every ruler knows our secret. What a turn of events. I thought I could keep it to myself, but fate had other plans.

Opaline points out the window. "They're currently being collected by the river, close to the mine. I saw them on my way back."

The mines are in the center of Tenacoro, surrounded by towering trees and the distant murmur of the river. Iron and other metals are the essence of the blades Tenacorians wield and the arrows they fashion for their hunts. Over countless years, the river has deposited these metals in the earth, making the ores rich, and extracting them is both challenging and rewarding.

Not that I would know because I've never seen them, but my father used to mention them a lot when he tried to teach me his craftsmanship.

As Queen Synadena speaks about the Crymzonians waiting for their orders, I envision the mines: a labyrinth of tunnels echoing with the rhythmic clinks of pickaxes against rocks.

That's when a new idea sparks in the back of my head.

"Metal," I say with a mischievous spark in my eyes. "We can make our blades even more formidable. What if we add fragments of those rocks to the metal mix? Imagine the strength and durability it could create!"

Everyone exchanges intrigued glances, caught up in the allure of my idea.

"These rocks could be the missing ingredient to elevate our power," I exclaim, my hands gesturing animatedly as if forging the weapons in the air. "We'll need to experiment, of course," I admit, my tone becoming more contemplative. "But imagine the damage our swords and arrows could do."

"You're forgetting one thing," Catalina says. "We don't have the time to test your idea. Otyx could already be on his way to us."

"What if there's another way to slow him down?" Cyrus asks, looking through the windowless arches out into the greenery.

"Like what?"

He spins his finger as if trying to unravel his thoughts into coherent sentences. "We already know that Crymzonians react to the Nullstone, and Queen Soulin is certain it will work on the Underworldlers. But does it affect people without magic?"

"No, it's designed as a last resort against magical creatures," Myra replies.

Cyrus claps his hands. "Exactly. The river outside leads straight to the Underworld. What if we poison it? Not literally poisoning it, just filling it with Nullstone? Perhaps that will give us time to re-forge already-made weapons and add the necessary Nullstone to them."

Why didn't I think of that? He's a genius.

"What about Oceris?" Queen Synadena asks, sitting back down on her throne. "We can't *poison* the water, not knowing if it might harm them."

Cyrus lowers his head. "I didn't think that far."

Catalina stops beside Cyrus to pet his back. "Great. But without testing the Nullstone on an Ocerian first, we won't be able to use your idea."

"Well, that settles it," Opaline says, snapping her fingers, yet no one moves. "What are we waiting for? Let's get those weapons going."

I approach the riverbank with cautious steps. The air is thick with the musky scent of foliage, and the distant sounds of exotic creatures echo through the trees. As I emerge into a clearing, followed by Cyrus, a sight unfolds I thought I would never witness.

Before me, soldiers clad in vibrant red armor stand in hesitant unity with warriors from Tenacoro, their attire a striking contrast—leaves and vines woven into a makeshift armor that blends seamlessly with the jungle's lush surroundings. The air hums with an unspoken tension, a delicate truce forged by necessity rather than camaraderie.

I observe the scene with curiosity and concern. With their divergent backgrounds, the soldiers exchange wary glances, each group uncertain of the other's intentions. Yet, a shared purpose draws them together—a common enemy, a looming threat that transcends the differences in their armor and traditions.

Amidst the uneasy alliance, a collaboration that speaks of desperation and innovation unfolds. The Crymzon soldiers, harnessing their magical powers, conjure flames that dance along the length of metallic swords and arrows. The heat emanating from the weapons creates a surreal glow as they keep their distance from the real threat—Nullstone. The Crymzonians' powers are useless if they come in contact with the shards, but that doesn't mean they can't use their magic to help speed up the creation of the needed weapons.

Beside them, Tenacorians clad in leaves and vines work with nimble fingers, adding carefully selected stone fragments to the almost molten metal. The clinking of stones against the red-hot blades and the sizzling sound the weapons make when submerged in water send shivers down my spine.

If my father could see in what horrendous way those blades are being modified with no concern about the quality, he would take it upon himself to re-forge every single sword.

But he's not here.

Nevertheless, I marvel at the unlikely partnership unfolding before me. It's proof of the primal instinct that overshadows the boundaries of kingdoms and cultures—the instinct to survive. As the metallic scent of heated swords mingles with the earthy aroma of Tenacoro, I sense a delicate harmony emerging from the discord.

The soldiers, despite their initial hesitations, find a rhythm. A silent communication develops between them, born out of necessity and the shared goal of defending their homes.

Is this how Escela was supposed to be before the different kingdoms stopped interacting with each other?

Amid the collaborative effort, I see the tiniest glimmer of hope. The once distinct groups can still become a unified force, blending their strengths to create something even the God of the Underworld doesn't see coming—a united land.

Witnessing the birth of a new alliance is terrifying and fulfilling because whatever happens next, no one can tell me we didn't try our best.

TWENTY-FOUR

QUEEN SOULIN

My magic has no limits—at least, that's what it feels like.

Since I restored the Heiligbaum and my connection to Khaos intensified my magic tenfold, I keep finding new ways to test what I can do with my powers. My mindset of preserving my magic has shifted to *there's no stopping me from trying*.

Still, it seems unreal to be able to meddle with everything surrounding me.

As I was cornered in Tenacoro's palace, I longed to escape the suffocating atmosphere. I felt like an unwanted guest, a pawn in a complex power game.

And they are right—I am a weapon, just not one that can be handled.

My desire for solitude intensified, and I attempted to distance myself from the fervent discussion with a subtle turn of my wrist. Little did I know that my unspoken plea triggered the magic within me. A delicate, invisible energy began to weave around me, responding to the urgency of my wish.

A shimmering veil of magic enveloped me like a second skin, rendering me invisible to the focused gazes of those around me. I stood there, waiting for them to chase after me, but no one moved. Instead, Catalina spoke of me like I was not even there. "What's her problem?"

Slowly, I crept closer to Cyrus, but his eyes didn't follow my movement. To test my theory, I waved my other hand right before his face—still no reaction.

I was invisible and apparently mute because no one turned their eyes to my whip either.

When Queen Synadena opened her mouth to respond to her, I took my chance and bolted through the open doors. I didn't stop running until I reached the path I took to get here.

I don't have to wait long for Storm to find me. Just like Adira, she can feel my presence, yet she circles aimlessly above me, her enormous eyes searching for me.

This is the first time my magic acted without me calling for it—no, the second time if I count the magical outburst at thirteen. Ringing with myself, I try to reverse the grip my magic has on me, and after a few tries, I feel the thinnest layer of magic peeling off my skin like a snake shedding.

Immediately, Storm touches down beside me when my body materializes again, and together, we lift into the sky.

"Do you trust me?" I ask as I press my palms firmly against her fuzz-covered body.

The humming vibrations Storm sends through my legs and palms into my body tell me everything I need to know, and my heart hurts. I don't deserve animals. Without hesitation, she agreed to let me try my newest chant on her, and I'm unsure if I can duplicate it again. Her trust in me is sickening and yet comforting all at once.

Channeling my magic, I close my eyes and envision us invisible. I can feel the powers creeping over my body and spreading through my fingers into Storm.

Her wings double flap as she feels my magic coating her, but she's back in her rhythm with the next beat, flying faster than ever before. My mind zones out as we fly under the beaming sun.

On my way out of Tenacoro's palace, I contemplated my next move. Finding Otyx is still at the top of my list, but there's another option I haven't considered yet.

My first thought was to search Librascendia for a resurrection spell. But what if the book in Librascendia has another way of reaching Otyx without further bloodshed? I've summoned him once, using forbidden magic. But what if I can reverse what I've done?

When I watch my kingdom appear on the horizon, I let out a loud sigh when it's still intact. The fear of finding Crymzon in ruins and Khaos' body buried under tons of stone settled in my bones the second I saw Eternitie in flames. Still, it doesn't make sense. Why destroy two kingdoms that have nothing to do with what's happening?

"Come in, fast," Conrad says, waving his hands at me as Storm lands on the East Tower.

"How can you see us?" I ask, jumping off Storm.

"You're not the only one who possesses magic," he replies, shrugging his shoulders as if it's obvious.

Could Myra see me in Tenacoro? If she did, she didn't lead it on.

But the bigger question is: how did Conrad know where I would land? It probably took him hours to reach the lookout over the city at his speed.

"Let's talk inside," he says, hurrying into the tower.

"What's going on?" I whisper, keeping my head low as I pursue him.

"Besides the Underworld breaching the surface, Emberix's resurrection, and that Otyx has lost his mind, everything is okay here," he mumbles, taking one careful step down the stairs after another.

"Who is Emberix?" I ask, watching Storm fold her wings to safely get through the door before I shut it with my magic.

"Dragons guard the souls in the Underworld. They're mostly small and no danger to us," he halts to catch his breath. "Not Emberix. Over the centuries, she fed off the sins floating through the Underworld like a beggar starving down food, and it strengthened her. To no surprise, she became Otyx's favorite. When it became obvious that she was large enough to reach the surface's crust, the Gods and Goddesses decided she was a threat."

Though I've never seen a breathing dragon, I can see a scale-covered body, sharp teeth, a long tail, and massive wings before my eyes.

"What did they do to her?" I ask, my heart racing because I can imagine where his story is going, and the thought of losing Adira is still too fresh. She was my favorite—not because Storm or the others have done anything to disappoint me, but because I raised her. She was my first Fighter Moth and the first who drilled herself through the hard outer shell of my heart.

"She was sentenced to eternal rest," Conrad says, using his hand on the wall to guide him.

Using *eternal rest* to describe her death sentence isn't better, even if we're talking about Death's pet.

"Did she try to reach the surface?" I ask.

He shakes his head. "That isn't the point. Emberix was dangerous."

My body heats. "But she did nothing to deserve that fate," I say, my voice sharp.

"I didn't say it was the right thing to do. I'm trying to tell you that Emberix is back, and she's angry."

Great. Not only have I angered a God, but his lovely fire-breathing dragon has awoken from her slumber, probably more infuriated than ever.

"Is there any good news?" I ask, trying to refocus on the actual issue.

"Crymzon is still standing," he says, shrugging his shoulders. "That's about it."

I'm waiting for the update I know he's ignoring at all costs. He doesn't want to talk about the glass cage I keep Khaos in to preserve him.

Conrad turns to me, pausing for a moment. "Why did you come back?"

"Because there's something I need to do," I reply, trying to focus on my newest mission instead of the pain in my chest.

When we finally reach the last step, I push past Conrad. "Take care of Storm while I'm gone," I say, picking up the pace to regain the lost time following Conrad.

"There's a faster way to get into Librascendia," Conrad says behind me just as I'm about to round a corner, and I come to a screeching halt. I turn around, and he smiles at me before I can voice my question.

"I'm way older than you. When I served your father, he wasn't careful with his secrets." His bright yet weathered eyes focus on me. "I know what is behind those doors and what you're searching for. I'm also aware that you won't listen to me, yet please remember my words when you're about to do the unthinkable: Blood Magic won't help you."

What am I supposed to say? Knowing that Conrad is conscious about what I'm searching for is unsettling. No one knows what I've done in that room besides Otyx and I—and Conrad, it seems like.

"Now, dear Soulin," he begins, "using magic to create a portal requires finesse and focus. It's not about forcing the arcane energies, but coaxing them to weave a passage between spaces."

With his wrinkled hand, he conjures a soft glow at his fingertips. I watch as he gracefully traces sigils in the air, inscribing invisible patterns that dance with his energy. The corridor responds to his command, and before us, a swirling portal materializes, revealing a glimpse into a room of forgotten books and ancient objects—Librascendia.

"Magic is like a language," he explains, his eyes reflecting the depth of his understanding. "You must speak to it with intention and respect. Now, try it yourself. Feel the energy around you."

The urge to storm off and leave him behind is pulling on every fiber of my body. "Don't talk to me like I'm a fool," I hiss, my eyes lingering on his hands that hold the portal open.

"Inexperience doesn't make you a fool—Ignorance does," he answers, lowering his arms slowly, and with every inch, the portal fades.

Eager yet apprehensive, I mimic his gestures. My hands tremble slightly with uncertainty as I attempt to channel the magic that lingers in my veins. The air hums with a subtle vibration, and a faint, translucent portal emerges, mirroring the one the old man had crafted.

Encouraged by my success, I step through the portal into the ancient study filled with dusty tomes and the soft smell of aged parchment. Shelves stacked with books bound in weathered leather and parchment surround me, and for a heartbeat, I can feel the silence overtaking me.

I can't be in here alone.

I turn to see Conrad still standing in the corridor, Storm unmoving behind him. He offers me a nod of approval, acknowledging the new ability he has shown me. However, as I wait for him to walk through the portal, I notice the solemnity in his eyes and his gentle smile.

"I've shown you the way," he says through the portal, his voice carrying a hint of melancholy. "Some paths are meant to be walked alone. Remember my words."

That's not what I want. Yet, with a sense of reverence, I follow the old man's guidance again. My hands move with an unnatural assurance as I trace the same sigils to close the portal. The passage between us dissipates like the morning mist, leaving me alone in Librascendia.

Conrad's figure lingers behind the dissipating magic, a silhouette against the backdrop of the red sandstone wall behind him. His eyes convey a mix of pride and farewell. As the portal closes completely, the room darkens, and I take a few deep breaths before I spin on my heels.

Something tells me that Conrad isn't the man I think he is. Besides being one of the few people on this planet to know about the location of Painite in Terminus, his magic was powerful enough to withstand mine when I tried to open the throne room's door. And the way he knew exactly why I came back to Crymzon without saying a single word—something is off.

Yet, the portal was the last evidence I needed to know that he's loyal to me and one of the best magic-wielders I'd ever seen.

Tapping my foot on the ground, I wait for the black substance to inch in my direction. After the twentieth tap, I still don't see the inky liquid pooling towards me.

Do I have to call for it? Was there something I did last time that activated the book to come to me? Does it feed off desperation because I have a lot of that pulsating through me right now?

"Come out, come out, wherever you are," I sing, my eyes fleeting over the thousands of books until my eyes land on something unusual that sends a chill down my spine.

TWENTY-FIVE

DEVANA

"What did I tell you about eavesdropping?" Opaline asks behind me, and I almost tumble into the river.

I must have lost track of time while I watched the Crymzonians working together with Tenacorians. I can't recall when I checked my surroundings the last time—was it a minute or an hour ago? It can't be long because the sun has barely started to dip high on the horizon.

A boy screams behind me, and instinctively, I grab the sword handle attached to my belt.

"He's just a boy," Cyrus says, holding his hands up, and when I finally turn my face toward the commotion, I freeze.

Opaline has her arms wrapped around a male—from the looks of it, an early teenager—as he tries to kick her feet out under her.

"Let me go!" he screams, winding his body almost out of her grip, but Opaline bites on her lip and reinforces her hold on him.

"Wait until I tell mother about this," he spits out, throwing his head back to hit her nose, but Opaline is faster and uses that moment to get a fist full of his long, coiled hair.

"I've warned you, Crystol," Opaline says right into his ear as she arches his neck. "You must monitor your surroundings."

With that, Opaline releases him, and I jump forward to catch the boy tumbling into my arms. Embarrassed, he pounces back and straightens his leaf and vein uniform before he opens his mouth to address me. "I didn't mean you any harm," he says, lifting the left corner of his mouth. "You just made it too easy to fight the temptation to scare you."

What is he talking about?

"I'm sorry about my brother's unusual behavior," Opaline says, grabbing him by the neck to pull him behind her. He lets out a groan. "He has a horrible way of introducing himself to new arrivals."

Ouch, that hurt, but Opaline is right. I'm a new arrival. After over twenty-five years of absence, I'm not familiar with Tenacoro anymore. It feels, sounds, and smells like home, but so does every burning blade my eyes were glued to just a minute ago.

My eyes dart back and forth between Opaline and Crystol, and their similarities strike me immediately.

"I've told you this isn't a game," Opaline says, pointing her finger at his face. "I need you to stay in the shelter until all this is over."

"I can help. I've been training." He flexes his arm, showing his muscles. "Please take me with you."

"If something happens to mother and me, you're all Tenacoro has left," Opaline says, pulling him closer. "I need you to stay put, just this time."

Listening to Opaline trying to convince her brother to stay behind is against everything we believe in. No Tenacorian gets left behind during a fight, no matter the age. And that shows me precisely that Opaline is scared. She knows that the probability of her return is slim, even slimmer now that Soulin won't join the fight. Without her magic, we're practically done for if those stones don't work.

"You look stronger than me," Cyrus laughs, getting closer to him. "Are you the youngest of your family?"

"And the smartest," Crystol replies, tapping his finger against his skull.

"I can see that," he answers, suppressing a smile. "How about you show me some of your moves?"

Crystol's eyes blaze with youthful enthusiasm as he rips himself free. "What do you want to see? I'm very good with a bow and arrow."

"Let's start there," Cyrus says, looking over at me as if searching for my permission. I nod and shake my head simultaneously because we don't have time to play around, but on the other hand, this might be the last time Crystol will be a boy if the battle is as bad as I think.

"Just a few minutes," Opaline says, bowing her head to Cyrus. "Thank you." Her last words are sincere.

I watch Cyrus move away from us alongside the boy until they're mere figures framed by the lush greenery surrounding them.

Crystol patiently guides Cyrus in the delicate art of wielding a bow and arrow. As the bowstring sings in the air, my gaze drifts back towards the distant metal clinking. The groups of soldiers toil tirelessly, forging swords that will soon find purpose in the crucible of the impending battle. The rhythmic symphony of magic and metal echoes through the jungle, a stark contrast to the serenity of the tutorial in archery.

Lost in my contemplation, my mind paints vivid scenes of an alternate reality. I envision a life where the Underworld doesn't cast its shadow across Escela. In this imagined world, Cyrus, now deeply engrossed in the art of archery, would have been content living a simple life as long as we were together. Crystol, devoid of the burden of impending conflict, would have enjoyed a carefree childhood, his laughter mingling with the rustle of leaves.

Yet, reality calls me back to the present. The distant clanging of metal is a persistent reminder of the storm on the horizon. As I continue to watch them, a bittersweet ache settles within my chest. The juxtaposition of innocence and impending turmoil plays out before me, an emotional curtain woven with threads of hope and despair.

"He's a good man," Opaline says, her eyes focused on them. "I hope we make it."

So do I and everyone who's preparing for war around us.

Cyrus' brow furrows in concentration as he aims the bow, and I can't stop looking at his handsome face. Beside him, Crystol's eyes gleam with determination to help him.

He's too young to witness what's coming. It's not fair—none of this is.

"I'm not here to judge, but he must be the worst hunter I've ever seen," Opaline giggles as Cyrus misses another leaf that fell from a tree.

"He for sure is, but I wouldn't change it for the world," I reply, my heart filling with warmth.

"I might not know you for long, but I'm happy for you," she says, watching her brother. "Some day, my time will come, and I'll find someone who makes me feel this way."

I never even thought about how lucky I am. Finding Cyrus was more than just a coincidence. Both of us fled our kingdoms without looking back. I would have never met him if my father hadn't taken me away from here.

An electric pulse runs through my body as I think of my father. I still haven't sought him out. It should have been the first thing to do when I set foot on the ground. But knowing my mother could lurk around any corner stopped me.

Would I recognize her? Is there a part of me that still remembers her even though I forgot what she looked like long ago? Is there an instinct that will tell me which woman birthed me?

"What is it?" Cyrus asks as he runs in my direction.

Lost in my thoughts, I didn't realize Crystol's lesson was over.

"Nothing," I say, rubbing my lips over each other. His eyes linger on my mouth, forcing me to stop moving them. "Seriously, I'm fine."

"No one is fine right now," Opaline whispers beside me. "You can tell us."

"It's my mother," I say, glaring at her.

There, it's out. What's the point of pretending anymore?

Opaline scrunches a brow. "Liora?"

The world spins around me as I take her name in. Liora. My mother.

I might have forgotten what she looks like, but I'll never forget her name.

"Is she still alive?" I whisper, fighting the panic attack that pushes its way through my stomach and up my throat.

Opaline looks at everything but me. "She is, but the version of the woman you once knew is far gone."

"What does that mean?" Cyrus asks, saving me from asking that same question.

"She now belongs to the Silent Sisters."

TWENTY-SIX

Avira

With a swift, determined motion, I burst through the door like a lightning strike. The room is void of color and painted in various shades of black. The walls, the bed, the bedding, and the dresser are all draped in an inky darkness that absorbs the very essence of light.

The impact of the door hitting the wall is loud enough to let the entire planet know that I've arrived, yet the solitary figure sitting on the bed is stoic, unmoving, as if carved from the shadows surrounding him. Curly locks of hair frame his gray face, and his shoulders, broad and statuesque, give an impression of strength despite the unsettling stillness that defines him.

My urgency propels me forward, navigating through the dark sea of the room until I stand before Khaos. His gaze is fixed upon the wall, devoid of any discernible emotion. It's as if his very essence has merged with the obscure atmosphere of the Underworld, rendering him an inert component.

Undeterred, I extend my hand, shaking it before his impassive face.

No reaction.

I snap my fingers in a futile attempt to break the eerie stillness, but Khaos remains unmoving, like a statue in the dimly lit room.

Frustration creeps up inside me as I contemplate how to snap him out of his trance. Determined to pierce through the veil of his detachment, I reach out, my fingers closing around his head. I encounter a disconcerting emptiness beneath my touch, a void that echoes with the absence of thought or emotion. It's as if the very core of his being has been hollowed out, leaving behind a shell of a man.

In my desperate attempt to elicit any response, I gaze into his vacant eyes, searching for a glimmer of recognition or life. Yet, his gaze remains fixed on the wall, indifferent to the surrounding commotion.

What is going on with him? Did I break him? Did I make a mistake when I stripped him of his former life?

I need him. Without him, my plan to lure out Soulin is null.

The room constricts, its darkness pressing against the edges of my perception. Determined not to succumb to the oppressive atmosphere, I withdraw my hands.

Fuck! How do I fix him? Where is Otyx when I need him? After all, Khaos is his soul and not mine. Is he aware that something is going on with him?

As if seeking answers in the shadows, I circle the room, examining every detail. The black bedspread clings to the mattress like a shroud, and the dresser stands as a monolith of obscurity, its contours barely distinguishable in the dim light. The air in the room is heavy with an otherworldly presence, a weight that presses down on my shoulders.

Then I feel it. One sin after another, they brush over my skin, testing me. I feel the heat wrath leaves in my stomach, the coolness that comes with envy, lust between my legs, and pride as I keep my head high and shoulders squared.

Every single one is tempting, like a lifeline I didn't know I needed to survive.

Returning to the motionless man on the bed, I consider my next move. The snapping of fingers, shaking, and even physical contact have failed to pierce through to him. An idea sparks in my mind—perhaps there's a way to bring light back into his eyes.

I rush toward the dresser, fumbling for a candle or any source of illumination. In my frantic search, my fingers brush against an orb stowed in a drawer. With a swift movement, I grab it, and suddenly, the room is bathed in a stark, blinding light as the orb begins to glow beneath my touch.

The transformation is instantaneous. The blackness retreats, revealing the room's features in stark clarity against the light.

Yet, Khaos remains unchanged. His gray skin, curly hair, and stoic countenance persist, unaffected by my attempt to bring him back.

There has to be something I can do.

I return to his side, my eyes scanning his unmoving form. The blinding light exposes every nuance of his features and the scar on his cheek. I wonder how he got it; when I saw his memories, all I could see was the Crymzon Queen.

I reach out again to touch his face and meet the same desolate void.

In the room's brilliance, I grapple with a disturbing realization—the shadows have merely masked the emptiness within him. The light banished the darkness that cloaked the room but failed to dispel the profound vacancy that grips his being.

Perhaps that's his problem. What if I stripped his memories, leaving nothing else behind? If Otyx forgot to let him pick a sin, maybe he hasn't found his purpose yet; without it, he's inactive.

When my palms seal around his head for a third time, anger floods my body.

I shouldn't be doing this alone. Otyx should be by my side, looking the same way at me as Khaos observed his Queen for years. His hands should be on my shoulder, guiding me on what to do next.

Instead, I'm all alone. And the most ridiculous part is, that's precisely what brought me here. I knew isolation before I ever set foot into the Underworld. My mother was so consumed with loving my father that there wasn't any room for me. She needed to produce an heir, so the throne didn't go to anyone outside her bloodline.

My nostrils flare as I feed my rage through my fingers into Khaos. That's what he should feel. He was Soulin's puppet. She didn't love him; she just wanted to keep him close in case everyone turned their backs on her. He was a backup for her to fall onto if her world collapsed.

It's freeing to let my emotions flow into him. Every heartache, every betrayal, every moment I felt like I wasn't enough flows through my body into his until his pupils dart in my direction, and I release him.

"There you are," I snarl, licking my lips. "I thought I broke you."

The edges around his eyes deepen as they darken. "I feel fine," he growls, cracking his neck.

"That's my man," I smile, stepping back to inspect my creation.

His entire demeanor has changed. He's still brutally handsome, but the light in his eyes has turned into something scary, almost deadly.

"There's something I need you to do, but first, we have to dress you properly," I say, sizing him up. "And I have just the right change in mind."

TWENTY-SEVEN

Queen Soulin

In the hallowed silence of Librascendia, I move with deliberate steps, my footsteps echoing against the red, time-worn stones.

At the end of the room, a sturdy wooden table holds a single black wax candle, its flame flickering with a spectral dance. I approach the table, drawn by the enigmatic presence of it. Its wavering light cast shadows that seem to reach out, whispering secrets hidden within the ancient walls.

Above the candle flame, in an inexplicable defiance of gravity, a single droplet of blood levitates, suspended in the air.

That can't be...

My eyes narrow as I recall the ritual I performed. The memory of summoning Otyx into the world of mortals floods back. Yet, as I delve into the recesses of my mind, a puzzle emerges—the candle's flame extinguished once I reached the God of the Underworld. I remember it as if it was just moments ago. So how come it's burning again?

My gaze fixates on the levitating droplet, its crimson hue almost fading into the wall's color. Under closer inspection, it seems to pulse with a life force of its own.

That's not how I remember leaving the candle behind. But I can't be sure because everything went so fast.

I reach out to touch the black wax. As my fingers graze its surface, I feel the subtle warmth emanating from the flame. The levitating droplet quivers as if responding to my proximity.

Without a doubt, I know it's my blood, and whatever it means, it's not good.

In an attempt to decipher the inexplicable, my thoughts go back to the book I consulted for the ritual—the reason I'm here. It showed me the war my ancestors fought against Otyx and helped me summon the same God. If it could direct me to the correct incantation to reach the God of the Underworld and open a way for him to reach the surface, it has to have a counterspell.

Turning away from the table, I navigate the labyrinthine aisles of towering bookshelves that hold the accumulated wisdom of ages. Dust motes dance in the air as I seek the volume that had guided me before.

"I need your help," I say, my eyes fleeting over the leather-bound spines and objects cluttering the shelves.

With each step, the library becomes alive, its knowledge pulsating through the shelves like a beat echoing in the chambers of a heart. I know it's here because I can feel its presence.

My hand closes around a weathered volume bound in cracked leather. I pull it from the shelf, the pages brittle with age. Embossed in faded gold, the title gleams in the library's muted light.

I don't know what exactly made me grab this book; sheer desperation seems to guide me now.

Opening the grimoire, a wave of confusion washes over me as I scan the pages. What had once been a repository of mystical knowledge is now a collection of empty sheets. The words that used to fill this book have vanished, leaving behind only the ghostly imprints of inkless parchment.

My brow furrows in bewilderment as I flip through the pages, each an empty void. With trembling hands, I toss the book to the ground and grab the one next to it, just to find more emptiness.

A revelation dawns upon me, sending shivers down my spine. The ancient and wise library has chosen to withhold its secrets. The pages of the grimoires, once a roadmap to the mystical, now mock me with their disobedience.

"No," I whisper, grabbing another book, then another. This can't be happening. I only did what the book told me to do. Without its guidance, I would have never been able to summon a God.

Turning away from the books, I return to the table. My eyes fixated on the black wax candle and the levitating droplet of blood. The flame continues its dance, casting ephemeral shadows that mirror my inner turmoil. Librascendia, a repository of untold wisdom, remains silent in the face of my inquiries, and I'm looking at the reason.

Blood Magic comes at a far greater cost than I was willing to pay. Not only did the incantation take Khaos from me, but it also doomed Escela by opening a path between the mortal world and the Underworld. And to rub my mistake in Librascendia decided I wasn't worthy of any more knowledge.

The levitating droplet, a poignant reminder of my backfired summoning, echoes in the room's silence.

No, I won't accept it—I won't accept that this is the end.

If I want to plead my case to Otyx, I must hurry before the other kingdoms start marching. I can't be held accountable for all the lives about to be lost.

Using my fingers, I extinguish the flame and close my eyes when my skin burns. That's when I feel the droplet splash on the back of my hand. As I rub the blood into my skin, I envision my next destination, and once the liquid is completely absorbed, I lift my arm to paint the sigils into the air.

My shoulders slump when I see the glass casket through the portal.

TWENTY-EIGHT

DEVANA

"**I**'m not going to see her," I say, shaking my head vividly.

Cyrus grabs my shoulders to stop me from pacing. His brown eyes search for my gaze, but I can't look at him. "Why not? I thought that's what you wanted. Your plan was to free those children, and going there to see her is your way in."

Yes, that was my plan until Otyx ripped a giant hole into our planet. Now, I can't think of anything better than to use his appearance as an excuse to avoid her.

"Opaline didn't say my mother is under the care of the Silent Sisters; she said *she belongs now to the Silent Sisters*. That's a tremendous difference," I say, shrugging him off, but he's stronger than expected. "Don't make me do this. Please don't."

"I'm never going to force you to do anything you don't desire. I'm just trying to tell you that this is important. You need that closure."

"No, I don't. I got my closure when she rejected me."

He puts his hands in the air to signal his defeat. "I'm not saying your father is a liar, but what if there's more to the story? Have you ever thought that this might not be the full truth?"

As much as I want to deny his questions, I can't. It has crossed my mind once or twice that maybe, just maybe, my father bent the truth like he does metal.

But what happens when I hear the other side of the story, and they don't overlap? There's no reason my father would do this to me.

Or is there?

Pressing my palms against my ears, I step away from him. "Stop messing with my head. I'm not going," I say, my heart heavy with the decision. Besides training to become Monsteress' assassin, I also made mental plans on how I would take out the Silent Sisters. I got obsessed with it the second my father told me about the place that was supposed to be my home.

"Fine, but at least let us rest," Cyrus says, watching Opaline and Crystol move toward the palace.

I want to tell him I'm not tired, but that's a lie. I haven't slept in days and am running on pure adrenaline.

His request to nap is my ticket to see my father—that is, if my childhood hut still stands after we abandoned it.

"What if we get attacked while we rest?" I ask, looking over at the soldiers who are halfway through the swords.

"We won't be any more prepared if we watch them reforge metal."

Fair point. I could use a minute to rest my legs and close my eyes.

I'm still amazed that since Soulin found out about our connection, I haven't felt the usual muscle ache I grew up with. Even though I've tried to stop my brain from making assumptions about what it could mean since there are more pressing matters at hand, in silent moments like this one, my mind circles back to the exact guess. I believe that ignoring our connection took a physical toll on me. It's as if my body tried to tell me it was missing something vital, and it wasn't able to communicate in any other way with me than through pain and weakness. But that would only make sense if Soulin felt the same, and that's a question I'll never ask her because my pride is preventing it.

There's also the possibility that I'm entirely wrong about this. A part of myself believes I was born this way to show me that even with daily unbearable pain, I can reach anything I set my mind to.

But that wouldn't explain why I suddenly feel *normal*.

Again, this is a matter I have to figure out after Otyx—if there is an *after*.

Through the dense jungle, I move with an ease that hints at my connection with the wilderness. Cyrus, trailing behind, struggles to match my agile pace as we navigate the verdant expanse. Shafts of sunlight pierce through the thick canopy, casting dappled patterns on the tangled undergrowth beneath our feet.

As we emerge into a clearing not too far from the palace, I halt, my eyes fixed on a colossal tree that rises majestically into the sky. Its trunk is gnarled, ancient, and seems to defy gravity as it soars toward the heavens. Perched within its lofty branches, a hut suspended in mid-air captures the essence of a bygone era that is still a distant memory in my head.

I turn to Cyrus. "This is it," I declare, my voice blending with nostalgia and reverence. "My childhood home."

I'm not sure what to make of his facial expression. It's excitement, sadness, and disbelief all at once. He rings with his emotions as if trying to figure out which should rule the others.

"How did you get up there?" he asks, still processing his feelings.

"I climbed," I say, stating the obvious. But I know what he means. How did my parents get me to our hut when I was too small to climb?

Cyrus laughs nervously. "I don't want to be rude, but is there another place to sleep?"

I narrow my eyes. "Is it not good enough for you?" I reply, teasing him.

I've never been ashamed of the hut I was born in, and his comment doesn't change that, but I've seen Eternitie. I've walked the halls of the Brass Palace. Cyrus is used to lots of room, servants, and no physical labor to get what he wants.

Tenacoro and even the Confines are different. If you want to survive, *you* can't sit still. From building a shelter to providing food and clothing, you must do everything yourself. If you're as lucky as I was, you grow up around people who take you in and slowly turn into friends and family.

"It's not the hut; it's the climb I'm worried about," Cyrus adds, mapping the tree trunk out as if he can put physical markers into its bark.

"Kids can do it," I say, and with an effortless grace, I begin to ascend the massive tree, nimble as a creature of the forest. I'm uncertain if it's my muscle memory helping me climb faster than ever or if it's the knowledge that I'm only feet away from seeing my father again.

"Kids are also not scared to fall to their death," Cyrus says, less accustomed to such arboreal pursuits, as he struggles to copy my elegance. He clutches at branches, his progress marked by determination and mild desperation.

After a challenging ascent, Cyrus finally reaches the hut, breathless. I'm already inside, welcoming him with a sad smile. "It's always a bit of a journey, but the view is worth it," I remark, gesturing towards the open windows that framed the jungle panorama.

As Cyrus catches his breath, he takes in the surroundings. The hut, crafted from a harmonious blend of vines and sturdy branches, merges seamlessly with the natural architecture of the tree.

"Where is he?" Cyrus asks, noticing my posture.

He knows exactly why I picked my childhood home to rest. Without stating my motive, he's aware I'm here to see my father.

"I don't know. Maybe he went out for a walk or to hunt," I say, pushing aside the lousy feeling that creeps up my spine.

I know he's well; otherwise, Erinna would have never found me at the coast before Eternitie. She dropped him off before she went searching for me.

"Perhaps he didn't come here because he thought your mother would be here," Cyrus replies, erasing my fear.

Why haven't I thought of that?

I wouldn't have come here if Opaline hadn't told me my mother was with the Silent Sisters.

"We'll find him, but right now, all I need is to close my eyes for a few minutes before I faint," he says, his eyes wandering past me.

"Just a few minutes," I repeat, already trying to find a location my father could have gone to.

I lead Cyrus through the interior, revealing a simple yet cozy two-room living space. The walls are made of vines, and the earthen floor bears the imprints of countless footsteps my family had taken in this home. The furniture, carved from resilient wood, radiates the warmth of memories etched into its grain.

"This is where I grew up," I muse, my fingers tracing the wall patterns.

As he absorbs the hut, I move towards one of the open window frames. Beyond the threshold, the jungle stretches endlessly, a sea of green that is nothing like the desert where my father settled down.

"I often wonder," I begin, digging my fingers into the wood, "what if I had never left? What if the rhythm of the jungle had been the only melody I ever knew?"

Cyrus joins me by the window. Together, we look out into the expanse.

"It's been over twenty years," I murmur, my gaze lingering on the unchanged landscape beyond the window. "No one has lived here since my departure." I point at our footprints on the dust-covered floor. "Time stands still here, frozen in a perpetual dance with the memories I left behind."

There's nothing Cyrus can say to slap me out of going down memory lane. While I suspected coming here was a bad idea, I had to. I needed to see with my own eyes what my father had sacrificed to keep me safe.

"I forgot how beautiful it is," I say, taking a deep breath.

Cyrus keeps quiet, and when I look over, I see him watching me, his lips slightly curled. "Indeed," he says as his eyes soften and his smile widens. "It's a stunning view."

It takes me a second to understand that he's not referring to the outdoors. I slap his shoulder before turning away from him. "You pick the worst timing," I say, unable to suppress a laugh.

"I'm sorry," he says, lowering his gaze.

"Don't be," I answer, gathering the bedding—all-natural fibers—with purposeful movements. The air carries the earthy fragrance of the surrounding flora, infusing the hut with the intoxicating scent of nature's embrace.

I unfurl the bedding, allowing it to billow momentarily in the gentle breeze that wafts through the open windows. As the fabric settles, dust particles, like tiny memories of my past, cling to the surface.

Undeterred, I grasp the corners of the bedding and shake it vigorously. The dust disperses into the air, catching rays of sunlight. As the dust scatters, I release the bedding from my grasp after a final, purposeful shake.

"I can sleep in the other room," Cyrus says, pointing to the wall.

"I need you here," I reply, my heart racing as I think about what lies on the other side of the wall—my parents' room. I could let him sleep there, especially since I know neither of my parents has used their bed in years, but I don't want to be alone.

"This might be our last chance—"

He presses his fingers against my mouth. "Don't say it."

I look up at his warm, brown eyes, and my knees wobble.

"How did we get here?" I ask after he takes his hand away. Slowly, I reach for his face and run my fingers over his stubbles.

"We climbed," he answers, mischief glinting in his eyes.

"You know what I mean," I say, smiling at him. "We were living just huts away from each other for a year. Why did we wait so long?"

He hesitates for a moment. "Because I was a coward," he finally says, his eyes resting on my lips. "When I was living with Liza, I hoped you would see through our charade. I was too scared to approach you because I thought you would think I wanted two women."

"You guys did an amazing job in fooling everyone," I snicker, thinking of all the times I saw them together, yet never touching each other. I should have known.

Climbing into bed, I point at the empty space beside me. "You coming?"

Cyrus jumps over me and almost falls off the bed. "It's a little small," he says, scooting closer to me. "My butt is hanging off the edge."

"Stop complaining," I reply, grabbing his arm to loop it under mine and around my waist.

We lay together, looking into the blue sky through the window.

As much as he doesn't want to acknowledge it, this might be our first and last time sharing a bed. And because of that, I can't just lay here and pretend everything will be fine.

TWENTY-NINE

QUEEN SOULIN

I hear the portal vaporize behind me as I step towards the thrones, as my eyes rest on the duplicate of the Crymzon Throne. It was meant to be for Khaos; he was supposed to sit there, staring at me with his playful grin.

My steps echo through the regal expanse, each footfall a solemn proclamation of my lone presence. The red sandstone walls seem to constrict around me, casting an air of suffocation over the once-grand chamber. The vastness of my kingdom, now confined within the narrow embrace of the throne room, mirrors the tumultuous emotions that swirl within me.

Approaching the imposing dais at the room's center, my eyes fixate on the glass casket, a vessel that holds a slumbering figure—the man I love. Behind the transparent barrier, he lays in a serene pose. Dark curls frame his face, and the scar on his left cheek.

As I stand before the glass, my emotions stir. Like coiled flames, anger flickers in the depths of my heart, fueled by the injustice that had befallen my King, and yet, intertwined with the rage, a current of profound sadness tugs at the corners of my heart. Khaos, who shared the triumphs and tribulations of my reign with me, is gone, and I'm responsible for it.

I press a hand against the cool surface of the glass, a futile attempt to bridge the distance that separates us. His frozen features only intensified the storm brewing within me. Once a symbol of sovereignty, the throne room now feels like a gilded cage, its walls closing in with each passing moment.

I can't breathe. It's too hard seeing him, knowing that he will never touch me again. He will never open his eyes again. He will never—

A subtle disturbance catches my attention—a delicate yet insistent noise emanating from the Silk Keep. As if drawn by an unseen force, I turn away from the glass casket and follow the noise with hesitant steps.

All of my moths big enough to cause such a noise should be in Tenacoro—that is, if Conrad followed my command.

Approaching the door that conceals the secret space, my curiosity mingles with the heaviness of my heart. With a deliberate motion, I push the door ajar, revealing a room bathed in the soft glow of concealed lanterns.

As the door swings open, my eyes widen. I step into the room, the air heavy with the enchanting fragrance of hundreds of tiny red moths that flutter about like living confetti. The walls pulse with the soft, rhythmic hum of delicate wings. As I venture further, my gaze fixates on the colossal presence of a horse-sized red moth in the corner, its wings spanned out.

"Adira?" I ask, frozen as I recognize the majestic creature before me.

It can't be.

She failed to answer my call when I opened the door to release my Fighter Moths. While she's never the first to step over the threshold, she's also never the last.

My mouth drops. Amid the crimson swarm, four smaller moths flit around Adira, their wings vibrant and freshly unfurled. My heart quickens with a mix of joy and disbelief. Against the natural order, *my* Adira must have given birth. But that's impossible. Moths lay eggs that turn into worm-like larvae before they start their metamorphosis. This process can take months to years and not a few days.

As I move closer to Adira, my hands trembling, I marvel at her. The smaller moths circle playfully around her, and I feel the gentle caress of their wings against my skin, a tender reminder of how much I love their touch.

Kneeling before the magnificent creature, I pressed my face against Adira's soft, velvety body. A surge of emotion wells within me, and I can't hold back the tears that now trace down my cheeks.

"I thought you were gone," I say, and my sobbing intensifies when Adira presses her wing against me as if she's trying to comfort me. "I thought I had lost you." Adira, her antennae twitching in response, exudes an aura of tranquil majesty.

As my sobs mingle with the rhythmic hum of wings, I think of the magic within me that was powerful enough to defy the laws of nature. I always knew it, but seeing Adira surrounded by her offspring was something I thought I would never witness.

Eventually, as my sobs subside, and the moths continue their fluttering dance, I open my eyes. My heart brims with a newfound understanding of the magic that courses through my veins as I rise from my knees.

Despite all the death my magic has brought to Escela, it has given life for once. For once, it wasn't destructive and cruel, but beautiful. It's a moment where my magic, against all odds, has birthed miracles in the form of delicate, crimson wings.

With a final, lingering gaze at Adira, I step back into the cascade of wings. "I need you to stay here and look after them. I'll be back as soon as possible."

Wiping my tears away, I walk back into the throne room, closing the door behind me before sealing it with magic. While my heart still aches so fucking bad from being in the same room with Khaos, it's also grateful to see Adira alive. This tiny flicker of hope was everything I needed to keep going.

I have to see this through. If it isn't for Khaos, I must do it for Adira.

THIRTY

AVIRA

In the quiet corner of a room I know all too well, threads of daylight stream through the window, casting a gentle glow over a wooden table. A needle dances in my skilled fingers, weaving an attire of transformation. Before me sits Khaos on my bed, his eyes following my every move.

"You are a tailor?" he asks, raising an eyebrow as he looks around the room I've called my home for almost a century.

"You know what's funny? I am," I say, looking up at him, but he doesn't seem amused, so I go into detail. "In my former life, I used to sew. I wasn't very good at it, but it was my escape from a world I wasn't welcome in."

Since my memories returned, my entire childhood trauma slammed into me like a bird falling out of the sky and onto the ground.

"That doesn't sound humorous," he replies, his face an icy mask.

"It is to me if you consider I didn't know I had this skill before living in Shadowmyre."

The room echoes with the soft cadence of stitching as silence settles between us. My eyes, focused yet reflective, survey the fabric before me, once a vibrant crimson that now whispers tales of time and tribulation. Khaos sits unmoving, his dark curls tousled, and his face etched with the shadows of a hardened past.

As my nimble fingers move, I decide to breathe new life into the gray canvas of the attire with a color that symbolizes growth, renewal, and the opposite of the Crymzon Queen's signature color—green. A choice deliberate and full of meaning, as if crafting this garment is a silent conversation between needle and thread, heart and soul, Conqueress and Queen. Without even saying a word, she will know my insult.

Once dull and lifeless, the fabric gradually transforms into a rich, earthy green as I add new fabric atop the old. The needle traces careful lines, forming the contours of a tailored masterpiece.

I can't wait to see her face when she sees him—the new Khaos.

My hands move with purpose, embellishing the garment with intricate details that mirror the complexities of the man beside me. Dark embroidery adorns the cuffs, a subtle nod to the shadows that now cling to him. A scarlet thread intertwines with the green, a reminder of the fiery spirit that still burns within but not for his Queen anymore.

The room falls into a tranquil hush as I put the fabric down to contemplate Khaos. I recognize the beauty in his darkness, the untold stories etched into the lines of his face. Determined to capture this essence, I add a touch of mystery—a hidden pocket, concealed within the folds of the fabric, for him to carry his secrets close.

Khaos, sensing the transformation underway, meets my gaze. A flicker of curiosity dances in his eyes, a silent question lingering in the air. Without saying a word, I continue, letting the garment speak the language of war and hate.

"What do you want?" he finally asks, pointing at the almost-finished suit. "My clothes are just fine." He looks down at himself.

"I thought it would be nice to give you a new outfit," I lie, following his gaze at the now colorless uniform pants and stained shirt he's wearing. Finding a discarded Crymzon uniform amongst the stacks of clothes in the room from which I get all my fabrics was too easy.

He shrugs his shoulders and leans back.

As the last stitches fall into place, I hold out the suit before me. There's beauty in stitching the fragments of a fractured soul together. All this time, I thought that by creating new clothes and holding the fabric tightly within my grasp as I crafted it to my desire, I would catch a glimpse of its history. But now, I know it's not about the past—it's about creating something we want to change into.

"Try it on," I say, holding it in his direction.

I intended to hand him his new suit and leave the room to give him some privacy, but he's faster. I can't move when Khaos deliberately undresses himself while holding my stare.

The gray garments, worn and weathered, cling to him with an air of resignation. He sheds the shirt, then his pants, and I watch every single movement, my eyes tracing the contours of his form.

Gods be damned! Why is he doing this to me?

Heat rushes between my legs as he steps out of his undergarments, freeing his cock.

"Put it on," I say, throwing the suit at him before storming out the door.

What the fuck is wrong with me? If I had stayed a second longer, I would have dug my nails into his skin while taking his cock in. I could feel lust rushing through me like a starving animal seeing prey.

But that can't happen. Even though Otyx and I are not on speaking terms right now, he's the one I want!

So, why am I feeling this way?

"Lust," a dark voice grumbles beside me, and when I look over my shoulder, I see Otyx in the shadows of my building. "It's one of the strongest sins out there, which I find ridiculous. Why punish people for their primal instincts? Reproduction is the reason we are all here. If it weren't for lust, the population would decrease drastically. Lust is all we are—until people added useless chores to their daily agenda."

"How long have you been following me?" I ask, trying to stop him from saying *lust* one more time because my body reacts to it every time it crosses his lips.

"Since the day you took my hand for the first time," he says, stepping onto the road. "Don't be embarrassed. You mortals are programmed to think of reproduction at all times."

"I'm not embarrassed," I answer, but the heat flushing my cheeks gives away my bluff.

"You could have had him," he says, smiling at me.

I cross my arms. "But I don't want him."

"I can smell your desperation," he replies, stepping closer. "Just say the word, and I *will* take you."

Otyx fucking knows I want him. Damn, I would be a fool not to. But I know what game he's playing, and I'm not done yet. "You can have me all you want once Soulin has paid for her mistake," I say, clenching my teeth.

The sky seems to darken when Otyx looms over me. "You should know by now that I can't interfere with fate," he says, his eyes darkening even further.

"Stop acting like I'm dying. I died a long time ago when you accepted my mother's offer," I growl at him, taking a step back. The heat I felt moments ago vanishes. "And besides, even if I die, I land right back in your arms. Isn't that what you want?"

He exhales sharply. "You still don't understand. I want you to live your life, and when it's your turn to come to me, I'll be waiting. But I don't want this," he says, lifting his arms to point out the mess around us.

My eyes wander over our surroundings, but I feel nothing when I see the smoke lingering in the mountains and the gray clouds encircling Starstrand. "That wasn't me," I state, pointing north.

I wondered where all the souls went, and from the looks of it, they found Eternitie.

"Please, stay with me," Otyx cuts in, stretching his hand out again.

I look at it, knowing what this hand is capable of. Yet, I want to feel it between my legs, around my throat, squeezing my ass. I want—

The door slams open between us, and I hold my breath, anticipation hanging in the space between us as Khaos steps into the light. His green suit, meticulously crafted, embraces him like a second skin. The tailored lines stress his frame, and the intricate details are magnificent.

Just as Khaos closes the last button, a subtle change unfolds. The vibrant green begins to drain as if a shadow creeps over the fabric, extinguishing its vitality.

A quiet gasp escapes my lips, my eyes widening in disbelief. My plan was almost perfect, but I didn't consider what would happen to the suit once a soul touches it.

"Please," Otyx repeats, but I can't take my eyes off Khaos.

Sensing the shift, Khaos furrows his brow. The green suit clings to him like a colorless echo of his former self. Determined not to let despair settle in, I reach for the needle I still hold in my hand—a slender instrument of possibility.

Walking over to him, I meet his gaze. Without explanation, I prick my finger with the needle, and a tiny bead of blood wells up. With deliberate intention, I allow the droplet to fall onto the suit, a crimson offering on the canvas of faded green.

I hold my breath as the blood touches the fabric. The green color, drained and diminished, stirs with newfound life as my blood seeps through the threads, each fiber absorbing the essence of my sacrifice. The suit, now vibrant green and pulsating, surges back to life. It spreads across the suit like a revitalizing force.

"That should help," I say, licking another droplet of blood off my finger.

"Avira, don't," Otyx says, watching me carefully as I straighten Khaos' collar.

"What is the difference between you and me?" I ask, cocking my head. "Your purpose is to collect doomed souls. Clearing Escela from sinful souls is mine. Don't you see? I'm helping you."

"You're destroying yourself," he snarls, his eyes moving to Khaos, then back to me. "This isn't who you are."

"You called me Conqueress for a reason."

"Is that what this is all about?" Otyx asks, shadows whirling around him. "You're doing all this because you're trying to live up to a name?"

"Of course not."

"I called you Conqueress because you're the only one who ever conquered my heart," he explains, tapping his fingers against his chest. "I know it's a dark one and barely functioning, but it's there and beating for *you*."

Goosebumps rise on my skin as I look at his chest. He's waiting for my answer...

I don't have one because I no longer know which feelings are real.

"I'm going to repeat it just one more time: once Soulin is dead, I'm all yours," I say after listening to the sins whispering their sweet melodies into my ear as I reach for Khaos' arm and pull him back to the palace behind me.

THIRTY-ONE

DEVANA

I can feel his erection press against my ass, and every time he moves his hips further away from me, I follow him.

Do I have to tell him I want him closer, or will he figure it out himself when he falls out of bed?

"I'm sorry. I can't control it," Cyrus whispers into my ear, and a shudder ripples through my body.

I don't want him to control himself.

"This could be our last night together," I whisper back, bumping my ass into him.

"Stop," he growls, moving another inch away, but I know I have him. If he moves further, he is going to slide off.

"I'm serious. If Soulin—"

"It's not the right time," he says, pulling the arm he has around me back to cover his crotch.

"There's never going to be a right time," I answer, feeling the coldness creeping into my skin where his arm was just seconds ago. The bed creaks under my weight as I turn to face him. "I just want to feel anything but hopelessness for a moment."

"But...what if you regret it later?" he whispers, his voice trailing off.

I know what I'm asking of him. I haven't forgotten about our last intimate encounter. Just the sheer touch of my hand around his dick was enough to make him erupt. But how do I tell him I liked it? How can I take his fear of disappointing me away because there's nothing better than knowing that just the sheer sight of me is enough to overstimulate him?

"I want to feel you inside me," I say, pressing my hand against his chest.

He reaches for me, and I grab his fingers to lead them under my shirt. His hand shakes when he comes in contact with my sensitive skin, which sends a shiver down my spine down to my core.

"Devana," he whispers between ragged breaths as I circle one of his fingers around my nipple.

"You feel so good," I pant, closing my eyes to concentrate on his touch.

It only takes a moment until his hand moves at its own accord. His gentle movements over my nipple make me buck against him, and before I can say anything else, he rolls in my direction, his weight pressing me into the bed.

I know he is scared; I can feel it by the way he hesitantly kisses me, but when I open my mouth to let him in, he grows bolder. With his entire palm, he squeezes my breast, and I don't have enough willpower to hold back the groan that escapes my throat.

The sound seems to have hit a nerve.

I don't know if it's his primal instinct taking over or if he's finally able to act out his dreams, but when I open my eyes, they're not the same warm eyes I'm used to. His eyes are clouded with lust.

Silently, I watch as he pulls his shirt over his head and lets it fall to the ground without breaking eye contact. He does the same to mine, and when my breasts jump free, he bites his lip, taking me in.

My breathing picks up, and my fingers itch to play with his body. Yet, I have to restrain myself. I don't want a foreplay. Teasing him more and accidentally forcing him to release too early again might break him, and I want this to be perfect—considering the circumstances.

The pleasure of his fingers caressing my aching nipples sends sparks between my legs.

"I want you now," I pant, opening my pants to slide it down. He stands up, pulls on the legs to free me of my last clothing before he draws out his cock and wiggles out of his pants.

My body clenches with the need to have him inside me. I want to reach forward to wrap my hand around his erection and feel his hardness against my skin. I can't stop shivering in anticipation, and it has nothing to do with the temperature in the room as his hand drifts down my sternum, tracing the line between my breasts.

I stare down my body as Cyrus centers himself between my legs, wraps a fist around his cock, and angles it down to drag the tip over my throbbing clit.

"Please," I whimper as he wets himself with my desire for him. I can't help but arch into him when his tip presses against my entrance.

Carefully, he shifts forward to press my body against the bed without crushing me with his weight.

As he leans down, I kiss him along the jaw to nip his earlobe. A shudder runs through his body when my teeth connect with his skin, and I let out a moan as he pushes into me slowly.

"Cyrus," I whisper into his ear, taking in every inch of him. "I want you to come inside me."

"Oh Gods," he moans as he stretches me with his cock, slowly picking up his pace. "You feel so fucking good."

I want to gasp because I've never *ever* heard him swear, yet, it's so wicked, I love it.

He sinks himself deeper, and the pulse between my legs intensifies, forcing me to dig my nails into his shoulder blades to stop myself from bucking into him.

This feels nothing like I imagined it would. I was prepared for discomfort or anything that would point out that lust is a sin. But this feels good—so good, I can barely catch my breath.

"Harder," I whisper, curling my legs around his hip to push him deeper inside me.

Cyrus shows no more hesitation as he pounds into me, his muffled groans filling my ear as I tilt my hips into the correct position to get him to rub the sensitive spot inside me.

With his fingers weaving tight through my hair, he thrusts into me harder and faster. His eyes are affixed to my breasts as they bounce up and down.

"You feel so good," Cyrus whispers between pants, his chest heaving as much as mine.

With every thrust, I can feel myself getting closer and closer to the feeling I know only from my own hands. My lower back tingles, and my muscles squeeze his dick as I try to prolong that feeling.

"Hurry," I pant, trying to suppress the desire to open my legs even wider to let more of him in.

"Come for me," Cyrus says as he keeps moving, drawing it out while every muscle of my body spasms as I cry and moan.

At the exact moment the wave of pleasure begins to erupt, he jerks back as a primal moan escapes his lips while his cum spurts into me in streams.

I lay entwined in Cyrus' legs as the tranquility surrounding us is abruptly shattered as distant horns blare, their mournful notes cutting through the trees.

My eyes snap open, my senses heightened by the urgency of the sound. Beside me, Cyrus stirs. The distant blare echoes through the jungle, signaling an impending upheaval.

"He's here," I say, scrambling out of bed. I'm taken aback when I realize it's nighttime.

As I feel for my jacket on the ground, my fingers brush against an unexpected weight in the pocket. With a curious frown, I retrieve a small metallic device, its edges cool against my skin. A rush of memory floods my mind—the gadget given to me by an old man in Eternitie. Since we escaped from Crymzon, I haven't taken my jacket off, so the Chrono-Locator felt like a part of my being.

I press a button on the device, and a holographic projection materializes above my palm. It unfolds like an intricate painting, revealing the detailed landscape of an entire kingdom—the Brass Palace, rolling hills, and a steaming city. The hologram holds a breathtaking beauty. Each detail is etched with precision as if plucked from the vivid dreams of an artist.

His gaze drawn to the hologram, Cyrus marvels at the spectacle. "What is this?" he asks, his voice an indistinct murmur.

I hesitate for a moment, blocking his view with my body. "An old man gave it to me." A hint of uncertainty lingers in my words as I press the button again and wait for his next question.

It never comes.

Guilt settles in the pit of my stomach as I stow the device back into my pocket. Faced with imminent uncertainty, the Chrono-Locator feels like a distraction, a fleeting glimpse into his kingdom how it used to be, and that's not what he needs right now. If we survive, I will give him the Chrono-Locator as a memory of his home.

The distant horns blare again, their urgency slicing through the air like a clarion call. We exchange a knowing look as we throw our clothes on. With a swift motion, I exit the hut perched among the trees, stepping into the moonlit night.

Cyrus emerges just seconds behind me, and we stare at the sky in anticipation of the arrival of an unseen force. The air crackles with tension, and a distant hum heralds the approach of wings soaring through the night sky. My eyes widen as I spot them, their silhouettes gliding through the wind.

Winged figures, their forms illuminated by the pale light of the moon, descend into Tenacoro.

"It's her," I say, pointing to their landing spot near the palace.

"It's not," Cyrus counters, pointing at another wave of winged figures in the sky. "Those are Starstrandians."

THIRTY-TWO

QUEEN SOULIN

"What's the plan?" Conrad asks as I portal myself back to the corridor I left him in.

"I don't have one," I answer, watching his eyebrows furrow.

"But you're planning something," he replies, petting Storm's head. "I can see it in your eyes."

It doesn't matter what I do next. Either Otyx is going to accept my plea and gives me Khaos back, or he kills me instantly and I'm reunited with him. Whatever I—or rather he—chooses will benefit me.

But I must stay alive because, without me, Crymzon will be overrun by magic as I break away as its vessel, dooming everyone inside it.

Would it be a bad thing, though? Crymzon is currently manless beside Conrad, my moths, and me. Everyone important presently lives in the tunnels beneath the prison outside the Crymzon Wall or in Tenacoro. If I go, they will end up without magic, but they will make it. I'm confident the other kingdoms will open their arms to take them in. Or they could rebuild, rock by rock.

"I've never thanked you for retrieving the Painite," I say, looking into his tired eyes. "You never deserved to be treated the way I treated you."

The smile I haven't seen on his face, but I'm so used to, comes back. For a split second, I thought I would never see it again. "You know how many children I have?" he asks, throwing me off.

I remember the exact number. 17.

"As a parent, you rarely hear a *thank you* or an apology," he continues, a light returning to his eyes. "Still, you're there for them, every day, every night, whenever they need you. You know what my favorite part about parenthood is?" He doesn't give me a second to respond. "The moment they realize, and I mean *really* realize, how loved they are."

"But I'm not your daughter," I correct him, shaking my head.

"Does it matter?"

My instinct is to say *yes*, yet I keep quiet and let his words sink in.

"I'll be by your side till the end," he adds, his smile turning into a wide grin.

"I can't ask that of you," I answer, stepping beside him to give Storm the same affection he's giving her.

"That's what I want," he counters, pulling his hand away. "I want to be by your side when you finally succeed."

I know better than trying to change this old man's decision. He's as dedicated to a cause as I am.

"Well then," I say, pressing my head against Storm's before I release her to sign the sigils into the air. "I hope you're as powerful as you made me believe."

I still don't know where he got the strength to keep me out of the throne room when I wanted to see Khaos, but I know it will be helpful.

Inhaling deeply, I clear my mind and envision the river parting Eternitie from Crymzon. When I open my eyes, I let out a scuffling noise as I see branches covered in leaves reach through the portal in our direction.

That's not where I want to go.

Shaking my hands, the portal vaporizes before me, and I repeat the process of channeling a new one. Again, I picture the river before my eyes...

Tenacoro appears.

"Ready?" he asks, marching through the portal before I can close it to try it anew.

"That's not where I want to go," I say, my eyes narrowing.

"Are you sure?" he asks, looking around. "It seems like this is exactly where you want to be, if you're honest with yourself."

I'm regretting inflating his ego by thanking him. At that moment, it felt like the right thing to do, but I'm not that type of person. Showing weakness doesn't come easy to me, and by opening up to Conrad, I realized that I'm still the easily annoyed Soulin I've always been.

"Of course, I'm certain," I bark, but when I hear the blaring noise rattling through the trees behind Conrad, I'm faster through the portal than I can say another word.

"What does it mean?" I ask Conrad, holding the portal open for another moment to let Storm through.

"It's some kind of alarm," he says, and I roll my eyes.

Seriously? That's clear as day because otherwise, I would have opened portal after portal until it showed me my true destination instead of ending up in Queen Synadena's domain.

Under the cloak of night, the jungle's dark depths conceal our movements. The chorus of nocturnal creatures harmonizes with the mysterious whispers that beckon me forward.

As I venture closer, Conrad and Storm following me silently, the murmurs grow louder, resonating through the dense foliage. My senses attune to the rhythm of the night, discerning the presence of others. Soon, the shadows yield to a moonlit clearing, revealing an unexpected assembly.

Before me stand the rulers of the other kingdoms—Queen Synadena and Queen Catalina—their regal figures outlined by the moon's soft glow. My keen eyes survey the scene. In front of the two leaders stand beings with blond hair, tall and ethereal, their wings stretching wide like alabaster feathers. Clad in silver armor that glints in the moonlight, they emanate an aura of celestial majesty.

What is Starstrand doing here? I thought Queen Caecilia was dead.

Hidden in the jungle's embrace, I observe the unfolding tableau. A calm conversation passes among the rulers, their voices a symphony of diplomacy and uncertainty.

As the dialogue unfolds, my instincts shift. The initial tension gives way to a realization—these Starstrandians don't impose a threat.

With a quiet signal to Conrad and Storm, I step out of the shadows and into the moonlit. "What's going on?" I ask.

My arrival is met with a brief hush as everyone turns their attention toward me. Conrad and Storm flank me.

"We heard that you're forming an army," a man says, stepping closer so I can get a better view of him. Blonde hair, blue eyes, muscles straining under his armor—that's literally the definition of every Starstrandian, and he isn't an exception.

"I'm Kieran Vale, King of Starstrand," he adds, sizing me up.

"And you will be a headless King if you take another step closer," I growl, returning his unpleasant stare.

"That's her way of welcoming new people," Opaline cuts in, jumping to his side before turning to me. Her eyes shoot ice at me as she gestures to me to calm down. "We were just discussing a new alliance. Please join us, Queen Soulin," she continues, smiling at Kieran.

My gaze is unwavering as I consider her words. Are they going to trust a Starstrandian who was appointed as their new ruler less than a few hours ago, if even?

"Continue," Queen Synadena says, looking at Kieran.

The new leader among the winged warriors, his silver armor gleaming in the moonlight, turns to her. "We seek an alliance, a union of kingdoms bound by mutual understanding and shared purpose to defeat the Underworld. Our wings will be useful in this war."

Synadena, attuned to the delicate balance of her kingdom, considers his proposition.

I know what she's thinking of. If Devana speaks the truth and Oceris joins us in the fight, it would be the first time all five kingdoms join forces—if she counts Catalina to represent her entire kingdom. Well, maybe my moths could retrieve some of her subjects after I left, but I'm confident they won't make outstanding soldiers.

No matter what he says, I don't trust him. I wasn't alive when Caecilia was crowned Queen of Starstrand, but I know that even though she was the rightful heir, it took her days to climb the throne.

So how did he do it? How did he persuade the other Starstrandians to become King?

Queen Synadena, with a regal nod, accepts the alliance, and Catalina mirrors her gesture before their eyes fall on me.

"Don't look at me," I say, shaking my head. "I won't join forces with someone I don't know." Synadena looks at me like she wants to throttle me. "It's not like you need my vote. It's two against one. Plus, I won't stick around."

"Then what are you doing here?" Catalina asks, crossing her arms.

I can't tell them that my magic involuntarily brought me here, and I, for sure, won't mention that I rushed through the portal because I thought they needed help.

"There's someone I need to check on before I go," I say, searching the crowd for Devana.

"That person isn't here," Synadena answers, glaring at me.

What did I do to her?

"If you won't join us, I would like you to leave," Catalina cuts in, a smile curving her lips.

Gods be damned. While I should loathe this woman for battling me every step of the way, I genuinely enjoy her feistiness.

Perhaps that's what Khaos saw in me.

Queen Synadena turns away from me and extends her hand to Kieran to seal the pact. Just as their palms touch, two figures tumble into the clearing, both out of breath.

"What did we miss?" Devana yells, holding her ribs as Cyrus crouches down beside her.

"Speaking of the devil." I gaze at their clothes. "Your shirt is on backward," I add, looking straight at Cyrus. His cheeks blush as he contemplates fixing his shirt or standing his ground.

"Starstrand is joining us," Queen Synadena says, releasing the new King.

Devana inhales and holds her breath to stop herself from gasping for air. Her eyes widen when she meets the newest King and confusion clouds her face.

"Kieran Vale, King of Starstrand," he says, lowering his head for a split second.

Devana leans away, and I know that gesture too well. She doesn't trust him either.

"What do you know so far?" Kieran asks, signaling his subjects, who have stood at attention since I entered the conversation, to take a break.

"One kingdom has fallen," Catalina says, holding her head high. "While everyone knows that the Underworld is the one who attacked both of our kingdoms, no one has actually seen the God. Eternitie didn't have a chance, but it seems yours did. We've heard that a Starstrandian and a dragon attacked Starstrand?" Her last sentence is more of a question than a statement.

"No Starstrandian would dare to attack their own home," Kieran counters, his eyes forming into slits. "I'm sorry to inform you that your source was incorrect. We were indeed attacked by a dragon, but it didn't have an owner."

My eyes dart to Devana, who's struggling to keep her mouth shut. Seeing her silent battle, I decide it's time to see what our connection is good for. Since I branded her with my handprint around her throat, I'm able to track her well-being and surroundings in case I need to find her.

Can I do more than that? There has to be an easier way to communicate with her.

Closing my eyes, I take a deep breath to clear my mind before surrendering to its vast expanse. Then, as if stepping out of my body, I reach out for her in my mind. The connection I feel, a tether woven of familiarity, beckons me to explore it.

Still concentrating on her, I delve into the recesses of my consciousness, seeking the thread that binds me to Devana. The warmth of our connection pulses like a steady heartbeat, guiding me through the intricacies of our mental realms.

Yet, as I reach out to bridge the gap, an unexpected resistance meets my efforts—a mental barrier, subtle yet formidable. Undeterred, I tap against the invisible wall, each gentle touch echoing through our shared connection like ripples across a still pond.

With determination in my mental touch, I seek to make myself noticeable, to send signals that traverse the intangible bridge between our minds. The warmth of Devana lingers just beyond reach, an elusive presence teasing my senses.

Let me in, I whisper to myself, persistently tapping against the barrier. To my surprise, the resistance softens, like a gate gradually creaking open. A surge of curiosity and anticipation wells within me as the barrier yields, allowing me access to the inner sanctum of Devana's mind.

The warmth I've sensed before envelopes me like a hug.

What are you doing to me? Devana's voice echoes through my head, and I cringe.

I open my eyes and meet hers. *You can feel me?* I ask without opening my mouth.

Her eyelids flutter as she stares at me. *What is going on? Get out of my head!*

I will once you tell me what you think of Kieran.

Her nostrils flare. *Why does it matter what I think? He's the new King. Great.*

I saw how you looked at him. All I want is the truth. What do you think of him?

Devana bites her lip. *He's lying. Satisfied?*

"Why isn't he attacking us, then?" Kieran asks in the distance as I let Devana's words settle.

"Maybe Otyx is aware of our preparations and knows how much damage those gems can do?" Queen Synadena answers, rubbing her chin.

"That doesn't make sense," Catalina cuts in. "If he would know, he could have attacked us before we completed them."

Why aren't you telling the others that he's a liar? I ask through the connection, watching Kieran tentatively.

Who's going to believe me? I'm not a royal. I'm a runaway, remember?

"Maybe we should wait it out? What's the worst that can happen?" Kieran asks, his white wings moving in the wind.

Catalina shakes her head in disbelief. "And what if the dragon comes back? It could burn this entire kingdom to the ground. Or the souls. It took them less than an hour to overrun Eternitie."

My eyes fly back to Devana. *If you don't tell them, I will.*

I can feel Devana's anger pulsing through the connection.

Don't.

Cyrus throws his hands in the air. "It doesn't matter where we go or what we do. If Otyx wants to find and eliminate us, no place on this planet is safe enough."

I shrug my shoulders. *Suit yourself.* Those are the last words I send through our connection before I reel my mind back in and use my magic to barricade it. Devana might not know how to get into my mind, but it's just a matter of time until she figures it out.

"I won't wait any longer. If anyone wants to join me, I'll be at Otyx's doorstep at sunrise," I say loudly to everyone.

I'm sick of waiting. Patience has never been my strength; since I have nothing to lose, it's even easier to live dangerously.

"It's all of us or none," Kieran says, his blue eyes flickering with a challenge. "Since you don't belong to our alliance, you're free to do as you please."

Opaline, who has been awfully quiet, makes her way to my side before turning to her mother. "I'm staying with her," she says, nodding at me.

Her mother looks at Opaline, her eyes soft. "Are you sure?"

That's something I didn't see coming. I thought it was *nice* to voice my departure this time instead of just vanishing, but I didn't expect anyone to accept my offer.

I should have known better.

"I know what I'm doing," she answers, looking at Catalina as if that's enough to win her over. I can see a flicker of fear in her eyes as she looks at her brother.

"They're staying," I say, crushing her thought process before Devana and Cyrus can answer. "Cyrus can't fight, and Devana will be in my way."

Silence.

"Good luck," Kieran says, and I realize what he's doing. He's trying to speed up my departure.

Opaline seems to deflate when she realizes it will only be the two of us, Conrad and Storm. Yet, she regains her confidence and nods. "Don't take too long," she says to her mother.

Without wording it, I know she realized what she agreed to.

Everyone knows that the front line never makes it out alive—never.

THIRTY-THREE

Avira

In the cavernous darkness of the room, shadows cling to the walls like the whispers of the sins surrounding me. I pace restlessly, my footsteps echoing in the silence that envelops the palace since I left Otyx behind in the streets. Beside me, Mordecai observes my movements with keen eyes, his serpentine tail swaying in anticipation. But he's not the only one watching me. Khaos, who claimed the bed again, stares at me occasionally while giving me the silent treatment.

He's waiting for my next move.

I should bring him to Crymzon to persuade Soulin to come out because I know it will work. And yet, I don't want to go there without the support of the other souls. I'm aware of who I am and what I can endure, which is why I know my wings are no match for the Queen's magic.

I feel the weight of uncertainty settle upon my shoulders. The air is heavy with unspoken tension, and as I pace, the dim light reveals glimpses of Mordecai's eyes on me.

"What?" I snarl after I can't take it any longer.

"Nothing," he replies, ripping his gaze off me to stare at a blank wall.

"Spit it out."

His eyes roll back as if trying to hold the words back. He caves. "Wouldn't it be easier to send her family to do the dirty work for you?"

Now, that's something I can work with.

"Go on," I say, forcing a smile onto my lips.

"I don't know how much you know about Crymzon, but their magic isn't as absolute as they think. Crymzon's magic has been weaning since the Queen killed her brother, father, and many Crymzonians inside the palace. In the attempt to cover up her mistake, they weren't very careful removing the blood off the ground before plastering new stones atop of it."

How have I never heard of this before?

"Spoiled blood drains their magic," I whisper, biting my lips.

"So you do know about it?" he asks, nodding at me.

No, I was guessing, but now I do.

"Anyway," he continues, interrupting my thoughts, "since the blood of her family still pollutes their soil as it seeps through the throne room's ground into the Underworld, it's a direct link to her brother and father."

"How do you know so much about Crymzon?"

Mordecai straightens. "I would be a horrible guard if I didn't keep tabs on where my souls go after Otyx requests them." He blows out a smoke puff through his nostrils. "King Obsidian was gone for a long time until he returned just days ago. Of course, his memories were stripped again, and he couldn't tell me where he had been or what he had done, but I could squeeze some details out of him. I guess he's easier to control through his remaining blood in Crymzon, and that's why Otyx chose him."

I shake my head. "Why are you telling me this now?"

"Because we're connected, remember? It's my duty to keep you safe."

Khaos chuckles, and it sends a fiery flare through my body. "Anything you want to add?"

"Why are you so obsessed with a mortal?"

Telling him he's speaking about the mortal he was head over heels for burns on my tongue, but I swallow it down. For my plan to work, he can't know who she is. Just his presence alone will be enough to drive her insane.

His scales shimmering in the muted glow, Mordecai tilts his head inquisitively as he waits for my response.

"That's something between her and I."

Suddenly, I cease pacing as I look out the window. The glass, revealing a panoramic view of Shadowmyre sprawling beneath, offers a glimpse into the world beyond the dark room. My breath catches as I witness a movement, a distant procession approaching the palace. Shrouded figures march with purpose toward me.

What took her so long to get here? I've expected her to come looking for me since the moment I burned Starstrand to the ground—figuratively speaking.

As I peer through the window, realization dawns upon me. It's not Soulin but the missing souls who strayed the moment Shadowmyre breached the surface. They are returning—and with them, the oppressing weight of their sins.

Sensing the shift in my aura, Mordecai lets out a low rumble, his eyes mirroring my internal turmoil. Only Khaos, attentive to my every movement, remains still yet again.

At the moment's stillness, I grapple with the sins that brush over me like the fingers of a ghostly specter. Like smoldering embers, Rage flickers within my chest, fueled by the betrayals and challenges I had faced in Starstrand and during Nekrojudex. Lust, an intoxicating scent in the air, hints at desires both whispered and unspoken. Envy, a bitter taste on my tongue paints the edges of my thoughts with shades of longing.

They're just in time. I have to go to her if Soulin doesn't want to come to me.

Yet, amid the tempest of emotions, I find myself patient and composed for the first time since I tied myself to Otyx.

As the procession draws nearer, my senses heighten. The sins swirling around me like pesky flies whisper sweet nothings into my ears, but I keep my thoughts under control. The window frames the approaching souls, now discernible as they ascend the palace steps.

"Is it time?" Khaos asks, looking over my shoulder.

I smile. "It is."

As the souls stream into the throne room, Khaos and I are already there waiting for them. My eyes meet theirs, searching for clues within the sea of faces. Some wear expressions of remorse, others defiance. The sins, however, continue to weave their ephemeral dance around me, reminding me of the complexities that rule this kingdom.

I step forward from the shadows of the throne into the dim light of the room. Now coiled by my side, Mordecai doesn't mirror my poised stance while Khaos stands behind the throne close to the bowl, still stained with my blood.

As I address them, a hush falls over the room, my voice carrying a weight that resonates in the stillness. "It's time to lay bare the sins that linger in the shadows. Let us remind those mortals how deadly sins are."

Rage, lust, and envy continue their dance around me, their presence a reminder of what I never had as a child, young adult, and even now. The other sins hum quietly in the background, waiting for their turn.

I, however, stand resolute, ready to navigate this untrained bunch of sinners against the only person standing between Otyx and me. Once Soulin is gone, I don't have to worry about someone trying to kill him because no one else is unhinged enough to approach him.

THIRTY-FOUR

DEVANA

D id Soulin really expect me to stay put after she invaded my
thoughts, told the new King to fuck off in front of the other
rulers, and left to fight Otyx by herself?

She should know better than telling a Tenacorian to avoid a fight.

"What are you doing?" Cyrus asks, following me loudly through the
low-hanging trees and bushes. While everyone was occupied with going
over war strategies, I took the opportunity to steal myself away. And it
almost worked.

"What does it look like?"

"Suicide," he answers right before a branch I just let go hits him square
in the face.

My first instinct is to check on him, but my muscles won't listen. "So,
what's your idea? Sit around and wait for the moment she gets herself
killed to watch me die in your arms?"

He rubs his face as guilt creeps up my stomach. Cyrus doesn't deserve
my anger. It's not his fault that I'm connected to the only individual who
no longer cares if she lives or dies.

Nevertheless, I need him to turn around.

"We could kidnap her and hold her hostage until the war is over," he replies, showing the red streak marking his face.

He has clearly thought this through, and his idea is actually...good—but just for her and my benefit.

I release another branch, but he ducks faster this time. "We need her magic. Without her, it's just a matter of time until the other kingdoms fall."

He stumbles after me. "That's why we have her army. Yes, she's powerful, but not as powerful as thousands of her men. No one will notice she's missing."

I stop in my tracks to face him. "What if you're wrong? Would you risk killing every soul on this planet to keep me safe?"

"What kind of question is that? Yes!"

"What about your sister? You're letting her fight. Why not me?"

The muscles in his jaw twitch. "My plan includes her."

His offer is tempting and something I haven't considered until now. However, it goes against everything I stand for. My father trained me my entire life not to turn away from a fight. He taught me it's essential to be vigilant and always ready.

I move quietly, my senses attuned to the subtle sounds and fragrances of Tenacoro. The moon still mutes the vibrant colors of greens and browns as I navigate the labyrinth of towering trees and tangled undergrowth.

Behind me, Cyrus trails cautiously, his footsteps measured as he attempts to keep pace with my stride. "What are you doing now?" he inquires, his voice a persistent murmur that cuts through the night.

Focused on my new mission, I spare him a glance. "For your plan to work, I need to make a tranquilizer dart," I reply.

My warrior's heart breaks as I speak those words aloud—but I'm also scared. I don't want to die.

Cyrus furrows his brow, a mixture of confusion and concern etching lines on his face. "What is that?"

I continue walking. "We need to subdue her without causing harm. A tranquilizer dart is the most humane way to do it."

Without hurting me, but that's the part I leave out. I'm unsure how I will react to putting Soulin to sleep. Maybe I'll feel just the poke, or perhaps it will also cloud my mind, forcing me to take an unwanted nap.

Still grappling with the unfamiliarity of the situation, Cyrus quickens his pace to match mine. "But how do you even know how to make one?"

My steps remain steady. "I've learned a few survival skills during my time in the Confines," I reply cryptically.

"Like killing the most powerful Queen in Escela?"

Darn it. I forgot how much I've told him. He knows about my past and why my father took me away from Tenacoro. He also knows why my father persisted in training me in the scorching heat of the desert until my already weak muscles were caving.

"We need to find a specific plant that will provide the necessary components," I add, my eyes scanning the ground. "She won't feel a thing, I promise."

It feels like we've been searching for hours when I recognize the telltale signs of the elusive plant I seek—a rare specimen with leaves that, when processed correctly, can yield a potent tranquilizing substance.

Cyrus, growing more anxious with each step, persists with his questions. "Are you sure about this? What if she knows what you're up to?"

I halt abruptly, my hand reaching out to pluck a vibrant leaf from the nearby plant. I turn to face him, a determined glint in my eyes. "This was your idea."

"I didn't mean to knock her out."

"You intended to approach her and nicely ask her if she would like to hide with us while the God responsible for her Soulmate's death kills more of her subjects?"

"Something like that," he mumbles, looking at my closed palm.

I blink my eyes. "I don't even know what to say to that," I answer after a few breaths.

How can an intelligent man like Cyrus be so...dumb? I've seen him build hideouts beneath huts with makeshift tools and help villagers in the Confines with solutions to almost all their problems by engineering something to help them. So how can the same man think we can talk the Crymzon Queen into hiding?

With the leaf in hand, I continue to gather various plants, berries, and roots, each chosen for its unique properties in crafting the perfect tranquilizer.

Cyrus reluctantly follows suit. "How do you know so much about these plants?"

I sigh. "There are things you don't know about me, about my past. I've been in situations where survival depended on resourcefulness. And right now, making this tranquilizer dart is our best chance."

As we reach a small clearing, I set about my task. I carefully strip the bark from a particular tree, revealing the inner fibers that serve as the dart's shaft.

"Do you even know how to use that thing?" he asks, eyeing the makeshift dart taking shape in my skilled hands.

I glance at him, a small smile playing on my lips. "I've used one before. It's not as complicated as it looks."

I keep working as Cyrus hovers nearby, unable to conceal his unease. "What if it doesn't work? What if she knows what we're up to?"

Finishing the dart with practiced precision, I rise to my feet. "This will work. Trust me."

Sometimes, I forget I only know him a little over a year because it feels like a lifetime.

"That's it?" Cyrus asks, looking at the two objects in my hands.

"You're insufferable," I reply, smiling at him. "If you don't stop asking me so many questions, I'll use it on you first."

"If this doesn't work, we will do it my way," he says, still eyeing my hands.

I'm almost intrigued to break the dart in the middle to see how he will approach Soulin. I would do it if the world wasn't falling apart around us.

"Now, let's find her," I say, carefully putting the dart and blow gun into my other pocket, far away from the Chrono-Locator. "There's one more thing. If it comes down to Escela or me, I need you to promise me you'll let me go."

I expect him to argue, to plead, even to knock me out to ensure I'm not going another step. Instead, his eyes fill with tears, and he blankly stares at me.

As we press on in pursuit of Soulin, the jungle gives way to a dried-out riverbed, the cracked earth a stark reminder of the once-flowing watercourse. Cyrus stares at me again, like he has done a lot the last hour, and I swallow. Following the meandering path of the parched riverbed, we discover fresh footprints imprinted on the hardened mud, evidence of recent passage.

The footprints lead us beyond Tenacoro, transitioning into the expansive red sands of the desert. As we trek forward, the low sun throws long shadows on the sand. Driven by reaching Soulin before she can make it to the Underworld, I ignore looking over my shoulder at everything I'm leaving behind.

"That's her," I say, pointing at a regal figure clad in crimson emerging in the distance, accompanied by a colossal moth that flutters its wings with majestic grace.

We conceal ourselves behind the skeletal remains of a once-mighty tree, its branches barren and twisted like dried leaves. From our covert vantage point, we observe Soulin standing alongside an old man, his weathered face reflecting a lifetime in the Crymzon desert, and Opaline with her Glimmarum.

"We won't be able to get close enough to her," Cyrus says. "She's going to see us."

It's almost impossible to stay unnoticed in the desert, but we have to try. With each step, we try to minimize our presence, expertly navigating between shadows and early sunlight—well, I do; Cyrus, not that much. As we draw closer, the landscape becomes our ally while we inch through the red sands like silent phantoms.

Time ebbs away, an hour passing in hushed breaths and shared glances. The old man, seemingly attuned to the surroundings, gazes in our direction a few times but doesn't notice us. Each time, I could feel my heart beating in my throat, yet we remained steadfast, our nerves unbending.

We stop behind another gnarled remains of a dead tree, just a hundred feet from the Queen and her entourage. I can see the outlines of the dark kingdom from here, which means we're running out of precious time. If we wait longer, she will be too close to the Underworld.

"I think we're close enough," I say, my fingers curling around the blowgun.

"We only have one try," Cyrus whispers, leaning against the tree to gasp silently for air.

"No pressure," I reply, feeling the same weight resting on my shoulders when I stood upon the Crymzon Wall to assassinate the Queen.

The shadows provide a sanctuary as I observe her movements. Her giant moth, its wings iridescent in the sunlight, hovers over her like a cloud. Now quite a few feet behind her, the old man struggles to keep her pace while Opaline covers the Queen as she trails her.

"Now or never," I whisper as I lean past the tree, holding the tranquilizer dart with steady hands.

Anxiety etched on his face, Cyrus whispers, "Are you sure this will work?"

I take a deep breath, my gaze never leaving Soulin. With a swift and practiced motion, I load the tranquilizer dart into a makeshift blowgun. I aim, waiting for just the right moment. When Opaline steps out of my way, I take a deep breath and release the dart.

The projectile sails through the air, finding its mark with precision.

Or it would have if Soulin hadn't countered it with a flick of her hand.

THIRTY-FIVE

Queen Soulin

This man never stops talking. At least, that's the Conrad I knew when he accompanied me to Terminus.

This version of Conrad I'm currently traveling with is nothing like the man from a week ago or even the one I witnessed for a few minutes after I thanked him. Since we started heading to the Underworld, he has barely opened his mouth.

"What is that thing called again?" I ask, looking at the lion that looks like a living carpet of green grass, who has been eyeing me like I'm its next snack.

"Verdant is my Glimmarum," Opaline answers, scratching its neck.

I narrow my eyes. "And...what does it do besides carrying someone around?" I ask, watching Conrad look down at me as he sits on its back.

"I guess he doesn't differ much from your moths," Opaline answers, pointing at Storm. "Glimmarums are our companies who imprint on us after birth. They bond themselves to us to bring solace and friendship. Carrying us is just a bonus."

If I didn't know better, I would think my moths are my Glimmarums. They are connected to me—not through a bond, but emotionally and through my magic. I wonder how my life would have played out if I had Adira already as a child or during the time I lost my entire family. Even though I was never alone, always surrounded by servants, maids, Myra, and Khaos, I felt lonely.

"What if he refuses to help you?" Opaline asks, ripping me out of my thoughts. She keeps circling back to this question as if she was hoping my answer would change.

"We have been over this. I won't give Otyx a choice."

Conrad shakes his head. "But you understand that—"

"Yes, I'm a mortal, and he's a God. I got it."

"I don't think you're thinking this through. You have nothing to offer."

I'm fucking aware of that. So why are those the only words Conrad keeps repeating since we left?

I huff. "But he doesn't know I come empty-handed."

"As I said, he's a God. He knows you're bluffing."

"I've been bluffing my entire life. Most people thought I was sending innocent children to prison to starve; they thought I killed my family to inherit the throne and even that my magic was as powerful as my father's while I had almost none. I'm good at making people believe the worst of me."

"It didn't work for me," Opaline cuts in, and I glare at her. Usually, this look is enough to bring my subjects to crumble to the ground. But not Opaline.

I scan the seemingly endless horizon, searching for signs beyond the vast sea of sand. The darkness clings to the desert like a shroud, revealing only the desolation of a landscape marked by a few skeletal remnants of trees, their twisted branches reaching desperately for the starlit sky.

Beside me, Opaline and Verdant walk with measured steps, their eyes reflecting my decision to go straight for Otyx. Storm, wings shimmering in the dim light, hovers above us with a watchful elegance while Conrad stares into the distance.

Amidst the quiet, a glimmer on the horizon catches my attention. I turn, my eyes tracing the slow ascent of a beautiful sunrise. The first rays of dawn paint the desert in hues of crimson and gold, casting a surreal glow upon the arid landscape.

As the sunrise unfolds behind me, I know the inevitable is coming closer and closer: war. Trying to keep my head clear, I avoid thinking about how this could play out.

"There's still time to turn around," Conrad says, sliding off the Glimmarum to stretch his legs.

He must have sensed the weight of the moment, and Storm, as if attuned to my emotions, flutters her wings with a subtle shift in demeanor.

Shaking my head, I continue my march, the red sunrise casting long shadows that dance in the shifting sands.

In the distance, as the sun begins its ascent, my keen eyes discern a foreboding sight. Black towers pierce the sky, their ominous presence rising from the depths like death reaching for the heavens. The Underworld, with its mysteries and shadows, looms on the horizon.

Just as I process the gravity of the looming towers, a faint whooshing noise whispers through the air. Instinctively, my hand moves precisely, activating the magic that courses through my veins. A shimmering barrier materializes, deflecting a dart that silently streaks toward me.

My senses heighten, my eyes narrowing toward the unseen assailant. Verdant whips around, its gaze sharp, and Storm hovers protectively, sensing the imminent threat.

"I wondered when they would show themselves," Conrad says, picking up the pointy dart dripping with an unknown substance.

Opaline comes to a halt beside him, taking the dart out of his hand. "It's a tranquilizer dart," she says, rolling it in her fingers.

I didn't even consider that someone from Tenacoro would follow us. They all had their tails between their legs when I asked them to join us. And to make matters worse, someone supposed to be an ally tried to immobilize me. I've never seen a sedative delivered through a weapon only as a drink or spell in Crymzon.

"Show yourself," I bark into the desert, my eyes focusing on the only dead tree surrounding us that could be used as a hiding place. The command echoes through the stillness, a regal decree in the heart of the crimson wasteland.

A beat passes, silence lingering. Then, from behind the tree, a woman and a man emerge, their figures cast in the hues of the rising sun. The woman, with long, dark braided hair and a complexion kissed by ebony, carries both a bow and arrow and a sword strapped to her hip. Her usual silver freckles glow like a blood splatter as the sun catches them.

Beside her, the man stands tall, his pale complexion contrasting the desert's warm tones. Wild brown hair frames his face, and a sprinkle of stubble adorns his jawline. A sword, inconsistent with his demeanor, hangs at his hip. I can't help but laugh at the sight, for I know that this man, despite his warrior's attire, isn't a fighter.

As Devana and Cyrus step forward, the sunrise casting long shadows across the red sands, both raise their hands in surrender.

"Ah, the shadows reveal its players," I remark. "Let me guess, you two are the only ones who followed us?"

Devana, her expression unwavering, speaks with a calm assurance. "We mean no harm."

Cyrus, his eyes portraying a hint of nervousness beneath the façade of confidence, nods in agreement. "We're just trying to save you."

Not again.

I know Cyrus saved my ass not once, but twice, since I took him prisoner. I wish I could say I don't need saving, but that would be a lie. Even though I need someone in my corner, I never expected Cyrus to be that person who comes through for me over and over again when it should be my Soulmate.

My gaze, sharp and discerning, flickers between the duo. I sense sincerity in their words, yet standing up against the God of the Underworld is my destiny. I've dug this hole and am the only one who can get us out of it again.

I lower my hands. "Shooting a fucking dart to sedate me is your approach to rescue me?"

As Devana and Cyrus draw closer within a respectful distance, the tension of the confrontation dissipates. Still, they keep their hands raised as a sign of deference. A contemplative demeanor replaces my laughter, and I regard them steadily.

"Yes, because asking you nicely to come with us and hide until all of this is over wasn't an option," Devana snarls, looking at Opaline for confirmation.

Cyrus lowers his arms. "You can't die," he says, his brows dropping. "I can't lose her."

He doesn't have to look at Devana to show me he's talking about her, and it stings. The feelings of loss, anger, and sadness gnaw on me because I know how he feels. Losing Khaos is the worst thing that ever happened to me. I felt the same way when my mother passed, but that was years ago, and I got my closure when I saw her on the battlefield beside my undead father.

Khaos, though, his loss is fresh and still pulsing through my heart like glass shards.

"I'll do my best," I reply, shrugging my shoulders. "I don't intend to die today, but if it needs to be done to save Escela from Otyx, I don't have another choice."

Or rather, if it needs to be done to be by Khaos' side again, I'll do it myself.

A growling noise escapes Verdant's throat, forcing the tiny hairs on my neck to stand. "What's wrong with him?" I ask Opaline, turning my face towards the sun like her Glimmarum.

As we stand there, the horizon towards Tenacoro stirs. Winged figures soar across the canvas of the waking sky, their forms radiant in the early light. Green griffins, majestic and proud, join them, their wings beating in harmony with the rhythm. Giant birds, their plumage as green as their kingdom, carried riders through the vast expanse above.

Beneath them, the red desert transformed into a bustling scene of four-legged jungle creatures in vibrant green, traversing the arid landscape as they carry people from other kingdoms.

Tears spring into Devana's eyes as she exchanges glances with Cyrus and Opaline. Conrad's weathered face is etched with stoic resolve as he surveys the panorama with a silent nod of approval.

Amid this kaleidoscope of movement and color, the realization dawns upon me. The other kingdoms have chosen to stand united against the impending threat. I can't believe it. When I gave the other rulers an ultimatum for my attack, I didn't think they would answer the call to unite against the God of the Underworld.

"They'll catch up," I say, turning my back to the newcomers to hide the tears prickling in my eyes. I can't let them see me like that, not now, not so close to the fight.

"Thank your mother for me," I whisper to Opaline, who has noticed my quick maneuver. We both know that without Synadena, we wouldn't have a backup steering for us. I'm aware that the Queen's motivation to ready the armies is her daughter, but I also know that's not the only reason. Even if Opaline had stayed with her, she would have come for me.

The decision to continue our march is unspoken but unanimous. They all turn as one and follow me silently, without exchanging a word. As we traverse the red desert, the sky behind us continues to swirl with feathers. The Starstrandians, griffins, and giant birds maintain a celestial escort, casting shadows on the floor as they fly above us. The jungle creatures' footfalls create a rhythmic beat that echoes the pulse of solidarity.

My heart quickens when I look at the looming towers, dark and foreboding, piercing the horizon like jagged teeth. As I take the first step, the air grows heavy with an ominous stillness.

There's no turning back now.

A quiet thought presses against my mind, one I've been trying to suppress. What if that's what Otyx wants? What if the Underworld is still unoccupied, and we leave our kingdoms unprotected behind by bringing every soldier, warrior, and animal able to fight with us?

"Where's Oceris?" Devana asks, her voice muffled.

"They'll come," Cyrus promises, but his tone isn't as confident as he thinks it is. If I can hear the slight tremble, Devana must have picked it up, too.

As we near the entrance to the Underworld, holding a collective breath, I feel their shared glances stabbing into my back. The time has come to confront the shadows that seek to devour our kingdoms and land.

United, we step over the threshold into the darkness, the sound of winged allies and jungle creatures following us.

THIRTY-SIX

AVIRA

No one ever tells you how boring it is to wait for a battle. Yes, there are all the signs of the impending conflict and the adrenaline rushing through your body as you stand by, but I imagined it would go faster and not drag on forever.

It has only been a few hours since the souls returned to Shadowmyre—hours that feel like an eternity.

I clap my hands, and the sound echoes through the throne room like thunder. "Let's go for a walk," I say to Khaos, who hasn't moved an inch since the souls cleared the room.

"What for?"

"I'm sick of sitting around."

That, and since we have so much time on our hands, I want to figure out what else my new powers can do besides reading people's memories, resurrecting dragons and souls, raising the Underworld to the surface, and calling upon the sins.

I lead the way through the double doors into the labyrinthine corridors of the palace, my footsteps echoing in the icy darkness. Khaos follows, his gaze flitting between the ominous architecture and me.

Since I got here, I haven't actually taken the time to pay attention to the palace. Every time I stepped into Otyx's home, I was either rushed or tried to escape.

As we venture down corridors I didn't know existed, my pace slows until I halt at the center of a long, dimly lit hallway. My eyes focus on an imposing giant black mirror resembling a sentinel reflecting the monochrome surroundings. It absorbs the shadows, amplifying the sense of foreboding permeating the palace.

My gaze lingers on the mirror, and a flicker of boredom crosses my features. The impending battle weighs on me, and the monotony of the black stone surroundings only heightens my restlessness. At that moment, a spark of inspiration seizes me. I turn to Khaos, a mischievous glint in my eyes.

"Watch closely," I say, my voice carrying a hint of playful command. With a graceful sweep of my hand, I summon the power within me, an energy that crackles and dances with a deadly force—the air hums with the resonance of my abilities.

Focusing on the mirror, I infuse it with my power. The giant black surface ripples, distortion giving way to a luminescent sheen. My intentions, veiled in mystery, unfold in the mirror's reflection.

As the distortion clears, the corridor transforms. The stone walls soften, replaced by the luxury of a grand room. Red, wavy hair cascades down the shoulders of a woman who steps into the frame, her form draped in a flowing dress of vibrant crimson. The room around her is shattered, remnants of once-elegant decor in pieces to her feet.

Curious, I observe my creation, watching as the red-haired figure moves with a grace that belies the destruction surrounding her. The woman in the mirror surveys the room, her expression a mix of weariness and determination.

Standing beside me, Khaos shifts his attention to his Queen, and my heart quickens. His eyes widen in recognition, and a knowing smile curves his lips. He watches her intently, as if deciphering her every step.

Does he recognize her? He must, according to his reaction.

"Who is she?" he asks, stepping closer to inspect the white strand of hair curling down over her face and chest.

"That's the person responsible for your death," I reply, trailing the cool surface of the mirror. "If I'm not mistaken, this used to be your room."

He looks over his shoulder at me, then at Soulin again. His eyes brighten again when she looks straight at him, confusion clouding her face as she stumbles back. It's as if she can see him.

"Why can't I remember her?" Khaos asks, smiling at her.

"Because she has done terrible things to you. I thought it would be better to start with a clean sleeve when you arrived, so I took your memories," I answer, watching Soulin squeeze her eyes shut before opening them back up abruptly. "And I want to give you something only a few souls get the chance to. I'm allowing you to destroy her."

Ringing with emotions, Khaos stares at his Queen as she forces her eyes shut again, digging her fingernails into her palms.

"Look at her. She can't even stand the sight of you," I say, dragging my fingernails over the frame.

"She can see me?"

"She can," I reply, keeping to myself that this isn't her present version. When I used my powers to create a window into the Crymzon Palace, I chose to show him the past, and my instinct didn't disappoint. "What do you say? Can I count on you?"

Together, we watch Soulin pace through the room, and just as she picks up a wooden piece of the ground to let her rage run free, I dissolve her reflection.

"What did she do to you?" he asks, his eyes still fixed on the mirror as if he can still see her.

The next lie slips so easily over my tongue that it doesn't even feel like one. "After killing you, she tried to overthrow the Underworld to become the most powerful being in Escela. You were just a hurdle in her way. I wanted to show her to you because knowing your opponent is crucial."

The softness in his eyes turns into heated anger. He doesn't need to know that by trying to kill Otyx, she killed him, or that it was never her intention to harm her Soulmate.

Still, I needed him to see her to understand his task. For a second, I thought he recognized her when I saw his smile—but it was rather the reaction any male gives Queen Soulin because of her magical beauty.

A smirk plays on my lips as I revel in the ability to unveil glimpses of the past, a power I must have harnessed from Otyx.

I decide to delve deeper into her past. With a focused gaze and a subtle twist of my wrist, I manipulate the mirror once again, urging it to unveil more layers of Soulin's history.

The reflection shimmers, revealing a scene of a battlefield, Khaos lying to her feet as she picks up a blood-crusted dagger to ram it into his chest. The following images show her triumphs and moments of vulnerability. Soulin emerges as a multifaceted character, her journey marked by courage and sacrifice. I only show Khaos what he needs to see—what I see.

Khaos, engrossed in the unfolding narrative, clenches his jaw. His eyes mirror the reflection's intensity, absorbing the complexity of emotions between him and Soulin.

He's almost there, I know it. He's so close to snapping.

Satisfied with the revelations, I withdraw my influence from the mirror. The scenes of the past gradually fade, leaving the giant black surface once again reflecting the cold, black-stoned corridor.

After the mirror reverts to its original state, I turn to him. "Do you remember her now?" I ask, drawing my eyebrows together and giving him the most innocent facial expression I can muster without giving my false pretense away.

"No, but I've seen enough," he replies, his jaw ticking. "What do you want me to do?"

THIRTY-SEVEN

DEVANA

The desert stretches endlessly under the now relentless sun, its red sands unyielding to the touch. How can it already be this scalding, and it's not even midday yet?

My eyes turn skyward and landward, awaiting the convergence of the winged Starstrandians and the oncoming force on foot. I scan the gathering. It isn't just mortals clad in crimson or green that stand in unified anticipation; scattered between them are also the majestic creatures of my home. Rhinos, gorillas, tigers, jaguars, and other animals, all larger than their ordinary counterparts, roam the sandy soon-to-be battlefield.

Yet, what truly captivates me is their shared trait—unlike Erinna, they're covered with lush green fur or skin.

As I marvel at the spectacle, a distant murmur permeates the air. The collective beat of wings echoes, heralding the arrival of the winged army in the sky. I turn my gaze skyward, and a hushed anticipation settles over the desert. The sky transforms into a kaleidoscope of colors as Starstrandians and Glimmarums soar above us. Red and green-clad warriors ride on the backs of giant birds, their green wings outstretched against the canvas of the intensifying daylight.

A seamless integration occurs as the winged army descends from the sky and the land-based forces approach on foot. Red, green, and silver blend into a harmonious spectrum, each color representing a facet of the united front.

The Glimmarums, chosen and unchosen, position themselves alongside their human warriors. Rhinos with emerald-hued hides, gorillas with moss-covered fur, and tigers and jaguars with glistening green stripes stand as guardians, each claiming a mortal.

My entire life, I wanted to be part of something that truly meant more than just the Confines community or being a Tenacorian. I realize that being a part of this union is the moment I've been waiting for. I'm one of the thousands standing beneath this beating sun, ready to defend all our kingdoms, and they rely on me because even if just one person retreats, it could be the beginning of the end.

The moment of stillness before the storm envelopes the assembly. The whispers and voices disappear entirely, and the wings above also fall silent.

Queen Synadena comes into view as she pushes through the ranks on the back of a massive green jaguar. Its golden eyes lock onto mine as the Queen raises a hand, a signal that ripples through the army behind her.

The winged army assembles to form a protective barrier in the skies while the soldiers on the ground and Glimmarums ready themselves. The red, green, and silver warriors, mortal and creature alike, stand shoulder to shoulder, the proof of the strength that emerges when disparate elements converge for a common cause.

"I can't tell you how long I've been waiting for this day," a familiar female voice blares behind me, and I spin around so fast I almost snap my neck.

"Liza!" Seeing her short, blonde hair, blue eyes, and wings—yes, she h as *wings*—force my heart to skip a beat. "You made it out in time!" I say, closing my arms around her frail body.

"Never thought you were a hugger," she says, rubbing my shoulder while leaning into me.

Replaying her words in my head, I step away from her. "You knew this day was coming?"

She lets out a quiet, uncomfortable laugh. "I'm not talking about the battle," she says, her eyes darkening momentarily before her gaze darts to Cyrus. "I'm talking about you two. You guys finally figured it out."

Cyrus points at himself, his cheeks and ears turning bright red. "We didn't—"

"Don't lie to me now," Liza says, swatting his hand as I playfully push against her shoulder. "I'm just messing with you guys. I guess this is my last attempt to lighten up your moods before everything goes down the drain."

A smile creeps up my face, and it feels incredible. I can't remember the last time I laughed naturally. I know it wasn't long ago, but it feels like forever.

"Have you been assigned yet?" Liza asks, looking us up and down.

"Assigned for what?" we ask at the same time.

"Don't tell me you're going in there by foot," she replies, craning her neck back. "Don't you have one of those Glimmarums?"

I do, but I can't bring it over me to drag her into this battle. First, even though we have spent little time together, I can't fathom putting her in harm's way more than I already have. Second, if I use her as my transportation, I know Cyrus will use his wings to stay with me, and fighting from above makes him an easier target because he doesn't have the necessary training.

"I've chosen not to use Erinna," I say, casting my eyes to the ground.

"That's up to you. But do you really think he will survive combat by foot?" Liza asks, glancing at Cyrus, who pretends to look deeply insulted.

I'm relieved that Liza knows him as well as I do, perhaps even better. They shared a hut for a year before Crymzonians captured us, and it shows that even though it was just a friendship between them, it was a good one.

Liza closes her eyes, her muscles relaxing as she takes a breath.

After dropping off the Lady of Fate at Starstrand, Cyrus went into detail about who Liza really was. I still can't wrap my head around it.

"Should I send him away? Is Cyrus going to die?" I whisper just for her to hear.

If she's a Fate, she already knows how this war will play out.

"He's going to be fine," she replies, her hands enclosing my arm as she opens her eyes.

"And my father?"

"He's still in Tenacoro, recovering from his time in Crymzon."

"And I?" I continue, pressing my lips together.

Her nails dig through the fabric of my jacket as she lowers her gaze, and her gesture is enough to tell me this won't end well for me.

I knew that when I set the course to follow Soulin. I knew the risk. My fate isn't in my hands; it's in Soulin's *and* mine.

Yet, it's unfair. No one should have their fate stripped from them because of the actions of another soul. If Soulin decides to die today, so be it, but I won't. I'm an excellent warrior.

There are so many dreams and life-altering events I thought I would experience in my lifetime, and all of them die with Liza's words. I'll never see my father again and never get to be the woman I always wanted to be. Not a warrior, but a mother. The dream of starting my own family was always far-fetched and impossible, but that changed when Cyrus stumbled into my room in Crymzon.

"Promise me you take good care of him," I say, curling my hand around hers.

"Always," she says, grabbing my neck to press her forehead against mine.

"What's going on?" Cyrus asks beside us.

As if caught in a lie, I jump back to face him. "I'm just really excited to see her," I say, tears forming as I look into his beautiful brown eyes.

It's a mystery to me how he has stayed so innocent through everything he has been through. Even though his life took a drastic turn from one day to another when he fled Eternitie, followed by the imprisonments, killing his father, watching his brother being carried away and Eternitie turn into cinder, he has stayed the same. There are no wrinkles around his eyes that point to worry, no hardness in his gaze or smile, and not even anger when someone upsets him.

"Pick your weapon," a soldier clad in red says to us, pointing at a rhino carrying a load of Nullstone-infused swords.

I've never been more thankful for an interruption than this one. I would have shared my fate with him if I had looked a second longer into Cyrus' eyes. But he can't know because even if we flee, Soulin will never agree to come with us, and once her time runs out, so will mine.

THIRTY-EIGHT

QUEEN SOULIN

Beneath the darkened sky above the Underworld, the earth trembles with a foreboding resonance as colossal tentacles, dark as the abyss, unfurl from the gaping holes surrounding the newest kingdom. The air vibrates with the groans of the earth as though protesting the intrusion from below. Each massive appendage snakes upward, reaching toward the heavens.

"What the fuck is that?" I ask, my eyes glued to the enormous suckers that cling to the dark buildings.

"I've seen nothing like it before," Myra replies, reading herself beside me with a sword. "It's not a dragon, is it?"

I better hope not! It can't be. But what else could come from the Underworld? It's clearly trying to break free from beneath the kingdom.

"Look over there," Opaline says, pointing into the distance where the river used to flow freely, now only a mere puddle. "I think it belongs to them."

Trying to keep the abomination of a creature in the corner of my eye to ensure it doesn't lash out in my direction, I follow her gaze. A blue wave rushes down the dried-out riverbed, but when I look closer, I realize it's not water; those are people. Dressed in silver and blue, an army marches in our direction, and right at the front, I see King Usiel. His skin, dark like the deepest night, is adorned with markings that glow with an inner radiance.

I hear the surprise in Devana's voice behind me. "They came."

Yeah, that's new. Oceris never, and I mean *never* comes to land, especially not during a battle.

My eyes dart back to the threat trying to break out underneath the Underworld. With a loud crack, another tentacle, massive and sinuous, surges from the subterranean depths, anchoring itself into the kingdom of Death. It wraps around the pillars of the Underworld, pulling with a strength that defies the laws of nature. The once-stable boundary between the worlds quivers under the immense force, threatening to crumble into the abyssal embrace beneath it.

But that makes little sense. If that beast belongs to Otyx, why is it threatening to tear that place apart? I thought it was trying to get out, but the longer I stare at it, the more the realization sets in that it's trying to drag the Underworld down with it.

Opaline is right.

As the creature continues its relentless pull, Usiel raises a silver-clad hand. A low hum, resonating with vibrating energy, rattles the sand beneath my feet. In response, the runes etched into the soldiers' skin glow brighter, as if attuning to the impending war.

With a silent command, the King signals his army forward. They move with purpose, their movements synchronized and yet somewhat sluggish, as if they had too much to drink. Each soldier wields weapons—swords that gleam and sharp-edged shields.

"What's wrong with them?" a Crymzonian near me asks.

"They're not used to having legs," a Tenacorian growls back, hitting two swords against each other. "If they keep that pace, they never make it in time."

I roll my eyes, but he's spot on. Through my magic, I was able to zoom in on them. Now, with my normal eyesight, they still have a long way before they reach us.

My head whips back to the creature as it lets out a guttural, primordial sound that reverberates through the very marrow of the earth. Its tentacles, relentless in their quest to pull the Underworld into the abyss, writhe and thrash against the black stones.

I should have researched the beasts lurking in the depths of the ocean. I know everything there is to know about the other kingdoms, so what stopped me from learning just a little about the kingdom beneath the waves?

Relaxing my fingers around the handle of my whip, I keep watching the beast do its thing. Perhaps if we wait a few more minutes, this will all be over before it even starts. If the creature gets a little more help, it might be strong enough to loosen the kingdom and plunge it back into the darkness.

Help—it needs help.

The high-pitched whistle I release through my lips is almost inaudible to my ears. That doesn't mean my beautiful moths won't sense it. Within a few seconds, the air around me quivers under the fluttering wings of my Fighter Moths. My heart swells seeing so many of my babies grown and well while others don't follow my call because they carry Tenacorians.

"Assist it," I say, pointing at the furling tentacles when Storm appears before me to lead the riderless moths. The arid breeze she brings with her plays with the tendrils of my hair.

From the scarlet grains of the desert emerge more giant moths, their wings a brilliant crimson that mirror the landscape. They unfurl gracefully from the sands, each wingbeat sending ripples through the air.

I watch the moths taking flight and ascending into the darkening sky above the Underworld. Like stained glass in the dying light, their wings carry them higher, creating a stark contrast against the deepening hues of twilight.

The moths, now a celestial squadron, gather above the towers of the Underworld. As they hover, a strange harmony unfolds—a delicate dance between the creatures of the desert and the enigmatic force pulling from beneath.

Undeterred and as a united front, my moths descend from their heights. With each gentle beat of their wings, they defy the downward pull. My heart races as I witness them pushing against the descending menace, a surreal alliance with the writhing tentacles below the Underworld. The dark towers, once static and foreboding, now quiver under the combined pressure.

It's still not enough.

Inhaling deeply, I dive into my powers to support my faithful animals. Their thin coat of fur glows as I let my magic flow into them, and I can feel the resistance of the Underworld beneath my touch.

Just a few more pushes, and it's over.

My gaze shifts from the darkening sky to the ground beneath me, seeking answers in the scarlet grains that cradle me. The sand moves away beneath me, and I know we're close.

That's when I hear it: screeching screams and the snapping of big teeth.

The blood in my veins freezes when I see the mighty wings appearing behind my moths who are desperately trying to get away. Their little flaps are nothing compared to the dragon chasing them, and I'm not fast enough to shield the ones already lost to its teeth.

"Come back," I yell, my eyes glued to the blonde woman steering the dragon.

THIRTY-NINE

Avira

Khaos is right where I want him—by my side and ready to give his Queen hell.

What did Soulin expect? She treated him worse than my mother ever treated me. I want to think it was a coincidence that she opened her legs for him just when she found out he was her Soulmate, but I know better. It was a decisive move, and a brilliant one at that.

It's not him she wants—it's the illusion of him she desires. It was never about Khaos but his loyalty, undivided devotion, and the feeling he gave her standing beside her.

I'm about to use this to my advantage. Soulin's moves are so calculated and predictable—and that's the reason I know she will crumble to my feet when she sees him.

"You can't ask that of me," Mordecai says, flashing his razor-sharp teeth.

"I'm not asking you to fight. I just need a lift," I reply, raising my voice.

"If you want to die so badly, go by foot. Enjoy your last seconds on this planet before her magic rips you into pieces."

I know he doesn't mean it. Mordecai has already tried to block the door with his massive body, pretending to sleep. I get he wants to see me live, but I can't honestly do that if Soulin is still breathing.

"I possess the power of a God," I say, reminding myself that I just meddled with time, something no mortal should be able to do.

"That means nothing," he snarls, his nostrils flaring. "I know you can feel it. If you listen closely, you can hear your heartbeat slowing down. It's preparing for—"

"Fine. I don't need you," I cut in, swatting my hand at him. "How would it look if I arrived on a small dragon?"

The hurt in Mordecai's eyes sends a painful flash through my heart, but I can't stop now.

"Emberix will do just fine." I turn to Khaos. "Come."

I don't look over my shoulder at Mordecai; instead, my eyes wander to the window at the formation lining up in the desert. Soulin answered my call but doesn't even know my best weapon yet.

Moving with determined grace, I step through the door, the golden fabric of my dress glimmering against the black stone surrounding me. Shadows cling to the intricate carvings on the walls, reminding me that Otyx is never far away.

Behind me, Khaos emerges from the room, his features etched with the anger I infused him with. As the door creaks closed, I turn, locking it securely.

My gaze meets his. "I can't have him interfere," I say, knowing I don't owe Khaos an explanation, but it makes me feel better.

He cocks an eyebrow. "Your relationship with this dragon is unhealthy," he replies, stating the obvious. "It's like watching a couple fight."

Together, we stride through the serpentine pathways I've gotten to know so well over the last couple of days.

Trying to ban Mordecai's words from my mind, I keep clenching my hands into fists.

How dare he leave me hanging like this? I thought we were in this together. He's bonded to me, for Otyx's sake!

But those are not the thoughts that turn my stomach around. It's the loud thumping in my chest that has gotten weaker with every hour. While it doesn't seem to affect me, it's a cause for concern. Otyx warned me he can feel my impending death, and Mordecai does, too.

I should be scared, but I don't believe in fate. Otyx had already broken his promise not to interfere with the mortal world when he brought me to Shadowmyre almost one hundred years ago. He will do it again; I just need to be patient.

As we approach the entrance, the grandeur of the palace unveils itself. The doors swing open, revealing a vast courtyard bathed in sunlight. The transition from the dimly lit corridors to the open expanse is an extreme juxtaposition, a metaphorical step from the shadows into the light.

That's what I am—shadow and light. I've been hiding long enough, and it's finally my time to shine—or rather, to outshine everyone else.

The courtyard, surrounded by the imposing architecture of the palace, comes alive with motion. Gray-skinned souls, draped in black and white garments, fill the space. Their heads bow in unison as a sign of deference, acknowledging my presence with a reverence that echoes louder than any words through the courtyard.

My heart pounds louder for a second when I see them standing in the exact spot where the arena once stood. The memory of the circular pit throws me back to the moment I thought I would drown in my memories.

Standing at the threshold between the palace and the courtyard, I raise my hand in a gesture for silence. The muted whispers fade, and an anticipatory hush settles over the assembled crowd again. I inhale deeply, summoning the strength of my convictions.

"My souls," I say, my voice resonating with authority that almost matches Otyx's. "The time we have prepared for is upon us. The war we have foreseen is no longer a distant specter; it stands at our doorstep. Today, we face a challenge that will define the course of our existence."

The souls listen intently, their eyes fixed on me like I'm their sun. I continue, "In the face of this impending conflict, I ask one thing of each and every one of you: to fight with your sin. Our sins are our greatest weapon."

As my words hang in the air, a murmur of agreement passes through the assembly. My gaze sweeps across the sea of faces, absorbing the shared commitment reflected in their eyes until my gaze lands on Ruby and Maeve standing close together, shaking their heads.

My expression hardens as I ignore their disbelief, and my voice grows more resolute. "There is one among them who must remain untouched. The woman with crimson hair," I declare, my eyes scanning the crowd, skipping my friends. "She's mine. Do not let the chaos of battle blind you because if I find out she was harmed by one of you, the Darklands will sound like a pleasant walk under the sun compared to what I will do to you." A subtle shift in the atmosphere hints at the gravity of my words.

I raise my hand, and with a piercing whistle that cuts through the air, I signal for attention as my gaze shifts skyward. A shadow sweeps across the open space, growing larger as a colossal figure descends from the heavens. Emberix, her wings outstretched and scales gleaming like obsidian, circles above before landing with a thunderous presence before me.

The crowd, their heads still bowed, tremble in her presence.

With a seamless grace, I climb onto the dragon's back, my silhouette against the sunlight creating a striking image of power and command. Emberix, responsive to my every nuance, awaits my guidance.

This is all I wanted from Mordecai. Was that too much to ask for?

"Today, we walk into battle," I declare, my voice carrying across the courtyard. "Let's show them what the Underworld is made of."

Their heads now lifted, the souls absorb my words. Throwing my fist into the air in a commanding gesture, Emberix responds to my unspoken command by unfurling her wings.

"Listen to my signal," I say with a last glance over my shoulder to Khaos, who's still standing at the threshold of the palace.

With a mighty flap of her wings, Emberix shoots into the sky, carrying me with her. Beneath me, my souls surge forward, flooding the courtyard like a tide of starving creatures. My lips curl into a smile as I watch them scatter, but it quickly dies when the ground beneath their feet shakes, throwing some of them to their hands and knees.

It's almost laughable how predictable Soulin is. Instead of blending into the crowd, she indeed wears her signature color like a bullseye on a target.

But she isn't the center of my attention right now. My undivided focus lies on the long tentacles reaching through the gaps between the crust and the Underworld.

Was Otyx hiding another creature down there that he forgot to tell me about? Might this be his way of showing off his power?

I circle the other towers of the palaces in Shadowmyre, recounting all the sins the Underworld has to offer to give the souls some time to weed out the weakest soldiers while I observe the animal trying to dig its way through the rock and sand.

It has to be a creature sent by the God. Nothing else can live in the Underworld besides the dead, and it's pretty apparent that this thing down there is too large to end up beneath Shadowmyre without being born there.

Deciding not to worry about it, I pet Emberix's neck to signal her to keep going.

While I was occupied with figuring out what the creature beneath Shadowmyre could mean, I didn't notice the giant moths finding purchase on the towers and buildings not far away from me.

For a split moment, I thought they must belong to Otyx, too, if it wasn't for their red wings. Nothing besides me has color in this place, and their red glow can only mean one thing—those are Soulin's creatures.

"Let's play a game," I say, leaning down to brush my hand against Emberix's cold scales. "Let's see how many you can catch."

My fingernails find a grip under the edges of her scales as she leaps forward, her mouth opened wide. The following snapping noise tells me there isn't much substance to those moths. I count as Emberix catches them, plucking them out of the sky one by one.

Nine, not bad.

The rest scatter; their little screeching screams are like music to my ears.

As I circle the Palace of Lust to see if there are any more, my mind goes straight to the Mother of Lust, who I thought was my birth mother for the longest time.

I wonder if she survived the fall. Well, I know, she did because everyone in Shadowmyre is already dead. Still, a little piece of me hoped it would eliminate her as one of the Seven without turning me into a Head of Sin.

The other six of the Seven still couldn't look me in the eye when I spotted them in the crowd. Since I let my grip on Isabella go, they know I'm not the same innocent soul I used to be. Plus, they know I haven't picked a sin yet, and I'm only one word away from requesting a battle by combat to get their throne.

When I circle Envy's palace for the third time, I decide I've given the souls long enough to reach the other armies.

Amidst the chaos of the raging battlefield, I land on Emberix with a grace that defies the turmoil below. The air hangs heavy with the taint of all seven sins, matching the backdrop to the crimson sands beneath us. As I step onto the ground, my eyes immediately lock onto the figure clad in regal crimson—Soulin.

The Queen, her long, wavy hair flowing like a cascade of blood over the silver freckles adorning her face, meets my gaze with a confident smile.

"Ah, the orchestrator of chaos graces my presence," I say, my voice carrying a melodic edge. "Do you remember what started this war, or has the sweetness of sin clouded your memory?"

Soulin, undeterred by my taunt, steps closer with unyielding confidence. "This war," she replies with a mocking grin, "was sparked by Otyx." Her eyes narrow. "Where is he? Has he sent you as his emissary of destruction?"

I burst into laughter, a sound that echoes with an eerie resonance across the battlefield. "Oh, my dear Soulin, he did more than send me. He unleashed me upon this planet, knowing the havoc I would wreak. I revel in the chaos it unfurls."

The fact that she still doesn't know who I am rubs me wrong. The mortals should have heard by now what I've done. Instead, she still thinks Otyx is behind all of this.

The Queen, though outwardly composed, senses my threat. To double down on it, Emberix growls in the background, and it's strong enough to shake the sand beneath my feet.

With a swift hand motion, Soulin conjures her magic to bind me in place as invisible tendrils close around my throat. I, however, counter the assault with my own powers, a dance of opposing forces that results in a stalemate. We stand locked in a silent struggle, our eyes fixed on each other, neither yielding nor gaining ground.

Emberix, restlessly waiting on my command, growls louder at the escalating tension. The battlefield, bathed in the hues of sin, becomes a stage for the power play between us. Yet, there is an unspoken understanding in our silent confrontation—a recognition of equality in our formidable abilities.

With a swipe of my fingers, I dismiss Emberix, sending her away with a silent command. Loyal and mighty, the creature soars into the sky and vanishes from sight.

Soulin, observing the act with a raised eyebrow, waits for my next move, still forcing her magic to constrict my throat.

She's strong—stronger than I expected. But so is Otyx's power coursing through me. I might be unable to free myself, but I don't need to. All I have to do is keep her as long as I can in place until...

I hear Emberix land beside me again and the boots hitting the sand.

A figure emerges from the dragon's shadows—a man with dark curls neatly brushed back, dressed in a green suit. His eyes gleam as he regards Soulin with a taunting smirk, and the magic pressing into my throat disappears.

FORTY

Devana

With every minute, I get more comfortable with my fate.

Fuck, I'm lying. I'm not okay. How can I be? Whatever I was doing the last two decades doesn't count as living. Training every day as an Ordinary while constantly looking over my shoulder to spot danger isn't a life. Everything that should be normal never was.

Yet, I'm sick of running. I'm sick of hiding. I want all of this to stop.

I don't have time to think about it any longer because before I can turn back to Cyrus to say my farewell in case it doesn't end well for me, as Liza predicted, the battlefield rages with the clash of swords and the repercussions of arrows. The suffocating feeling of sins settles in my bones as Cyrus and I fight side by side against the formidable souls. The enemy, their gray skin a blend of the black and white of their attire, advances with an unfaltering perseverance that sends shivers through the tinted desert and my body.

With my rock shards-infused sword, I was given moves with a fluidity born of years of combat training. Wielding the sword is second nature to me.

I can't say the same about Cyrus.

Amid the chaos, my movements are a symphony of deadly precision. With each swing of my blade, rock shards slash through the air, finding their mark among the approaching souls.

As we press forward, my limbs begin to feel the weariness of prolonged usage I know all too well. The sand beneath my feet seems to conspire against me, pulling on my limbs like it's trying to swallow me.

The pain only fuels my anger.

I've come too far to give up. Yes, I'm connected to Soulin, but that doesn't mean I must go down with her.

Amid the clash of steel and the swirl of red dust, I find myself surrounded by souls, Cyrus nowhere in sight. My every movement is a dance of survival, each swing of my sword a calculated response to the encroaching threat.

Cyrus' figure flashes into my view behind the souls encircling me, and I can read in his stiff movement that he's overwhelmed. In that moment, as a gray-skinned warrior lunges at him, my reflexes kick in. With a swift motion, I drop my sword, grab my bow, and unleash an arrow, the projectile finding the attacker's throat. Before the surrounding souls can attack, I pick the sword back up and turn on my heels, trying to determine which one will come at me first.

"Thank you," Cyrus yells, but his voice drowns between the screams and metal meeting metal.

As the skirmish goes on, my muscle fatigue becomes more pronounced. The relentless assault takes a toll on my body, and the pain that once haunted me daily resurfaces with each swing of my sword. Still, I fight on, drawing strength from the memories of my training and the future I want for myself.

My gaze keeps falling back on Cyrus, and my breath hitches when I realize he's not fighting by himself anymore. A silver-skinned woman with horns protruding from her blue-silver hair stands beside him.

Sylvora is back, and with her, the bird-like figure, and the vine-covered feline.

Where did they come from, and why are they here?

"Run!" I yell at Cyrus, searching for a gap between my attackers to get to him, but it's useless.

Sylvora leans in and whispers something into his ear. His eyes go wide as he lowers his sword, leaving him defenseless.

They are here to take him, just like they did to his brother. Sylvora is lacing his brain with sweet lies, and I know how this will end; her words are pure venom.

"Cyrus!" I scream, stabbing for the soul between us, but it counters my attack, sending me stumbling backward.

I need to get to him! Now!

Rotating around myself again and again, I search for an exit. Someone has to make a move. I turn again, and that's when I sense someone approaching me from behind, a dagger poised for a lethal strike. Just as the blade is about to descend, I twist my body in a swift motion to evade the attack.

The soul, caught off guard by my reflexes, stumbles and falls to the ground and...vanishes.

Before I can comprehend the situation, I survey the remaining attackers, my breaths labored and my limbs heavy.

They are all gone.

My heart pounds so loud in my chest that I can't hear what Cyrus is screaming at me. His face looks delighted, almost happy, as he pushes past Sylvora to get to me.

Frozen in place, I survey my surroundings while waiting for Cyrus to reach me. Among the remaining people, I don't see any souls from the Underworld, just Tenacorians, Crymzonians, Starstrandians, and a figure clad in glorious red in the middle of the chaos—Queen Soulin.

"We did it!" Cyrus screams, lifting me off my feet. My breath is heavy, and my body is aching as I look over his shoulder at the creatures behind him.

"I don't understand," I whisper, not letting Sylvora out of my sight.

He kisses me before letting me back down. "They came to help us," he says, his eyes shining with excitement.

No.

I saw her purring something into his ear. Is this what she can do? Did her words change our reality, making us believe we won?

Frantically, my gaze falls back on Soulin and then at the woman before her.

"It's her," I whisper, my eyes scanning the scene. The blonde, winged woman is back with her dragon and—

"Shit!" I say, retreating. My back collides with Cyrus, and he holds me tight.

His grip tightens when he follows my gaze. "Is that—"

FORTY-ONE

QUEEN SOULIN

Amidst the red sands and black rocky expanse, the battlefield is painted red. My eyes, fierce and unyielding, lock onto the woman before me—Otyx's favorite soul.

I get it. Compared to the other souls, this woman shines bright in her golden dress, a slim face surrounded by blonde hair, and a childish body. She looks like a delicate star, ready to bring destruction if provoked.

Yet, I still don't understand what trick he uses to make her appear...well, alive. Her skin is still vibrant, and her eyes and hair are colorful. The only thing that seems to be as lifeless as everyone else is her heart. But that won't stop me from snapping her neck to get to her owner. If Otyx thinks he can stop me with a child, he's mistaken.

Did it cross my mind thinking about what happens to the souls if we—hmm, killing isn't the right word—eliminate them? It did, for a brief moment, and I've concluded that it's none of my business. I have no problem with letting them crumble to the ground so they can crawl back to their God. As long as they stay down to give me a clear path, I'll be fine.

As the tension peaks between the woman and me, her dragon lands beside her. When it took off, I was prepared to split my magic to shield myself from its attack, but it never came.

Instead, a shadow shifts behind the woman, and a man emerges, his silhouette a haunting echo of familiarity. His dark curls that usually frame his face are slicked back, and the scar on his cheek has faded but is still visible. Yet, his presence is different, like a ghostly apparition that doesn't belong in the land of the living.

My gaze narrows as I recognize the spectral figure. It's him—the man with whom I've shared battles, laughter, and the quiet moments that stitch together the only reason I'm still standing. His armor, once a regal crimson of our shared kingdom, has taken on a ghastly hue of green. His skin, drained of vitality, bore the pallor of the lifeless.

A moment of disbelief grips me as Khaos grins at me with a viciousness that sends shivers down my spine. The battlefield, already laden with the weight of death, now holds an additional specter—the man I had once known, changed into a phantom that straddles the realms of life and death.

I thought seeing my father on the battlefield in Terminus, or my mother just outside the Crymzon Wall shattered my heart, but seeing Khaos tops them.

He's this...being because of me. I made him into this faded version of himself when I rammed that Nullstone into Otyx's chest.

My heart, for a fleeting moment, ceases its rhythmic dance. The world around me blurs as the gravity of the encounter unfurls before me. Sensing the disturbance, the opposing woman seizes the opportunity to her advantage, launching a swift and calculated strike.

In that breathless moment, torn between the past and the present, I return my focus to her. The clash of our powers echoes through the battlefield as the woman and I engage in a dance of magic and strategy. Each strike reverberates with an ear-shattering noise as we collide.

"I thought you would like to see him again," the woman snarls, her brow cocked. "He makes quite the fine addition to the Underworld, don't you think?"

Meanwhile, Khaos lingers on the periphery of the confrontation, coming to a halt beside the woman. His eyes, once filled with life, now hold a vacant yet deadly stare that pierces through my mental defenses. His presence cast a shadow on the battlefield, an unsettling reminder of a connection I fractured by summoning Otyx.

"Who are you?" I ask, watching her reach out a hand to press her palm against his gray cheek.

If she lays a finger on him, I'm going to rip that fucking bitch into shreds.

"You know my mother. Well, no, you knew her," she muses, trailing her finger up and down just inches from his face. "Let's see if you can guess who she was."

"Don't fucking touch him," I growl, doubling down on my magic, and to my surprise, she stumbles back.

I summon more of my reserved strength deep within my bones. It feels like my body is on fire, and I'm so close to burning out, but I don't care. Crimson ribbons of magic swirl around me, pulsating to my heartbeat as I swiftly dodge one of her strikes and redirect her own power back at her.

"That's impossible," the woman spits out while wiping blood out of the corner of her mouth. Her power, paired with mine, must have felt like a really nasty blow.

Khaos, his malevolent grin turning into a glare of defiance, recoils as I turn the tables.

"Who are you?" I bellow again, my eyes darting between her and Khaos.

"Conqueress," she says, readying herself to fight back, and that's the moment I realize she thought by using Khaos against me, she would weaken me. She planned to dangle him before me to force me to my knees.

Apparently, she didn't know that his sight does the complete opposite. I can feel his presence caressing my skin the way it used to.

"I'm giving you one more chance, *Conqueress*," I say, spitting out her name like poison. "Hand Khaos over, take your other souls, and retreat. I promise you, we will find a way for our kingdoms to live beside each other after I speak to Otyx."

This is not the plan I had in mind when the battle started, but I know it's doable. It has to be because there is no way I can return the Underworld to its rightful place. Even if I could, I wouldn't. Khaos is here because his new kingdom is above the surface. If Otyx submerges the Underworld again, I won't be able to see him—at least not until I die.

"You still don't get it, do you?" Conqueress asks, a grin on her face. "I won't leave until you're dead." She hits me with another wave of power, but it feels like a gentle brush.

"That makes no fucking sense. If I die, I'll be bound to the Underworld just like you are," I say, shaking my head. "Is that what you want?"

"Oh, I'm not dead," she replies, observing me as I study her.

I guess her colorfulness isn't Oryx's doing after all. Who would have thought?

"Let me change that," I bark, unleashing every ounce of my magic that sizzles through me like molten lava. A wall of crimson magic rushes in her direction, and just as it's about to hit the final blow, darkness forms before Conqueress, shielding her from my deadly attack.

A recurring thudding noise forces me to look away from her briefly. My eyes widen when I watch the souls engaged in battle with the united army hit the ground before their bodies disintegrate.

Did I do that? Did I lose control?

"That's enough," a dark male voice bellows from within the darkness, and my eyes dart back to the spot where Khaos stands. His eyes are on me, and my insides twist as I watch him fade away. Within a heartbeat, he's gone, and another figure stands in his place.

The chilling pull of envy, the sly whispers of greed, and the haunting echoes of wrath echo in the air as I try to keep my composure.

He's gone again.

Once the darkness clears, my heart splits in half when I see him. Unnatural abs, wings formed from shadows and death, the dark crown sitting upon his empty eye sockets—Otyx, the God of the Underworld.

FORTY-TWO

AVIRA

I knew he would come! I was confident he would, even though he kept repeating that he couldn't mess with fate.

He just did.

By shielding me from Soulin's brutal attack, he saved me, doing the one thing he told me he couldn't do.

That also means I'm free.

Just a few seconds ago was the moment I would have died. I defeated death. Or rather, I was saved by Death.

Soulin's eyes tinge with tears as she looks at my God. "It's me you want. I'm right here." She throws her hands in the air, signaling she's not a threat. "Just take me and leave Escela alone."

"I never wanted this to happen," Otyx replies, not even glancing at me as he moves closer to the Queen, who looks confused.

She shakes her head, raising her arms even higher. "I surrender," she says, lowering her head. "You went too far. I can't do this anymore."

"The hell you are," a man's voice bellows from behind her, and when I look over her shoulder, I see a tall, brown-haired man snatching an arrow out of a woman's shoulder strap before pushing her to the side to grab her bow.

Who is he, and what is he doing? Does he really think an arrow is enough to hurt a God?

"I surrender," Soulin repeats before she growls over her shoulder, "Stay out of this, Cyrus."

I finally have her where I want her. She's giving up. When Khaos halted beside me for a moment, I wasn't sure about it, but all she needed was a push in the right direction to show her how fast he could disappear again.

"You can't fucking do this, Soulin! You can't give up!" the man yells behind her as a woman with braided black hair tackles him to take her bow back. "Please, you can't do this!"

A smile forms on my lips as my eyes wander back to the Queen. "Really? You give up?"

More people stream in behind her. Judging by their attire, most of them are more royals.

"Get on your knees," I snarl, pressing myself against Otyx to show them who they are messing with. I'm not a nobody anymore. I'm Avira, the woman who conquered Otyx's heart, resurrected a dragon, raised the Underworld to the surface, and I'm about to become a Queen slayer.

Summoning my magic, I lift my arm to release it even though Soulin isn't following my direction, and when I'm about to let it go, Otyx pushes my arm down. "Avira. I need you to calm down. It's not her time."

Her time...Did he just say it's not *her* time?

It must be because I'm the one executing her in the next seconds. I need him to stop lecturing and start supporting me.

Another female steps beside Soulin, and I don't need a reminder of who she is. "Avira?" she asks, squinting her eyes together. "How is that possible?"

She recognized me. Good for her.

I chuckle, absorbing my power again to entertain Queen Synadena for a minute or two.

"Surprised to see me?" I ask, lifting my head to the sky to show off my profile. "I bet you didn't expect me here."

"Your mother said you died," Queen Synadena whispers, lowering her two swords. "But you don't look like them."

I know she means the other souls by *them*.

"What are you doing?" Her question is so genuine that it almost breaks my heart. Well, it would if I still had one that reacts to anything other than sins.

"Did you know?" I ask her, locking eyes. "Did you know the Queen of Starstrand offered the soul of her only daughter to save her king?"

The confusion in the Queen's eyes speaks louder than words.

"Did anyone know?" I bark into the sky, trying to reach as many listening ears as possible.

The silence following is deafening.

They must be lying. There's no way no one is aware of what happened to me. I need them to know, otherwise, I have nothing to use against them.

"I'm so sorry," Queen Synadena whispers, her eyebrows almost touching each other. "If I would have known what you were going through—"

"You would have what? Rescued me?"

"I would have," she says, her hands curling into fists.

"Stop!" I yell, unleashing my powers on her. "Stop lying! I'm sick of everyone lying to me!"

The Queen falls backward onto the ground, and I'm surprised when I see her fingertips move. Within the next heartbeat, an elderly woman with long gray hair falls on her knees beside her, checking her pulse before exhaling with relief.

"She's okay," the woman says to someone who must be the Queen's daughter.

If I wanted to kill her, she would be dead. But this isn't about her; it never was.

And just when I thought the woman helping Queen Synadena was the oldest person on this planet, an ancient man walks over to the couple to help her to her feet. "Get your soul under control, or I will," he barks, steadying the Queen.

"So, we meet again," I purr, remembering his icy facial expression as Emberix tried to break into Crymzon. The laugh escaping my throat is so dark, I can't believe it's coming from me. "Let me guess, you also don't know what happened to me?"

"What are you doing, Conrad?" Queen Soulin asks, making her way to him, but he ignores her.

The man builds himself up, handing the Queen to the other woman. "I know exactly what happened to you. I was there."

FORTY-THREE

Queen Soulin

I don't know what's going on anymore.

If I heard Otyx correctly, he isn't the one invading our planet—it's Avira, the former Princess of Starstrand, and she's doing all this because of her mother, Queen Caecilia.

Devana was right, after all. The attack on Starstrand was personal. And that's also the reason Otyx didn't seek me out the second the Underworld emerged.

Still, I'm responsible for Khaos' death, and I was the one using Blood Magic that allowed Avira to raise the Underworld.

But how did she do it? How is she so powerful as a mortal? And why did she say we both can't coexist in Escela? I never even met that woman before. What could be the reason for her personal agenda against me?

Conrad closes in on Avira, and I silently follow him to hear his next words. "Your mother loved you with all her heart. That's why she kept you locked away in Starstrand. After your birth, she got paranoid that something horrible could happen to you."

"That's not love," Avira snarls, biting her lip. "She exchanged my soul for my father's. If she really wanted to keep me safe, she would have never plotted my death."

Conrad shakes his head. "She believed she could bring him back to you. All she wanted was her family back together—for *you*."

"It doesn't matter what she believed," Avira barks back. "Don't you see what my mother did to me? And *she*?" Her bony finger points in my direction. "She tried to take the only being from me who loves me for who I am."

What? I did no such thing. I didn't even know she existed until...

My eyes wander to Otyx, then back to her.

Are you fucking kidding me?

"And I paid the price, didn't I?" I mumble back, trying to envision Khaos not as the vicious man who stood on this battlefield, but as the man who was excited about our Connection Ceremony. "I only summoned him because he took everything from me. My family, my magic, and he kept marching back into my life, bringing destruction and death with him. If he would have left me alone, I would have never done what I did."

"Did you never ask yourself why another kingdom's God is so fixated on yours? Did it ever cross your mind that by using your magic to heal injuries and cheat death, he would come after the souls you owe him?"

"What is she talking about?" I ask the God standing beside her.

His jaw ticks before he inhales deeply. "I'm responsible for restoring the balance between life and death," he replies. "That means every few thousand years, I must collect the souls that got away."

This is what all this is about? The reason Otyx attacked one of my ancestors and didn't return until my reign started? Haven't I given him enough souls with my magical outburst?

"You sent my brother," I hiss, recalling his black eyes and pale skin. "You even resurrected my mother and father."

Otyx raises a hand, waving a finger at me. "You were off limits," he corrects, holding my stare.

"Off limits? My brother tried to kill me," I reply, pulling the long, red sleeve up to show him the scar his blade left on me. "And my mother..." my voice cracks.

"I've learned from my mistake," Otyx cuts in, lowering his head.

"Cut the bullshit," Conrad says beside me, stepping in front of me. "You got what you came for, and now it's your time to call all your souls back and leave us alone."

Damn.

I've never seen that side of Conrad. I knew something changed in his demeanor the last few days...but damn.

Then it hits me what he's saying.

No. Otyx can't leave. If he goes, he will take Khaos with him.

"How dare you raise your voice against my God?" Avira growls, who has been silently watching the exchange while clinging to Otyx.

"Don't mess with me, girl" Conrad snarls back, and I can see the exact moment Avira snaps.

I'm not fast enough to counter the darkness she sends flying Conrad's way. It hits him square on, and I must protect my face from the blast. The air crackles with energy as the darkness intensifies, searing and burning Conrad. Peeking through my fingers, I witness that her power is strong enough to peel Conrad's skin clean off his bones—if he had any.

Conrad's charred outer layer falls away, revealing a radiant light, and my breath hitches when a stunning woman unveils herself.

With cascading red locks that tumble down her shoulders over her curvaceous form, the woman emerges with an otherworldly grace. The red sand beneath her feet shimmers in response to the energy emanating from her as she steps out of the old man's shell.

"I should have known," Otyx says through clenched teeth. "You always had a thing for hiding in plain sight."

"I learned from the best," Lunra replies, her eyes scanning me before she directs her gaze back to the God.

I don't want to know what she means by that because I'm still trying to wrap my head around why I couldn't remember Conrad when we first met. He was never a *real* person. Everything he had told me about being my father's trustee to his family was a big, fat lie. All this time, I commanded my Goddess—*my Goddess*—around like a servant, and she took it.

Lunra was the one who helped me find the Painite and brought it back to Crymzon to feed it to the Heiligbaum. She was the one sealing the throne room with enough magic that I couldn't break through. She's also the one who manipulated my portal to send me to Tenacoro instead of directly to the Underworld.

All the signs were there, and I ignored them.

Otyx stares at Lunra for a long time. Eventually, he breaks his gaze from her and looks at Avira. "It's time," he says, holding his hand in her direction.

Avira eyes his hand wearily but doesn't grab it.

What is she waiting for?

"Wait," I say, breaking the silent moment between them. "What do I need to do to get Khaos back?"

"There's nothing I can do," Otyx replies, not taking his eyes off Avira.

My stomach twists and my heart leaps. There must be a loophole because I can't continue without him.

All the verbal info dump from every conversation I ever had circulates through my head until it focuses on something Avira said.

Her mother offered her soul in exchange for her father's.

My brain redirects to a different conversation I had with Lunra beneath the burning tree.

If the connection between two Soulmates is strong enough to withstand death, the lowborn could potentially carry the weight of the Crymzon Throne.

"That's it then?" I ask, gliding my sleeved hand into the pocket of my pants. "You're returning to the Underworld, and then what?"

"You won't see me again until your time has come," he replies, confirming what I already suspected. Otyx wants to go back to the way his kingdom was. He will return his kingdom back to the world below, taking Khaos with him.

My eyes rest on Avira, who is still struggling with the decision to grab his hand or keep fighting. Her rage brought them here, and I'm willing to bet she doesn't like disappointments. After all, I'm still alive.

After an eternity, she lowers her head and reaches for his hand. Avira made her choice, and I can't accept it.

I look over my shoulder at Devana, who is pressed against Cyrus, and form the words *I'm sorry* with my lips. I mean them, I really do, but I'm not fit to be Crymzon's Queen. I never was. Whatever I touch dies.

Pulling out the Nullstone dagger I've stored in my pocket for the God, I lift it into the sky and bolt forward. I know my chances of killing Otyx are slim, but he's occupied by Avira. Reaching for my magic, I use it to help me move even faster.

But I don't aim for Otyx.

All this time, I thought he was going after me, punishing me for my actions. Even though I still hate him, it's not his fault that my kingdom is tainted with death. It's his duty to keep the scales even, and as much as it sucks, I get it.

My blade points at Avira, rushing through the air at record speed.

Revenge is never pretty. It's petty if we're completely honest. Yet, she's a mortal and wronged me, making her the perfect contestant for what I'm about to do.

"A soul for a soul!" I scream, thinking about Khaos. This would make all our dreams come true. Avira could spend eternity with Otyx; he would finally leave Escela alone, and I would get Khaos back.

I force the dagger down on her, aiming straight for her head because her heart is turned away from me. That's when she sees me. Clinging onto Otyx, her hand shoots in my direction, grabbing my wrist.

She's strong, stronger than she was minutes ago.

For a heartbeat, we struggle, the blade getting closer and closer to her. I can see the anger in her eyes as she digs into Otyx's arm. My eyes dart to her connection to the God, and it hits me she's currently absorbing his power to overthrow me.

And then, the blade turns, and I let out a gasp when she rams it into my heart as hard as she can.

FORTY-FOUR

AVIRA

My fingers tremble as I press the dagger deeper into her chest. It's her own damn fault. I chose to go with Otyx, so why did she have to launch at me?

Then I remember her words: *A soul for a soul.*

She tried to sacrifice me to get Khaos back, knowing it might not work. But she did it anyway, putting all her strength into her last move.

"What did you do?" Otyx asks beside me, taking his other hand to release my grip. I feel the strength of his fingers uncurling mine as he detaches himself from me.

I look up, searching the crowd that has formed behind Soulin. I expected them to look triumphant because I finally ended the terrible reign of the Crymzon Queen, the tyrant of Escela. Instead, I'm met with mortified stares, gasping mouths, and tears.

Not too far away, I can hear a man shouting a name over and over again. "Devana. Hang in there! I got you! Devana!" The man holds a woman against his chest, her arms and legs dangling to the ground like a marionette without strings.

Otyx steps behind Soulin, grabbing her under her arms before he gently lets her down.

"Why do you take her side?" I snarl, my heart pounding with anger. "It wasn't my fault. She attacked me, and I just defended myself."

What am I missing here? Why is he tending to her and not to me? He should ask me if I'm okay. Instead, he hovers over Soulin, ignoring me.

"I told you what would happen. Your fate was clear, and you kept ignoring my warnings. On top of that, you used my power to your advantage. Without it, you know it would have been you."

I can't believe what is coming out of his mouth. Is he serious? "You rather wanted to see me dead?"

"I want you by my side," he barks back, inspecting the dagger in her chest that keeps rising and falling with her shallow breaths. "I know it's selfish, but I can't help it."

And here is why he didn't protect me from Soulin a second time. I know he could have, but his longing for me was too intense. If Soulin had been successful, I would have had no choice but to return to Shadowmyre.

So many thoughts rush through my head, and I slowly realize that my revenge on my mother and Soulin doesn't change what I want.

It didn't matter if she was alive or dead for me to be with Otyx. Because that's what I want; that's all I wanted since raising the Underworld to the surface. I only wanted to show Otyx how life would be in sunlight—together. I wanted to show him he doesn't have to hide in the shadows, far away from anything living.

Yet, that's who he is. He tried to tell me he wanted to go back to how everything was. I just didn't listen.

"Can you fix her?" I whisper, finally realizing that the actual monster walking the surface is *me*.

"It's too late," Otyx replies, wiping a tear from Soulin's eye away before he lifts his head to look at me.

FORTY-FIVE

QUEEN SOULIN

The red desert stretches infinitely beneath me as my consciousness, untethered from the confines of my physical form, detaches itself. The people surrounding Otyx, blurred shadows against the crimson expanse, don't move a muscle as they watch him. They also seem unaware of my ethereal presence that lingers in their midst.

I observe myself lying on the sand, a mere shell of my former self, while the quiet vibrations of my last breaths resonate through the air. My heartbeat, once a steady rhythm of life, now echoes in my disembodied awareness, each thud a reminder of the fading connection to the living.

That's when Myra's braided gray hair catches my attention as she steps forward, tears streaming down her face. I approach her, my steps silent on the red desert sand. Myra extends a hand toward me as if she can see me, but her fingers pass through me like a fleeting whisper.

"I'm sorry it had to end this way," I whisper, my voice carried by the gentle breeze that sweeps across the desolate landscape. Myra, immersed in her own reality, remains oblivious to me as she lets out a gut-wrenching scream.

As she continues to scream, I find myself drawn toward another figure—a shadowy silhouette that materializes from thin air. Unaware of the impending end, this woman carries an air of quiet acceptance.

I watch as the shadowy figure navigates the red desert, her steps deliberate. The impending departure of us hangs in the air like an unspoken truth, and I feel a profound empathy for the woman who is about to face the inevitable with me.

The shadowy figure's features become more precise with each step, revealing a face with silver freckles. Her eyes, pools of darkness, reflect sadness.

"I'm sorry," I whisper as Devana pauses beside me, her gaze turning toward the horizon before it moves to her unmoving body in Cyrus' arms as he screams at her to hold on.

"I thought I had more time," Devana says, her eyes not leaving Cyrus. "Do you think he's going to be okay?"

As our final moments unfold, I watch him with a mix of sorrow and reverence. "Not for a long, long time," I answer, closing my eyes. "I'm so incredibly sorry."

I don't know how often I have to say it for her to believe it. All I wanted was Khaos back. Instead, I killed another person who didn't deserve to die.

In the silence that follows next, I extend a hand toward Devana. "I want to hate you so freaking much, but I can't," she says, grabbing my hand. "I was the one who shot the arrow at your coronation," she whispers beside me, squeezing me.

Her confession should enrage me, yet I feel nothing but understanding. To the outside world, I must have looked like a madwoman. Only Myra knew my actual plans, about all the people I safely harbored beneath the prison, me trying to restore the Heiligbaum to stop my entire kingdom from falling apart, and my internal struggle with the loss of my family.

"Back then, I didn't know we were connected," she continues, her eyes moving to my body on the ground. "I trained my entire life to assassinate you, just to find out that my fate was bound to yours all this time. Quite ironic, isn't it?"

Just as I want to answer her, my attention gets sucked in by Queen Synadena, who builds herself up before the God of the Underworld.

What is she doing?

"Take me instead," Synadena says, hammering her fist against her chest. "If it's *a soul for a soul*, take mine and let them live."

No, I can't let this happen. Synadena can't give her life up for mine.

Devana's nails bite into my skin as we watch Otyx rise to his feet. "Is that what you want?"

"No, she doesn't," Opaline screeches, rushing to her mother to grab her arm. "What are you doing?"

"The right thing," she answers, cupping her daughter's face.

"You can't go," Opaline says through tears. "I need you. Crystol needs you."

"Oh, my dear child. You have everything you need," Queen Synadena says, wiping away Opaline's tears. "I've lived a long and happy life. It's time for a change."

"You can't do this to us!" Opaline screams, pushing herself away from her mother. "I won't let you."

"Please take care of your brother," the Queen says, reaching for her daughter again. I expect Opaline to pull back again. Instead, she leans into her, pressing her wet face into her chest.

"Some day, you two will understand why I had to go."

Panic grips me as I watch Synadena take a step back. She can't do this to her children and kingdom. If she sacrifices herself for me, Opaline will never forgive me. Hell, I'll never forgive myself.

The knot forming in my throat threatens to suffocate me. I rip myself away from Devana and stop right before the Queen. "Don't do this. Please. Just let me go. You can't pay for my mistakes!" I turn to Devana, the only person who can see me. "Tell her. Please tell her not to do it."

Devana just stands there, watching Cyrus now kneeling on the ground with her unmoving body. "It was always her plan," she says, slowly shaking her head. "She knew."

"Knew what?"

"She knew she would never make it out of this alive."

"What are you talking about?" I yell at her as I step in front of Otyx. His eyes lock onto mine. "You can see me," I whisper, waving my hand before his face. He follows my movement. "Tell her to stop this."

"I can't," he replies without moving his lips. "Her time started ticking weeks ago."

This is insane. I can't let this happen.

"What do you mean?" I ask, my eyes darting to Synadena.

"She's dying," he answers, looking at her. "She has been great at covering it up, but she can feel that she doesn't have much time left."

Can Gods lie? They must, because this can't be further from the truth. Synadena looks fine. She looks young...for her age.

"Take me," Synadena repeats, and I feel her breath on my neck as she stops behind me. When I turn, her eyes go straight through me.

I pull my arms back to push her away, but before I can touch her, a dark hand reaches through my chest into hers, and the most excruciating pain curses through my head, forcing me to double down. Pressing my hands against my temples, a high-pitched noise rings in my ears, drowning out Devana's screams in the distance.

Then, everything goes dark.

FORTY-SIX

DEVANA

Escaping death by a few heartbeats freaking hurts. I always thought dying would be the most painful part, but no, it's living.

"You're back!" Cyrus whispers into my ear, pressing me so hard against his chest that my ribs are about to crack. "You're alive!"

"It doesn't feel like it," I reply, trying to move, but every fiber in my body is on fire. It's a burning sensation that spreads through my entire body until it reaches my heart, where it settles in deeply.

"It hurts so bad," I whisper, tears stinging in my eyes.

I've dealt with pain before. I've conquered it every day despite the severity. But this throbbing sensation is new.

Cyrus looks up and searches the crowd before us. "Something is wrong with her!"

I hear the terror in his voice as he tries to lift me to bring me closer.

Against my better judgment, I turn my head to the side, and my eyes land on the two women motionless on the ground.

Reality slams into me.

"Synadena," I whisper, tossing myself to the side and out of his arms. With a thud, I land on all four, and it takes everything out of me to start crawling. It hurts; everything hurts. Each movement is an agonizing struggle, the grains of sand biting into my palms as I press forward.

"Let me help you," Cyrus says behind me, carefully lifting me to my feet, but he isn't cautious enough because my muscles ache and strain under his action.

As we approach, the heat radiating from the desert intensifies, amplifying the physical toll on my weary body. The air shimmers with the mirage of life, a cruel illusion contrasting the harsh reality before us.

The two women, their forms sprawled on the unforgiving ground, come into focus as we draw near. My breath is shallow, each inhalation a struggle against the oppressive heat. The sight of the lifeless figures stirs conflicting emotions within me—relief at my survival, yet an overwhelming weight of guilt that settles in the pit of my stomach.

Clenching my teeth together, I lean into him, and for a fleeting moment, I forget my discomfort when I see Opaline hunched over her mother's face. I've never seen a Tenacorian cry. To be honest, I thought I was the only one. But Opaline's tears are thick as they roll down her face onto her mother's.

Glistening with sweat and grit, I reach the side of Synadena. "Let me go," I whisper to Cyrus. The ground beneath my hands is searing as he lowers me, but the fire of my determination burns brighter. With every ounce of strength I can muster, I cradle her face in my hands, seeking any sign of life.

"This wasn't supposed to happen," I say, still searching for a heartbeat I know I'll never find. "I'm so sorry."

Opaline's eyes dart to me, and a shiver runs through me when I see the coldness in her eyes. Another rush of guilt surges through me as I realize the sacrifice she made for my survival. Queen Synadena gave her life so that Soulin and I could live.

Tears blur my vision as I survey the face of the fallen warrior, feeling the grief that emanates from the stillness surrounding her. My breath catches in my throat as I trace the contours of Synadena's face to memorize each feature.

Caught between the agony of survival and the sorrow of loss, I close my eyes, allowing the tears to trace a path down my dusty cheeks. My grip tightens on her lifeless body, my lifeline tethered to the memory of the woman who gave everything—my Queen.

I cringe when a soft hand wipes the tears off my face, and when I open my eyes, I look straight into Opaline's warm, brown eyes. "I might never understand why she did it, but I know she had her reasons. As much as it hurts, I must believe in that."

My throat burns as I try to form words. "It's a debt I'll never be able to repay," I croak, and the guilt that tries to settle deep into my heart eases a little. But that doesn't last long because, in the next moment, another wave of sorrow rushes through me, contracting every muscle in my body. The pain is so intense that I bite my lip to redirect it without success.

I don't understand. Why am I hurting so much?

My eyes wander to the other person who laid motionless beside Synadena moments ago.

Soulin moved.

She sits in the sand, her knees pressed to her face and her arms curled around her legs.

Another wave of grief sweeps through my muscles, immobilizing me.

"Soulin?" I whisper, letting go of Synadena when I regain control over my body.

She doesn't respond.

I don't need Cyrus' help this time to get closer to her. Within two labored breaths, I'm beside her, pressing my trembling hand against her back. A shockwave of guilt, grief, and heartbreak slams into me, knocking me almost unconscious.

It's not my pain I'm feeling—it's hers. Perhaps some tiny portion belongs to me, but the rest is all hers.

"Soulin," I repeat, finding strength in my voice.

From what I'm feeling through our connection, I know Soulin doesn't have the energy to face me.

"She's gone," she mumbles, her voice cracking. "She did this for me. But that means I'll never see Khaos again."

Every emotion Soulin feels rushes through me, and I must pull my hand away to decrease the amount.

"The Nullstone," Cyrus whispers behind me, and I follow his gaze to the blade almost buried in the sand beside her. "She doesn't have any magic left."

That's how she does it. Soulin conceals her emotions and pain behind a thick layer of magic. That explains why she never felt our connection before, and I was burdened with it.

"You'll see them again," I whisper, my hand lingering just inches from her back. I want to touch her. I want her to know she isn't alone. But my body is exhausted, and I don't know if I can take another punch of her emotions.

"No matter what I do, people die around me," Soulin says, grabbing her legs even tighter.

I thought nothing would beat finding out that I'm connected to the Crymzon Queen, but seeing her like this literally breaks my heart. It almost seems like years and years of emotions are finally grabbing hold of her, beating every unshed tear out of her at this very moment.

Another pair of feet appears beside me. "You were like a daughter to her," Opaline says, kneeling beside us. I'm thankful when she reaches out for Soulin, something I can't do without going through her intensified state of mind. "I really, *really* dislike you right now, but I could never hate you," she adds, her voice thick. "Scratch that. I will hate you if you let her death be in vain."

Soulin stiffens under her touch as those words leave her lips. Damn, I even straightened myself.

But Opaline is right.

Getting a second chance—and I mean a *real, almost dying and coming back alive* chance—is unheard of. Synadena gave us what no one else was willing to give.

And why should they? No one else is responsible for us once we reach adulthood.

Without another word, Soulin drags her silken glove over her face before she twists her upper body to face us. "There's nothing I can say to turn back time," she says, her eyes red and face swollen from tears. "But I promise you I'll do everything in my power to give back what your mother gave us."

Opaline's jawline ticks as she watches Soulin intently. "I know," she whispers, petting her on the back.

As I watch their exchange, my mouth dries. Opaline entered the battle as a mother-daughter duo and emerged as a Queen. As her kingdom demands, she's the next heir to Tenacoro's throne, which means she's my Queen now.

Just as I open my mouth to say something, another wave of heartbreak washes over me, and I can see in Soulin's scrunched facial expression that she's trying to keep herself under control. Her eyes lock onto mine and without a word, she knows what I'm feeling.

"My magic should return in a couple of hours. Once it's back, I'll ensure you'll never feel my pain again," she says, pressing her lips into a thin line.

I want to say that it's ok to miss him, or time will heal your wounds, but I know nothing about Soulmate Connections. Whatever Khaos and Soulin had was even stronger than what I feel for Cyrus.

Whatever I say, there's nothing to help ease her pain. Perhaps we both have to learn to live with it.

FORTY-SEVEN

QUEEN SOULIN

Nausea floods my body when Otyx pulls the dagger out of my chest before pressing his hand against the open wound to heal me. I try to assist him, but my magic is gone. Every fiber usually occupied by it seems filled with more emotions than I thought possible.

I was so close to being reunited with Khaos.

But what's worse, Synadena gave her life to save Devana and me.

As I ring with my mental burdens, I barely notice what's happening around me until Devana and Opaline talk to me. Before I turned to face them, I let my eyes wander over the dark towers of the places and the streets of the Underworld before me.

There's a chance he's right there, watching me. I just want to see him one last time because I never got to say goodbye.

Opaline's words ring in my ears as I stand on unsteady feet.

I will hate you if you let her death be in vain.

That's precisely what I did for a moment. While I was in that upright fetal position, I thought about ways of making it back to Khaos. He consumes my every thought, every breath, and every desire I have. Thinking of a life without him in it doesn't seem worth living.

Yet, I can't let my friend down. Even after rejecting Opaline for years, she picked up right where we left off.

Maybe there is more out there than just a Soulmate Connection. Perhaps that's why Lunra blessed Devana, connecting her to me. What if this was her way of telling me I'll be okay as long as I have her?

The thought seems bizarre, but with every passing heartbeat, it grows on me.

When I search the crowd for Lunra, I have to find out, to my bittersweet disappointment, that she isn't here anymore. The only reminder of her appearance is the old skin of Conrad submerging slowly under the shifting sand.

How did I not catch on to her disguise? All the signs were there. Still, I didn't know this was something Gods and Goddesses could do. What if more of them walk this planet, and we don't even know who they are?

As I breathe in the smoldering heat of the desert, something I thought I would never do again, my breath hitches when Myra walks in my direction, her hands curled into fists. "How could you?" she barks, shoving me, and grabs me by my shoulders when she realizes I'm not steady enough. Yet, the anger in her eyes is real. "Do you know what you've done?"

Oh, I know. If she refers to the part where Synadena is now dead and Khaos is still not beside us, *I know.*

"I had to try," I answer, lowering my head.

"Try what?"

"To bring *him* back," I whisper because I'm aware of how childish my reason is.

The anger in her eyes turns into the same heartbreaking sadness I'm currently experiencing.

I didn't think of Myra when I pulled the dagger out of my pocket and aimed for Avira. And I should have. After what happened to Khaos, I'm all she has left—and she's all I have left in Crymzon.

"Then let me do this for you," she replies after a long, silent moment.

My pounding heart seizes when those words circle through my head and finally catch meaning.

My mouth pops open as I stare at her, then behind me where Otyx stands beside Avira. Are they watching us for their entertainment? Haven't they seen enough?

"A soul for a soul," Myra says, stepping out of my way, but I regain control over my body and move before her.

"No, you don't have to do that. I'll be fine. We'll be fine," I say, holding her by her shoulders to stop her from moving any closer to the God.

"Please let me go, Soulin. I've fulfilled your mother's wish. I raised you and gave you all the love I had. But now it's my time to be with Elia again. She's waiting."

"But I need you," I whisper, my stomach so tight I wonder if I'll ever feel anything but this nauseating feeling of loss.

"You haven't needed me for quite some time," she responds, cupping my face. "And that's okay. That's what every mother, biological or not, wants for her child. I'm so proud of you," she says, squeezing my cheeks. "The only thing you're missing is to experience what I had. And I know you were so close, but fate always had the upper hand. Hopefully, this time, you have more people in your corner to help you."

She looks over her shoulder at the various people enclosing us. That's when I realize I don't have to hide anymore. Those people have now seen me at my worst. They have seen my vulnerable side, my struggle without magic, and how much I miss Khaos.

"Please let me do this for you."

"You can't ask that of me. I can't be the one responsible for your death, too."

"My death will never be your burden," she says, her face softening. "I'm going freely. I just need to know that you'll be alright."

What does she want to hear from me? That I'll gladly trade her for Khaos? That I'm going to be okay because I have him in return?

"I'll make sure of it," Devana says, stepping into my peripheral vision.

"Stay out of this," I bark at her, and Myra pinches my cheek, forcing me to redirect my agitation at her. "What was that for?"

"She's just trying to help," Myra answers, her brows drawn together.

Mumbling under my breath, I release one hand to rub my cheek. How can such a small pinch be so painful?

Just as I release the other hand, Myra takes that opportunity to hug me, pressing me tightly against her. "Please, let them in," she whispers into my ear before letting me go.

What does that even mean? Let who in?

Myra slowly sways me to the side, out of her way, and I want to retaliate again, but my brain tells me she's made up her mind. Yet, I should do more. I should pull her back and leave with her, but the longing to see Khaos again is stronger.

"I'm ready when you are," Myra says directed at Otyx.

I hold my breath, waiting for him to dismiss her. Instead, he closes the remaining distance between them and looks down at her.

"I can't guarantee that he'll be the person you remember. Once a soul departs their body, the mind fractures the longer it's outside its host."

She looks over her shoulder at me before facing him again. "If you trick me, I'll haunt you forever," she warns, flashing her teeth.

"I just told you the risk. I can't promise you he's going to be the person you knew," he says firmly, and my eyes dart to Avira.

Why isn't she stepping in? Just a few minutes ago, she killed me without remorse, and now she's acting like all of this isn't happening. I know something is brewing inside her because her face hardened at Otyx's words, and her knuckles are so white from digging her nails into her palms that I'm waiting to hear her fingers break.

"It's a risk I'm willing to take," Myra finally says.

I bolt forward, but Otyx's hand is faster. With practiced ease, his hand dives into her chest, touching her heart.

While I wasn't fast enough to intervene, I'm right there to catch her body before she can hit the ground. I'm surprised at how light Myra is as I let her down gently.

The same feeling of helplessness I felt when I held Khaos washes over me. But when I see the smile slowly dying on her face, I know I must let her go. This is what she wanted. After fifteen years of living without Elia, she's finally able to reunite with the love of her life.

Still, it doesn't hurt any less knowing that she's forever gone. I'll never be able to see her again.

Holding on to her tightly, Otyx's voice swirls through my mind.

I can't guarantee that he'll be the person you remember.

I'm unsure what it means, but I'm about to discover how true Otyx's statement is.

FORTY-EIGHT

Avira

I don't know which part snapped me out of the trance I've been in for far too long.

I remember flying into the Cloud Palace to kill my mother.

No, wait. It started when I offered my blood to help Otyx heal as the only mortal praying to him. After his overwhelming power coursed through my body, I drained Khaos of his memories and turned him into a weapon. I painfully remember how I treated Mordecai and how I forced my insecurities onto Otyx, accusing him of not supporting me.

The memories are so vibrant and cruel that I almost double over.

And then there's the moment I saw the horror in Soulin's eyes as I took advantage of her Soulmate and the force I used—borrowed from Otyx—to ram that dagger into her heart.

How do all of my recent actions make me better than her? Soulin acted out of hate and pure powerlessness to save her kingdom from further destruction. She didn't know then that the God was done collecting souls.

But I did.

I knew it was over, but I still harmed her in the worst possible way. I found pleasure in her suffering.

"Mortals are not designed to carry the power of Gods," I whisper to myself, remembering the words Otyx spoke repeatedly.

I thought he kept repeating it because I'm weak, but it's not my weakness he was referring to—it was my emotions.

His power is one thing, but I'm prone to succumb to the sins as a mortal. Those dark desires tangled themselves around my being, squeezing out every cruel part inside me I didn't know I had. How else can I explain what I've done?

Still, I didn't find my way back to myself until I watched the selfless acts of Queen Synadena and the other woman. It catapulted me back to when my mother offered my soul to Otyx. Her desperate attempt to get my father back clouded her rational thinking. She really thought she could have it all—save my father and get me back.

And I wish she could have.

Even though my father is long gone, bringing the Underworld to the surface could have been my chance to reunite with my mother. All of this could have been a dream coming true.

Instead, I killed her.

"It won't work," I whisper repeatedly, and I don't feel my nails biting into my palms until I draw blood.

The last bargain, the woman's soul for Khaos', won't work. I know he's too far gone because I'm the one who messed with his soul. I've corrupted him irreversibly.

He'll be in the same state—perhaps worse—my father was in when Otyx returned his soul to his body.

My eyes glide over the battlefield sprawled out before me. Hundreds of warriors and soldiers fell during the few minutes the fight lasted. These fallen souls would still be alive if I hadn't acted out of pure hate.

I'm at fault—no one else.

Wrath bubbles up inside me, but it isn't directed at anyone but me.

"Please take the memories from me," I say, tears stinging in my eyes as I look up at Otyx, who has been standing silently beside me after stopping that poor woman's heart.

He looks down at me, his lips a thin line. "If I do, there's no going back."

I know I'm taking the easy way out if Otyx agrees. Plus, erasing my memories again would mean losing the part of me that makes me, well, *me*.

I guess that's not the truth, either. Even after I lost my past when grabbing his hand for the first time, I remained almost the same person I was at the surface.

So what changed?

Was it the oppressing weight of the sins, his power rushing through my veins, or the betrayals that kept piling up?

"I'm the definition of a doomed soul. Look at what I've done," I say, pointing at the bloodshed before us. "And my mother—" my voice breaks off.

The memory of her facial expression when she realized I was going to kill her moves to the front of my brain. I didn't hesitate to take her out. She had so much to say, and I acted irrationally.

Hoping the pain will stop the memory, I grab my hair and pull on it. It doesn't.

It would be easier to point fingers again and accuse Otyx of not stopping me or Soulin from trying to overthrow him. But Otyx tried to redirect me. He offered his hand the chance to retreat multiple times, and I was too arrogant to take it. I thought it was my purpose to get revenge for him.

Soulin looks up at us, and the initial thought of cutting her down for just breathing vaporizes when I see the tears in her eyes.

"What will happen to her if you agree to her plea?" she asks, still kneeling beside the old woman.

My eyes rest on the woman she clutches to her chest, but Soulin's gaze lingers on me.

"She'll become a part of the Underworld. But this time, she won't be able to stay a mortal."

She's not talking about the woman who sacrificed herself for her Soulmate. She was referring to me!

Soulin shakes her head.

Why does she care what will happen to me? I've done horrible things. Isn't she the least concerned about finding out how much damage I've caused to her Soulmate because that should be her primary focus?

Perhaps it's me who wants to know how he's doing because I know I'm responsible for the state he's going to be in—he's probably already in right now.

"What if she stays with me in Crymzon?" she asks, lifting herself off the ground.

"What?" That's all I can get out as I search her face for any clues of a hidden agenda. "Why?"

She can't be serious.

I *literally* just killed her! Well, almost. She was still battling with her last breaths when Otyx intervened. Still, attempted murder doesn't sound any better.

"Because I know how it feels to be suffocated by guilt. I've been where you're now; perhaps I can help you find peace with it." She shakes her head. "I'm not saying I'm the best at coping with my emotions, but you can do it. I can help you."

Has she forgotten why we're here? Partially because of me—well, mostly—but she also played a role in why I came to the surface.

We're both equally monstrous, and as much as I want to believe her that things can get better if I let her take me with her, that's not what I want.

I break the silence that presses down on us. "I can't accept your offer," I answer slowly, mentally walking through my options.

I can go back to Shadowmyre, leaving everything I did behind. Or, I can...

After what I've done, no other option is available to me. At least there is no option that will keep Escela safe because I can't promise I won't succumb to the sins again.

My breath catches as I look into Otyx's dark eyes. "I would like to come home," I say, stretching my hand toward him. "If you have me."

Inhaling sharply, I close my eyes and wait for his touch. A heartbeat passes, then another.

Confused, I open my eyes to look up at him.

"I need you to look at me when I do this," he says, unfurling his wings. "I need your permission to take your soul. Are you sure you don't want the life you've been dreaming of...how did you say it: *away from the darkness and shadows?*"

Doubt pushes its way into my mind again. Is he trying to convince me to stay? Is this his way of saying he thinks I don't belong to Shadowmyre anymore because of what I've done or because he wants me to stay with Soulin?

"Look at me," Otyx says, his fingers stopping just inches from my face. "My love for you is not easily broken. Believe me, I want nothing more than to have you by my side, but it would be selfish of me to exploit you while you're most vulnerable. I'll patiently wait for you if you desire to live on the surface. I've waited almost a century and will wait hundreds more if I have to."

My knees almost buckle as I take his words in. He already wanted me before I exchanged my first word with him. I made a mark on his heart before setting foot into the Underworld.

Still, he's giving me the opportunity to experience the life that was stolen from me.

I know I could endure a mortal life weighted down by my fresh memories; I could find a way to live with the guilt and embarrassment of the horror I unleashed on Escela and find my path to redemption alongside Soulin.

But I don't want to.

My name will go down in history, no matter what. I'll be known as the Queen Slayer, Conqueress, maybe even Death's mistress, and I could make peace with it.

But the thought of trying to build a life without Otyx is too much.

Just when I think I'm in control of my emotions again, my mother's face appears before me. The horror, the betrayal, the pure love she felt for me in the split second before I commanded Emberix to unleash her fire on her burns into my memory like a glowing piece of charcoal.

If I had listened to her...if I had taken just a moment to let her explain...

"Please make it stop," I plead, my hand now trembling before him as I fight tears. "I want to go home."

I don't care if this is the cowardly way to rid myself of those memories. I need it to stop because I wasn't myself when I did all those horrific things. The sins tricked me into using them to feel invincible. And it felt amazing and freeing—until it's now time to pay the price.

Without another word, Otyx leans down, his wings forming a sheltering cocoon around us.

"I got you," he says as I feel the coldness of his touch on my hand.

It's not the same warm touch I'd felt when he caressed my skin in my room. This is the touch of a God, his powers deadly enough to drain the life out of me. I feel the warmth pouring out of every fiber of my body into his hand, and my eyes widen when I watch my color neutralize into a soft gray.

Just when I think he's done, I see my mother's face again. Squeezing my eyes shut, I fight against the image until I hear a soft, murmuring voice in the back of my head.

"I won't take all your memories," Otyx says.

The compassion in his voice pushes the figure torturing my mind to the side, and I can see glimpses of my memories as he carefully sorts through them, taking and leaving some. With every decision he makes, I feel my body getting lighter as my anxiety and pain ease.

Then, I feel Otyx retreat out of my mind, leaving it...clear.

"How are you feeling?" Otyx whispers as he holds my hand.

"I...where...what happened?" I stammer, noticing his wings pressed firmly against me, enclosing us in a cocoon.

"Everything will be just as it was," he whispers, touching my cheek.

I don't understand. What is going on?

I close my eyes and return to the last thing I remember: Otyx taking my hand. Me telling him I want to go home. His skin on mine as we make love. Me reaching out my hand to ask the God for a dance. The moment I find out Netherius isn't Netherius at all. Emberix beneath the ground, a glow surrounding her. Mordecai trying to help me out of a dark pit and single images of him by my side. Ruby bursting into my room. Endless hours of using the sewing machine. Again, Otyx reaching out his hand to grab mine.

Then, there's darkness until...

An image of my mother and father appears before my eyes, both of them laughing as they pull me into a tight hug.

When I open my eyes, I'm confused. I don't remember why I'm in the ballroom of Shadowmyre, cradled against Otyx's chest as he sits on his throne. "I got you," he whispers, and the words sound familiar and yet new.

"What's going on?" I ask, cupping his face. The worry creasing his facial expression eases when our skin connects.

"We're home," he answers, leaning down to kiss me softly.

FORTY-NINE

Khaos

I awake with a violent gasp, my chest heaving as if starved for air. My consciousness emerges from the depths of a hazy slumber, and my disorientation lingers in the space between dreams and reality.

How long have I been asleep?

As I attempt to sit up, a searing pain shoots through my head, and my hand instinctively goes to the source of the ache.

A dull thud echoes as my hand collides with something unyielding. My eyes widen in confusion as my surroundings come into focus. Cold glass meets my touch, and a shiver runs down my spine as I trace the smooth, unbroken surface. Panic flickers in my chest when I realize I'm enclosed in a glass cage.

Frantically, I struggle to sit up, but a sharp pain jolts through my head once more, my skull protesting the abrupt movement. The confined space of my prison becomes apparent as I extend my limbs, each movement restricted by the transparent enclosure.

Barely able to catch my breath, I steady my breathing, my exhalations forming a foggy film on the glassy surface. Panic grips me, an unseen force tightening its hold as I survey my surroundings. The air within feels dense, a harbinger of the looming threat of suffocation.

With trembling fingers, I explore the edges of the glass, desperately searching for any sign of an opening. My digits dance along the smooth surface, feeling the coldness beneath my touch, but no crevice or latch presents itself. Frustration and urgency etch lines on my face as I continue my futile exploration.

As the oxygen within the glass enclosure grows scarce, my gasps intensify. My attempts to find an escape route become more desperate, the film of fog on the glass now blurring my vision. The sense of confinement weighs on me, the transparent walls closing in as I grapple with the reality of my predicament.

I'm going to die.

My heart pounds in my chest, a relentless drumbeat that underscores my rising panic. A surge of wrath courses through my veins, and an unexplained fury fuels my determination to break free. Drawing strength from the depths of my desperation, I raise my fists and slam them against the glass.

The resounding thuds echo in the confined space as I unleash my frustration, each blow a declaration of my fight against the inexplicable imprisonment. My screams reverberate within the glass, a symphony of wrath and confusion that resonates in the silent void.

How did I get here?

Images flicker before my eyes—fragmented glimpses of a battle, faces blurred by the haze of memory. I strain to piece together the fractured scenes, but they slip through my grasp like sand. The intensity of the images matches the ferocity of my pounding fists, a maelstrom of emotions that swirl within the claustrophobic enclosure.

With each scream and thud, my lungs burn, starved of the life-giving oxygen that rapidly depletes. My vision blurs at the edges, a darkening tunnel closing in on the periphery of my awareness.

The pounding in my head subsides, replaced by an eerie calm that settles over me. My gasps for air become softer, the fog on the glass dissipating into nothingness.

The images of battle fade into my mind's recesses, leaving a sense of surrender behind.

What did I do to deserve this?

One image appears in the center of my mind. A woman draped in a red, flowy dress, her curls the same color as the fabric aside one silver strain. Her lips curl into a smile, sending silver freckles dancing over her cheeks as we lock eyes.

Warmth spreads through my body when I watch her step towards me. As I look at her, it's like wrath comes in the form of heat.

Biting my lip, I slam my fists against the glass one last time, and a chuckle escapes my throat when I hear a crack.

FIFTY

Queen Soulin

I dragged out the moment as long as possible because I didn't know if Khaos would walk down one of those streets searching for me in the desert before the Underworld.

The longer I wait, the more I realize his soul and body are two completely different parts of him. If his soul returned to him, he must be at home.

But I'm terrified to return to Crymzon.

"Do we really have to accompany her?" Cyrus whispers behind me as we make our way to find Storm amid the battlefield. I've tried to call out for her, but she didn't respond.

"Be quiet. She can hear us," Devana replies in a calm voice. "We'll leave as soon as I know she's okay."

My instincts are to turn on my heels and bark at them, yet I don't want to scare them away. I need them for what's to come.

I was so used to being shadowed by Myra until she found refuge beneath the prison. After that, Conrad—or rather, Lunra—took over for her. Until this day, I never had to be alone.

Also, I'm purposely not mentioning Khaos because I'm afraid to remember being close to him. What if the version of *my* Khaos doesn't exist anymore? What if his death changed him, and I realize that Myra's sacrifice was for nothing?

No, it can't be meaningless. Even if he's different, I'll find a way to make this work. I must!

As much as I want to, I can't send Devana and Cyrus away. Among all the Crymzonians marching south to head back to Crymzon, those two are the only ones who actually got to know me.

Isn't that ironic?

The man I imprisoned to lure out his father's secrets, who killed said father to save me, and the woman who wanted me dead since the moment we took our first breath together, grew on me.

"Remember when I told you I would never leave your side?" Cyrus asks, and bile rises in my throat when I hear his sickening love talk.

Here it comes. He's trying to tell her he would never leave her, and yet he's silently asking for permission to do so to see his sister.

"Go check on her," Devana answers, and I suppress a smile. Of course, she lets him go because no one wants a clingy woman.

I roll my eyes as I hear the smack of lips parting and Cyrus rushing away from us.

"You know there was nothing I could do," I say, my eyes wandering over the lifeless bodies spread over the dunes once Cyrus is out of earshot. "When I got to Eternitie, I barely had time to get Catalina out of there."

If I had my magic, I would free their souls. Even though I know Otyx will claim them, I still believe that setting them free gives them the slightest chance of being reborn. Instead of doing that part myself, I watch a select few of my soldiers go to work on their fellow Crymzonians while the other kingdoms retrieve their fallen to give them their burial accustomed to their kingdom.

"I never said it was your fault," Devana answers, treading through the sand beside me. "Thank you," she adds, and I abruptly halt.

"For what?"

"I don't know how you ended up in Eternitie when your own life was falling apart, yet you were there and rescued Catalina."

Gratitude always felt like a weakness, and the same goes for apologies, but hearing those words out of her mouth sends a fuzzy feeling through me I'm not accustomed to.

I keep my head high, dodging body parts and soldiers left and right as I give her the silent treatment.

Receiving recognition is one thing, but what do I say in return? Every word, every sentence coming to my mind sounds either extremely cocky or way over the top.

"Do you want to talk about it?" Devana asks, bending down to close the eyelids of a woman staring into the sky. She holds her hand over her face for a second as she mumbles a prayer before letting go of her.

"Stop acting like we're friends," I snarl, irritation burning inside me.

"I know you're scared," she answers, stopping. "Without your magic, you can't hide your feelings and mind behind that thick wall of yours."

"Ok, I'm sorry," I say, twisting to look at her. "Is that what you want to hear? Are we good now?"

"You know, I can do this all day," she replies, raising a brow. "I have infinite patience when it comes to dealing with your emotions because I've been living with them my entire life. And that's also why I know whatever you're feeling right now is not directed at me. So, spit it out before I dig through your mind to find it."

Is that possible? Can she read my thoughts?

"What if he changed?" I whisper just loud enough for her to hear.

Her facial expression goes from a challenging stare to a blank canvas until her eyebrows droop. "We all do," she answers, slightly shaking her head. "You're not the same person you were when all this started. But I get it. Change is scary, but it shouldn't hold you back from fighting for the things you love."

That's a very vague answer. *When all this started* could mean when we were born, when I leveled the throne room, or when we set foot into this war. Yet, I know what she's trying to say.

"I know that. But what if he doesn't remember me?" I ask, refining my question. It sounds petty because I should feel happy to see him again. Yet, I don't think I can handle it if he rejects me.

"If that's the case, we'll figure it out," Devana replies, not downplaying my worry. "He handled your salty ass for years, so I'm sure you can manage getting used to the new Khaos. We won't find out until you see him again."

I stop in my tracks as panic creeps up my spine, settling in my bones.

"What is it?" Devana asks, rushing to my side. "What's wrong?"

She's just as on edge as I am.

"That's not your emotion," she says, grabbing my arm as another wave of panic rushes through me. "I can feel it, too."

"Oh, shit!" I whisper, searching our surroundings frantically.

I don't have magic. I can't bring us back.

"I need a Crymzonian," I mutter, looking past Devana, but none of my crimson-clad soldiers are in sight.

"For what?"

"The glass cage," I reply.

The confusion clouding her face tells me she has no clue what I'm talking about. "Before I left Crymzon, I put Khaos into an airtight glass cage. I thought I could preserve him, but now that he's breathing again, he's going to run out of oxygen," I add, my breath coming out in quick puffs as I imagine the agony he must be in.

Devana's eyes widen. "You did what?" Without waiting for an answer, her gaze searches the desert, and comes to the same conclusion I came to. We're alone.

I still haven't found Storm. If I find her, she could help me to get back.

I don't want to believe she could be one of the moths that was plucked out of the sky by the dragon. To add to that, I still don't have my fucking magic back. I'm stranded.

"Do you trust me?" Devana asks, releasing my arm to grab the feather bound around her neck underneath the metal choker to hide my handprint.

"I...I don't know," I whisper back.

"Well, you don't have another chance," she answers, blowing into the quill.

I don't know what to expect from her questionable action, but a griffin falling out of the sky wasn't any of my mental options.

"Hop on," she commands, climbing her Glimmarum, and I look at her outreached hand. "Now!"

Swallowing my pride, I grab her hand and fall into place behind her, my thick thighs enclosing her muscular frame.

"Hold on tight," she says, and I search for anything to hang on to. Clenching my teeth, I wrap my arms around her waist and stare awkwardly to the side to avoid my breath brushing over her neck.

This is my confirmation that I'm a wicked person. Just a few days ago, I asked the same of Catalina, and back then, I snickered as she had to follow my instructions.

It's just a ride, nothing more. Yet, it feels good to be so close to her. Devana feels familiar, like a piece of me that has been missing and finally found its place.

She didn't kid when she said to hold on tight. The griffin leaps into the cloudless sky, its wings, a magnificent fusion of eagle and lion, easily cut through the air. Beneath us, the red desert stretches endlessly. Its vastness is only interrupted by a few small, empty villages and the towering red wall surrounding Crymzon.

Just as we make it over the Crymzon Wall to the courtyard, the griffin navigates with a deft twist through a set of open doors, revealing the grand entrance hall.

I leap off the griffin's back, my gaze fixed on the throne room. Devana dismounts as well, but I don't wait for her. Without a word, I sprint through the entrance hall, my flowing hair trailing behind me like a crimson comet.

I abruptly stop when I reach the double doors, and the air grows tense as my eyes land on the dais at the room's center.

Oh, shit!

The glass coffin is shattered into a thousand glimmering pieces. My heart skips a beat as dread and anticipation grip me.

Khaos was supposed to rest within that glass cage—but it's empty. My breath catches in my throat as I move closer, each step echoing through the silent hall.

Devana, trailing behind, confronts me with a question that's hanging heavy in the air. "Where is he?"

I don't know.

"Stay here," I order, my voice commanding obedience. With determination etched across my face, I retrace my steps through the entrance hall, ascending towards the palace's inner sanctums.

FIFTY-ONE

QUEEN SOULIN

I don't know where he could be. It didn't take us long to get here, but even those few minutes could have been enough for him to escape.

Up the ornate corridors, I ascend, passing chambers and tapestries I have paid no mind to in years. It's different this time. Memories intertwine with the stones of the palace, and I find myself drawn to the room that pains me the most—the room where Khaos asked me to stay with him so he could wake up beside me; the room where we shared our first night; the room we used to sneak into as children.

The door creaks open, revealing a space filled with the echoes of passion and loss.

As I close the door, enveloped by the room's intimate ambiance, a figure emerges from the shadows, and my heart seizes.

Khaos steps forward with an enigmatic smile. The air in the room crackles as my eyes wander over the new clothes he must have put on without the massive black stain on his chest and the brutally handsome face I've missed so damn much.

"I knew you would come," he whispers, his voice a melodic cadence that resonates with my deepest emotions. I move towards him, my eyes never leaving his. "Why can't I remember anything?"

My stomach drops.

Nothing? Is every memory we ever share lost?

"I thought I lost you," I admit, my voice a tender murmur. "I really fucked up this time."

His smile falters, and for a moment, I thought I could see the malicious smile he gave me on the battlefield, the one that shattered my heart.

"The last thing I remember is you screaming my name, followed by darkness pulling me down. Then there was this woman." My body stiffens. "There was something wrong with her. It was like...like she was made of nightmares and darkness. When she touched me—" My nails bite into my palms. "All I could feel was misery. I tried to fight her, to get her out of my head, and the next thing I remember is waking up in that glass confinement."

There's no easy way to say it, so I just go for it. "You died."

I watch as multiple emotions cross his face. It's something between disbelief, horror, surprise, and sadness.

It's my time to come clean and see how strong our Connection is—if it's still there. "I used Blood Magic to summon the God of the Underworld," I begin, wetting my dry lips for the following words. "And when I stabbed him with a Nullstone, you came rushing into the room. I don't know how, but whatever I did to Otyx killed you."

I swallow hard and wait. As much as I want to plead my case, I can't turn back time to make him understand I wouldn't have done it if I knew it would harm him. It was my fault and mine alone.

He shakes his head and looks at his hands as if seeing them for the first time. "So what am I now? A ghost?"

Under different circumstances, I would laugh, but nothing is amusing right now.

"Myra traded her soul for yours," I add, knowing that this could be the last words I ever say to him because he won't be able to forgive me after everything I just told him.

Khaos' face goes blank. "What do you mean?"

I take in a deep breath. "She offered her soul to Otyx in return for yours. That's why you can't remember anything. Your soul departed to the Underworld. And that's how you ended up surrounded by glass because I couldn't let you go."

I step towards him, and he backs away, his eyes on mine. "What else?"

My heart hammers so loudly that I could barely hear him. "Queen Synadena did the same for Devana and me."

His tense muscles relax, and his face softens as he looks at me. I can feel him leaning in my direction, ready to embrace and comfort me, so I lift my hand. "Which was also my fault," I add, hindering him from doing something he could regret later. He needs the truth—all of it. "That woman who touched you, I tried to kill her to offer her soul in return for yours. Instead of succeeding, she rammed a dagger into me."

Coming clean is the scariest thing I've ever done. It's terrifying because I know there is nothing I can do to make any of my actions sound any less cruel.

"Myra is dead?" he repeats, tears welling in his eyes.

I nod, my throat too closed up to answer.

"Did she feel pain?"

The burning sensation in my throat spreads into my chest. "When I caught her, she was smiling," I croak out, remembering the slight curl of her lips. "She was excited to see Elia again."

Fuck. How is everything I'm saying pointing back at me for killing someone?

Khaos wipes his face, taking the time he needs to digest everything I just told him. The thought of him never forgiving me crosses my mind again...and stays. As much as it hurts to look at him, knowing he'll never trust me again, I can't look away.

That's when I feel a twinge of responsibility growing inside me. I must return to the throne room to tell Devana that Khaos is here. She's probably already worried and searching for me.

Taking that excuse, I lower my gaze and take a step backward. "You can have this room," I say, taking another step.

"Where are you going?"

My standard answer, *there's something I need to do,* doesn't come out. Instead, I opt to tell him. "I left Devana behind in the throne room. She must be worried by now."

His eyes squeeze into slits. "Devana?"

Oh, please don't tell me I have to explain to him who she is.

He shakes his head. "She can wait," he whispers, and my eyes fly up to him as he closes the distance between us to embrace me.

For a moment, time stands still.

"I don't understand," I whisper after a few deep inhales, pressing my face into his chest to take in his familiar scent. "You're not supposed to forgive me."

He kisses the top of my head. "If I know something, Soulin SinClaret, it's that everything you do is to protect your people. You've saved thousands of lives by building the tunnels under the prison. You tried to eliminate a God to get your kingdom and its people out of his grasp. And you tried to give your life in return for mine." He squeezes me harder. "You're not cruel or unlovable; fate just doesn't enjoy seeing you prevail."

FIFTY-TWO

QUEEN SOULIN

When I look up, his lips press against mine before I can say another word.

He feels so good. The fear I had just moments ago vaporizes as he pushes his tongue into my mouth, and I can taste his longing for me.

"I've missed you," I whisper as we break apart, studying his eyes. He still gives me the same tender expression I'm so used to.

How does he do it?

"I'm here to stay," he whispers back, trailing his hand down my back until he reaches my ass. "And there's something I'm dying to recreate. But this time, it will feel so much better."

Holding me tight, he pushes me backward until my back hits the wall, and I know exactly what he means as my mind throws me back into the water chamber.

Pinning me with his hips, he slides his fingers over the buttons of my shirt, opening them one by one.

"That's new," he says, trying to tug on the fabric to free my breast, but it won't budge. He takes a step back to look at me. "Since when do you wear pants?"

"I don't think you're in the position to judge," I laugh, slowly peeling myself out of the sleeves. His eyes linger on my breasts as I pull the fabric down and over my ass. "I've never seen you trying to fight in a dress. Do you know how impractical they are?"

He throws his head back, laughing. "I wasn't judging," he grins, his eyes darkening. "But I love a challenge," he adds, stopping before me.

The warmth of his touch on my bare skin feels incredible.

"Now, where were we?" he growls into my ear, pressing his erection against me.

Without self-control, I rip his shirt open, and my eyes land on his chest, searching for the scar I know I'll find. My gaze wanders over his muscles to his heart, and I let out a quiet gasp.

"Where did it go?" I whisper, tracing the invisible mark on his chest I can still see before my eyes, but not on him.

"I don't know," he answers, shrugging his shoulders. "Do you miss it?"

"No," I reply, thinking of the hole in his chest when I found him in Terminus. That was the moment I realized I needed him more than air. Seeing him on the ground broke something inside me.

He cocks his head. "So, what's stopping you?"

I don't know. Maybe because I still can't believe he's real and right before me, or perhaps this could be a sign from Otyx that he's finally done with me by releasing him.

"Nothing," I growl, digging my fingers into his belt to pull him closer. "Can I make a request?"

He groans. "It depends."

"I want you to look at me when you get yours," I say with a wicked smile. "I want to look into your face as you come inside me."

His cock switches in response to my words.

"What will you do if I don't?" he growls as I open his buckle and let his pants drop.

"Then we have to do it again and again until you can finally obey my commands."

FIFTY-THREE

Devana

U gh.

I wish I hadn't gone searching for Soulin. Luckily, I located her, and by the sounds, she found Khaos, and everything was more than acceptable between them. I also took that cue to know it was my time to leave. They made up, so I know she'll be fine.

"Bring me to my father," I say to Erinna as I reach her in the entrance hall. Even she thought we would be here for a while because she found a comfortable spot behind a pillar to lie down. Or perhaps she smelled my scent because if my memory serves me correctly, it's the same spot I woke up on after the Crymzon Soldiers raided our village and brought us here.

I can still feel the terror I felt back then, but this time, I also feel gratitude. While Soulin's magic was gone, I could see glimpses and pieces of her memories. A lot of them make little sense, but one thought stuck out. She didn't send her soldiers to kill or torture us; she sent them to capture us before the army of Undead King Keres sent could slaughter us to make us like them.

Soulin saved us—in her horrible, twisted way.

I'm still combing through the bits and pieces of her memories to understand her better as Erinna takes us where I told her to.

The wind whistles past me as Erinna propels us forward with powerful strokes of her wings, closer to Tenacoro.

As we glide through the clouds, a distant sound reaches my ears—a rhythmic beating of wings. Instinctively, I tighten my grip on Erinna's feathers and search for a place to hide, but the blue sky above and the desert below offer no refuge.

Could it be the dragon?

I try to recall the moment the Underworld submerged again after the God grabbed Avira's hand. He lifted her into the sky and carried her away, followed by the creature beneath the Underworld pulling the kingdom down into the abyss. The dragon followed just in time before the monstrous hole in the ground closed back up, leaving stained black rock behind until the sand slowly covered it up.

My eyes scan the sky, and soon, moths emerge on the distant horizon, carrying an entourage of soldiers. A moment of tension grips me as I wonder if they are allies or adversaries. The war has ended, alliances could have shifted, and the once united forces now dispersed into uncertainty.

My heart pounds with worry as the colossal moths approach. I have no more fight in me—not today.

To my relief, the airborne soldiers pay no heed to my griffin or me. They continue their trajectory without acknowledgment, their wings casting fleeting shadows over the sand below. As the last of them disappear into the distance, I exhale.

Sensing the tension, Erinna lets out a low, reassuring rumble as she picks up speed. With ease, we descend toward the emerald expanse unfolding beneath us, a mosaic of vibrant flora, winding rivers, and crystal blue lagoons.

I'm not surprised to see most of the lagoons in use. Even though I've never set foot in one, I know of its healing powers.

We glide over the dense jungle canopy until an ancient rock ruin appears on the outskirts of the kingdom. The crumbling stones stand sentinel, overlooking the ocean beyond. With an intuitive sense of finding my father, Erinna begins to steer towards the ancient structure.

A moment of indecision grips me. The memories tied to those ruins are laden with misery—whoever enters that building never returns.

I hesitate, my fingers tracing the feathers of Erinna's neck. "What are you doing?" I ask, clearing my throat as nervousness creeps up my stomach when I see the place my mother had chosen for me after she found me too weak.

Yet, before I can fully process my emotions, instinct takes over. I gently guide Erinna away from the ruins, steering us back toward the kingdom's heart.

Did I tell Erinna to find my mother instead of my father? Have I misspoken?

As we approach the palace, its towering spires and the river below come into view. I can't deny the knot forming in my stomach. The palace also holds joyous and painful memories—memories of a mother who ruled with an iron will and a father who sought to find a normal path for their daughter.

I direct Erinna to a landing pad near the palace gates with measured precision. My griffin touches down, and the bustling sounds of the kingdom reach my ears as I dismount, feeling the weight of my armor as I take in the familiar surroundings.

I hesitate at the palace entrance, a moment of internal conflict warring within me. Erinna stands beside me, her presence a silent support. I wrestle with the desire to climb back onto Erinna and reunite with my father, and the fear of confronting the unresolved issues that linger between my mother and me.

In a decisive move, I choose to delay that confrontation. With a final glance back at the ancient ruins on the outskirts, I lead Erinna through the palace doors, weaving through the bustling entrance hall. The air is thick with the fragrance of exotic blooms and the murmur of courtiers going about their duties.

I navigate the corridors, my thoughts a whirlwind of emotions. I'm not ready to face my mother, to delve into the complexities of our relationship that have been strained by duty and destiny. Yet, she's all I can think about.

As I ascend the grand staircase, a servant approaches, bowing respectfully. "The queen awaits you in the throne room," he announces, and I nod hesitantly.

How did she know I was coming? I made the choice just minutes ago to avoid my mother.

A sense of urgency pushes me forward as I follow the servant, each step echoing in the cavernous hallways. The throne room looms ahead, its colossal doors imposing and ornate. As they are pushed open for me, I'm met with a sight that stirs conflicting emotions. Opaline, the new Queen, sits regally on the throne, her gaze steady.

"I didn't expect to see you so soon," Opaline says, dropping her stony mask as the doors close behind me. Her face softens, and her mouth slightly curls. "Are you here to stay?"

"I'm here because I can't find my father," I reply, immediately regretting my words. That shouldn't have been the first thing I said to the woman whose mother sacrificed herself for me.

Opaline must have sensed my unease because she stands up from the beautiful throne, naturally grown of vines, and walks in my direction.

"What's the greatest achievement for a warrior?" she asks, catching me off guard.

"Dying in battle?" I ask, my brain not processing her sudden subject change fast enough.

She tilts her head from side to side. "Fighting for what they believe in," she finally says, halting before me. "And that's what my mother did—always. I knew the day would come when she left us—sooner than later. After my father passed away, her health declined. But she left something behind," she says, circling me. "You gave her death a purpose. With your life, she extended hers. Plus, she united our land with a single handshake. And that's what I'm going to hold on to."

Tears spring into my eyes again, and I don't care if I'm a Tenacorian. I've held in my emotions for far too long, and if this isn't the right time to let them flow, I don't know when it is.

Opaline comes back around and hugs me. "It's okay," she whispers, rubbing my shoulder. "We'll be okay."

How can she be so sure?

"Have you told him?" I whisper, thinking of her brother as guilt creeps into my stomach.

"I didn't have to because he was there," she replies, letting me go. "Yeah, I didn't notice it either. He did well hiding amidst the airborne Glimmarums. He's lucky he didn't get hurt, because otherwise, I would have grounded him until he's at least three hundred," she adds, whirling around to head back to her throne. "It will take him some time to understand everything he has seen, but he'll come around."

Opaline lets herself down on the vines, looking out the open windows into the jungle.

"About your father. The last time he was spotted, he was going towards the Silent Sisters," she says, her voice trailing off.

"Why would he go there?"

"I think you know the answer," Opaline replies without looking at me.

FIFTY-FOUR

Otyx

I forgot how amazing she feels. Her skin beneath my touch is soft and better than any sin.

"Are you ready?" I whisper into her ear, marveling at Avira through the mirror before us.

"Are you not concerned about what the souls think of you when they see me at your side as you announce the contestants?"

Otyx shrugs. "Why should I? This is my kingdom. I get to do whatever I want."

Technically, it's incorrect, considering Nekrojudex still demands a winner to pick a House of Sin, but I'm about to change that.

"I wish I were as cocky as you are sometimes," she smirks, flattening the beautiful black fabric that brings out her almost white complexion.

I have to say, I miss seeing her in colorful garments, her golden hair, and red lips. But since she traded her mortal life for an eternity with me, I can't complain. For once, someone chose me.

I grin back at her. "I know that side of you exists. Just give it time, my Fallen Angel. You'll get it back."

She raises an eyebrow. "Is that what I need to do to bring you to your knees?" she whispers, coming closer. Her chest presses against my stomach as she looks up at me, her eyes gleaming with mischief. "Do you want me to do bad things? Does that turn you on?"

"Only if you do them to me," I smirk back, and my breath hitches when I feel her fingers gliding under my skirt and between my legs. The pressure she applies is enough to make my knees wobble for a second as she moves my cock in her fist. "I'll be damned. You're already hungry for more?"

The sparkle in her eyes tells me I'm right.

"Just the tip," she pants through ragged breaths. "The souls can wait."

They may, but Nekrojudex clearly won't because I feel it tugging on me.

As long as Nekrojudex has been around, I always thought there wasn't a loophole to get out of it until Avira found one. I never considered what would happen if a mortal took part in the trials. After all, this is the realm of doomed souls, not the living. Therefore, Nekrojudex registered her as a mortal, and when she died, it demanded a new winner.

I'm glad it couldn't detect that Avira is still with me. It would have taken her from me if she had to pick a House. I guess I could have still visited her daily, but I like her by my side, or rather, the grip she has around my cock.

Straining against the pull Nekrojudex has on me, I swing her around and press her against the mirror. "And what if I want my cock all the way up inside your pussy? So deep that you can't think of anything but me?"

Ripping her new skirt off her body, I'm not surprised she doesn't wear any undergarments beneath it. My hand finds its way between her thighs, and I can feel the wetness coating my fingers.

Pressing her naked butt against me, she brushes my skirt to the side until she can feel my dick at her entrance. "Don't make me wait," she purrs, arching her back.

Fuck! How am I supposed to say *no* to her?

FIFTY-FIVE

DEVANA

I pace through my childhood hut, my brain hurting from overthinking. I knew this moment would eventually come, and I had over twenty years to break my head about it. Now that the confrontation with my mother is here, I don't feel as confident with all the rehearsed sentences I wanted to throw at her as I thought I would.

A grunting noise outside the hut makes me stop in my tracks. Is that a man?

After the day's events, I should have been more careful and kept the sword close I tossed somewhere in the corner. Yet, I don't feel threatened. Tenacoro is a safe place—safer than the Confines or any other kingdom.

When I hear the mumbling voice outside the door, I can't help but giggle. "Why a tree?" the voice stammers. "Who thought putting a hut into a tree would be a great idea?"

Cyrus appears before me, his hair a sweaty mess, his clothes dirty, and his face smeared with something that looks like oil and rust.

"Hey there," I say, smirking at him.

He immediately straightens when he sees me. "I'll get used to it," he replies, breathless. "But a tree? Really?"

"You have wings. Use them," I answer, still laughing.

Cyrus shakes his head. "But what if they are taken from me? I can't rely on them. If I want to be with you, I have to adapt."

Adapt? Now that's new.

"I'm not going to stay here," I reply, scanning the hut. "I just didn't know where else to go."

"I feel the same way," Cyrus says, leaning against the wall to catch his breath. "Restoring Eternitie is going to take a while. Nevertheless, it doesn't feel like home anymore. Catalina says I'm welcome to stay, but I can't."

"Because of what happened to your father and brother?"

"Because of you," he answers, looking deep into my eyes. "I'm going to help Catalina rebuild, and then I'll go wherever you are."

I shake my head. "I can't expect that of you."

He steps forward, taking my hands in his. "Home is where you are."

"But your sister—"

"Doesn't need me. Plus, we can always visit her. So, where do you want to go?"

"I'm still trying to find my father," I say, knowing his next question before he can say it. "He's with the Silent Sisters."

Cyrus' face is an open book. "Your mother?"

Slowly, I nod, feeling my hands getting clammy. "I can't face her alone," I add, squeezing his hands. "I-I don't know what I'll do when I see her. She—"

Cyrus pulls me into his arms to cut me off. "Then let's go," he declares, letting go of me.

"There's just one more thing I must do." I walk to my jacket, which is hung over the wooden chair in the corner that used to carry my father's armor. Reaching into the pocket, I pull out the Chrono-Locator. "This was given to me, and until today, I didn't know what it was for. Back then, I thought he gave it to me to give me hope. Now I know it was never meant for me."

I release the cold metal into his palm.

"What's that?"

I press the button to project the map. "It looks like a blueprint of Eternitie. Perhaps it can help you during the reconstruction."

Cyrus' eyes wander over the unscathed kingdom until his eyes fall onto the Brass Palace. "Who gave this to you?"

"Uh…" I put my finger on the training ground and retraced the steps I took to the street, where I found the towering buildings and the small workshop with the tall man. "It was right…"

I lean in closer to show him the small building filled with gadgets, but it's not there. "I swear it was right here," I add, pointing at an empty spot on the map.

I don't understand. Where did the shop go?

Cyrus presses the button again, and the hologram vanishes. "Maybe the map was created before the building you're looking for was built," he says, sensing my unease.

That's possible, yet I can't shake the feeling that it was purposefully left out.

Cyrus stuffs the device into his pocket before grinning at me. "Thank you so much. This will help tremendously," he says, grabbing my jacket to push me out the door. "Let's go before you change your mind again."

FIFTY-SIX

DEVANA

N o. No. No.

I don't want to step into those ruins. The silence surrounding the place haunts me, and I'm not even inside yet.

Instead of using Erinna, we walked to the edge of the jungle, where the dense foliage meets the rocky shore. I gaze at the weathered remnants of a forgotten building, a palpable silence enveloping the air. The usual symphony of nature, the rustle of leaves, and the distant waves crashing against the shore are all silenced, as if nature holds its breath with me.

My footsteps are muffled against the moss-covered ground, exposing none of the usual sounds associated with exploration. I hesitate before the entrance, crossing my arms over my upset stomach. Beside me, Cyrus offers a reassuring squeeze on my arm, a silent gesture of support that anchors my resolve.

I need to do this. Now or never!

As we step into the shadowy interior of the ruins, the silence persists. Shafts of pale light filter through holes in the ceiling, illuminating a labyrinth of ancient chambers and corridors. The air within is heavy with the weight of unspoken words, sending a shiver down my spine.

This place feels as oppressive as I imagined it in my countless dreams. How could my mother have wanted this for me?

Determined, I press forward, the rhythmic thuds of our muted footsteps guiding me through the corridors. As we delve deeper, a distant sound pierces the quiet—a high-pitched child's scream filled with urgency. It shatters the silence, reverberating through the stone chambers like a clap of thunder. My breath catches in my throat and my senses heighten by the unexpected disturbance.

Ignoring the instinct to flee, I bolt toward the piercing scream. Cyrus, keeping pace, casts a concerned glance my way but says nothing. Our muted footsteps quicken, leading us through a maze of ancient stones and forgotten corridors.

Finally, I burst into a dimly lit room, and the source of the child's distress makes me stop in my tracks. A woman, her back turned to me, lingers over a body whose tiny feet kick beneath her.

"Get off her!" I scream, unsheathed the sword attached to my hips.

The woman, her silhouette familiar yet distorted in the low light, looks up from the child she was tormenting. Her eyes turn to me, and a moment of recognition flickers in the depths of her gaze.

"Stop!" I yell again, my initial panic replaced by confusion and anger.

The woman, rising from her stance over the child, squares her shoulders, and I can feel Cyrus' gaze bouncing back and forth between us.

"Devana?" the woman asks, her voice a measured tone that holds both authority and a trace of maternal concern as she searches my face.

I nod in acknowledgment but remain silent. The air between us crackles with unspoken words, a tension born from years of unaddressed grievances.

I, however, am not ready to yield to her. I meet my mother's gaze, a silent defiance lingering in my eyes. "Step away from her," I command, my voice carrying a firmness that hints at the anger boiling inside me.

The child beneath her looks up with innocent curiosity, still caught in fits of little screams as my mother raises her hands. "It's not what you think it is," she says, slowly stepping away from the little girl on the ground.

It takes me far too long to realize what's going on. The child's scream was not a cry of fear but a joyous laughter emanating from the sheer delight of being tickled.

As I take in the sight before me, my breaths come in ragged gasps. My mother, her features softened by time and maternal affection, wears a smile that mirrors the child's infectious joy.

"I heard a scream, I thought..." I begin, my voice trailing off as my eyes search my mother's face for an explanation.

My mother, understanding the gravity of the misunderstanding, steps forward, a mix of amusement and tenderness in her expression.

"It was only laughter," she reassures, her voice a soothing melody in the stillness of the ruins. Sensing the shift in attention, the child gazes up at us with wide-eyed innocence.

As the initial shock subsides, I slowly lower the sword. Cyrus, standing at a respectful distance, observes our reunion quietly.

"It's been too long," my mother whispers, her earth-colored eyes conveying a depth of emotion that words can only partially capture. Still trying to process the unexpected encounter, I nod in silent agreement.

She reaches out for me even though she's ten feet away. "Your father told me how grown and beautiful you are," she says, her voice hitching.

"I can see where she gets it from," Cyrus chimes in, and the gaze I throw at him makes him stumble back. "I'm sorry. Not my turn," he adds, stepping back into the shadows.

"Where is my father?" I ask, returning my eyes to hers. "What have you done to him?"

I can't help but notice our similarities. She's tall, lean but muscular, and her hair looks exactly like mine. The only difference is the soft wrinkles around her mouth and eyes and missing freckles.

"Is that why you're here?" she replies, and I can practically hear her heartbreak.

"Where is he?" I repeat, my nostrils flaring as I try to keep my temper under control.

"I don't think you'd believe me if I told you the truth," she answers, tilting her head.

"Try me."

"I sent him to the lagoon again because he wasn't feeling well."

On any other day, I wouldn't have believed her. Yet, I remember what he looked like when Soulin released him. My father looked on the verge of death after being trapped without water and food for several days.

"I can bring you to him," she says, holding a hand out to the child to help it to its feet.

When their hands touch, I can't take it any longer. That little hand was supposed to be mine. Instead, she's assisting a stranger like it's hers.

"Devana?" Cyrus yells after me as I bolt through the corridors, trying to recall our path.

After running for minutes like my life depended on it, I can see the light at the end of the tunnel. The air burns in my lungs as I sprint the last stretch, and I'm just a few feet away from freedom when I collide with a boulder of a man.

"Whoa, whoa, whoa. Slow down," a deep male voice says, grabbing me by the shoulders to stop me from tipping over. "Devana?"

Why is everyone so surprised to see me?

"What happened?" my father asks, enclosing me. "Did someone hurt you?" He holds me away from himself to scan my body. Then his eyes follow the way I came from. "You saw her, didn't you?"

My throat and chest are so closed up that I feel like I'll choke on my own words if I try to respond.

"Hear me out," my father says, pulling me back against his chest. "I was wrong."

Excuse me?

"I made a huge mistake."

"What mistake?" I ask, trying to wiggle myself out of his grip. Behind me, I can hear Cyrus coming to a screeching halt.

"I was wrong to take you away from here," he finally says, applying more pressure on my body. "All your mother wanted was the best for you. Just like I did. I thought the Silent Sisters were terrible—"

"They are! I know what they do to those children!"

"And what is that?"

"They strip them of their identity and treat them like shit."

"Do you really think Queen Synadena would allow that?"

I swallow.

He doesn't know yet. He doesn't know that the Queen gave her life for mine because he wasn't there when we marched against the Underworld.

"But that's what you told me," I whisper.

"And I was wrong," he repeats. "I didn't know the Silent Sisters raised your mother. Their job is to raise and support the most powerful individuals in Tenacoro, not the weak. Liora always had your best interest in mind. She wanted to ensure you have everything you need to understand your special connection and its meaning."

"Stop lying," I say, my voice thick with tears.

"He's telling the truth," Liora says behind me. "After you left, I tried to follow you, but after years of searching, I returned to my roots. I thought if you ever come looking for me, you would start here."

"Please let me go," I whisper. Reluctantly, my father does as I say. Taking a few deep breaths, I slowly turn, my gaze landing on my mother. "That child." I point at the ruins. "What were you doing with her?"

"We were playing," she responds, lowering her gaze. "She arrived just a few days ago and was missing her parents. So I told her I would send for them. Instead, she asked me if I would like to play the game she used to play with her mother when she was sad."

"Tickling," I say, finishing her thought.

She nods, still not looking up. "Yes."

My father walks around me to stand beside my mother, and without further words, I know. Forgiving her was an option I never thought I would have, but now, there's nothing to forgive. She isn't the monster I made her out to be. If I'm being honest, I'm proud. I would have sought her out years ago if I had known what the Silent Sisters really do.

For a moment, I considered redirecting that hurt toward my father, but to what good? We all have suffered enough. Because of my father's misinformation, and my mother not explaining her decision correctly, we spent almost thirty years apart.

I can't take it any longer.

"Do you...like walks?" I ask carefully, searching for my mother's eyes.

When she raises her head, I watch a tear roll over her cheek. "I do," she replies, holding back more tears.

"What do you think about kids?" I ask Cyrus after my walk.

"They are cute," Cyrus replies carefully, his eyebrows drawn together.

My eyes wander to the children playing before us in a room as big as Soulin's throne room. I tilt my head from one side to another. "What do you think about living here?"

"As Silent Sisters? I don't think I'll pass their qualifications," he laughs, shrugging his shoulders.

I join his laughter until I find the courage to keep going. "I want to support these children. Just look at them. Don't they make you happy? Can't you see us helping to raise them?"

After a long talk with my mother, I know I've spent my entire life running away from everything good for me and toward danger and misery. And that's precisely why I want to stay. It will take us some time to get used to each other, and time won't be able to fill the years we have lost, but we can start fresh, making new memories.

The silence between us is unbearable.

"How many children are we talking about?"

I clear my throat. "We can start with about a dozen," I say, grinning at him. "I mean, if my mother and the other Sisters allow it."

A hard swallow follows Cyrus' cough. He looks at me, then at the building blending into the dense greenery we're in.

"Why not? Let's do it," he replies, grabbing my hand to pull me closer, and I can't help but lean into him.

FIFTY-SEVEN

Queen Soulin

"What happened to our secret ceremony?" Khaos asks, carefully pulling a new suit out of our closet.

"After rebuilding Eternitie and lending Tenacoro my army, moths, and Nullstone for the battle, I thought it was just fair to get some presents in return."

Rebuilding is so much harder than destroying. There, I said it, and I mean it.

Catalina, the woman she is, didn't ask for my help to restore her kingdom, but rubbing my magic into her face and seeing her city up and running again in less than a day was worth it. I guess it could be seen as a little thank you for all the horrible things I've done to her family. No, scratch that; I still think her father was an ass and deserved to die.

"That's it? You just want payment for your generosity of a war you brought to Escela?"

Damn, that still stings when he words it like that.

"I enjoy showing you off, okay?" I reply, looking out the window.

Khaos whips around. "What did you say?"

"I said I thought it would be nice to start a new leaf with the other kingdoms," I lie, scrunching my face.

"Oh no, I heard you the first time," he replies, and my eyes flutter over to him as I see clothes flying to the ground in the corner of my eye. "So, what's your favorite part about me? I have to make sure I present myself correctly."

"Put your clothes on," I laugh, closing the last button on my dress. "We're already late."

"It won't take long," he growls, stepping over his clothes to get to me.

I smirk back at him. "Then make it count," I say, grabbing a moth clip off my dresser and walking out of the room. I force the door shut behind me before he can follow. Giggling, I stand there, leaning against the wall as I count.

"184," I count just as the door finally creaks open, and there he is, stepping through with a quiet confidence that catches my breath.

Dressed in a rich crimson suit, his black hair cascades in untamed curls into his face, Khaos steps before me. Half of the scar on his left cheek is covered by the beard he has been growing. His eyes wander over me like I'm the juiciest piece of meat he has ever seen.

I follow his gaze to my own attire, a breathtaking red silken dress adorned with crystals and moths. It matches the hue of his suit with an uncanny harmony, as if the threads of fate had woven our garments in tandem.

"I'm sorry Storm hasn't returned yet," he says, and my heart leaps.

He knows as well as I do that she won't. I've waited days and even returned to the desert looking for her—without finding a trace. If she were still alive, she would have come home. Or perhaps, the salty moth she is, she decided it was her to roam free. I hope it's the latter, and I'll see her again someday, but I won't know until then.

Khaos shifts his weight. "But Adira will be there with Stormy and her other offspring," he says, and those words ease the pain in my chest.

"Stormy will be the death of me," I reply, recalling the last time I tried to break one of Adira's babies in. "She has a good chance of living up to Storm's name and attitude."

Chuckling, I hook my arm into his, and we start walking.

Together, we climb the long, broad steps lined with a throng of people. The air is thick with anticipation, the hum of whispered conversations filling the space as we ascend towards the grand cathedral that stands as a beacon of our Goddess against the skyline.

At the entrance, soldiers flank the towering doors, and with a synchronized push, the doors swing open, revealing a room filled to the rim with people. The collective hush that falls over the crowd heightens the atmosphere of expectancy. I look over the sea of faces and stop after seeing all the other rulers, plus Devana and Cyrus, present.

"They all came," Khaos whispers, hooking my arm into his.

They indeed did.

As we approach the center of the room, the Heiligbaum, casting a surreal glow that dances upon the faces of the assembled crowd, stands surrounded by water at the far end. The flames flicker with a breathtaking brilliance, and the water encircling the tree seems to stand still.

The crowd before us parts, creating a path leading to the cathedral's heart. We follow the illuminated trail hand in hand, our footsteps echoing in the grand chamber. Whispers of awe and curiosity accompany our walk, yet I remain focused on the Heiligbaum.

Flashes of my past rush through my mind. An image of little Khaos materializes as I saw him for the first time readying my horse. The smile he gave me was warm and so childish, and still the same smile currently marking his face.

I try to remember if I had realized back then that he'd be the one burying himself deeply into my heart. When I met him, I wasn't looking for love, just adventure.

I gaze at him.

He gave me both—love and adventure.

Reaching the water's edge surrounding the burning tree, I hesitate momentarily. My gown shimmers with crystals that catch the tree's fiery glow, mirroring the flames' luminescence. Khaos' crimson suit seems to resonate with the intensity of the burning branches, creating an illusion of intertwining destinies.

Khaos leans into me. "Are you getting cold feet?"

I huff. "No. I just want to remember this moment forever," I whisper back, marveling at his face, which is much older than my head's version.

"Don't get sentimental on me now," he grins, winking at me.

With a shared breath, we step into the water, its surface cool beneath my feet. The water, now knee-deep, cradles our reflections as we press forward. Ripples diffuse from our steps, creating a visual symphony that portrays the pulsating energy within the cathedral.

When we reach the Heiligbaum's platform, a voice echoes through the vast room, resonating from an unseen source. "Welcome," it whispers in a harmonious cadence. The crowd, captivated by it, remains hushed, their collective gaze fixed upon us. I turn to face Khaos and tighten my grip on his hands.

Beside us, a figure materializes, radiating a beauty that transcends mortal comprehension. The onlookers gasp as the stunning presence takes form—Lunra, Goddess of the Moon and Love.

The Goddess extends her arms, addressing the room with a voice like a gentle breeze. "Greetings, people of Escela," she begins. As she continues, the flames seem to respond, flickering with the intensity of my beating heart. "It is time to celebrate the Soulmate Connection that binds these two souls," she declares.

Turning her attention to us, her eyes acknowledge us with warmth. "Before the divine flame, pledge your loyalty to each other and the kingdom you're destined to rule," she instructs.

She's cutting right to the chase.

Lunra guides us through words of ancient significance that hold the weight of commitment and union. As we repeat the vows, our voices reverberate through the cathedral, each syllable carrying the promise of eternal devotion. The words, a binding incantation, curl around us like soft feathers.

With the vows spoken, the Goddess gestures towards the Heiligbaum, its flames dancing with an intensified brilliance. "Touch the sacred flame together, and let your Soulmate Connection be sealed," she proclaims.

"Now, that's a dealbreaker," Khaos says, furrowing his brows.

"Shut up," I laugh, pulling his hand, still entwined with mine, towards the tree. As our fingertips brush the fiery trunk, a surge of energy passes through our hands, intertwining our souls in a mystical union.

I thought I couldn't give him more. I was wrong. As our Soulmate Connection seals, I can feel his touch on my hand and his presence inside my head. It's like we're the same person, yet two completely different individuals.

His love for me slams into my consciousness like a magical blast, and I hope he can feel the same on his end.

The room, momentarily hushed, erupts into a celebration as the crowd witnesses the culmination of a divine Soulmate Ceremony, which has never been done before in front of other kingdoms. Applause and cheers ricochet through the cathedral, the joyous symphony of approval filling the air.

"We did it," Khaos whispers, forcing a smile on his lips to cover the emotions rushing through my veins like lava.

"Your love withstood death," Lunra says, only directed at us, and my mouth goes dry. "Don't take it for granted."

Your love withstood death.

Didn't she tell me it was impossible? I know she did, but we made it. Both of us defied Otyx, and both of us are still here to tell the tale.

"Thank you for everything," I whisper, looking into Lunra's warm eyes, and that's when I see it. The eye color might not be the same, but without a doubt, those are Conrad's eyes.

I should have known; I should have sensed her presence whenever Conrad was around me, but I didn't. That doesn't change the fact that I miss him.

"I'm never far," Lunra whispers back, her lips stretching into the wide smile the old man used to give me.

The Goddess, her divine presence still palpable, bestows a nod of approval upon us before fading into the shimmering glow of the Heiligbaum.

Khaos squeezes my hands. "What did she mean by *your love withstood death*?"

I put on the biggest smile I can muster. "I'll explain it to you later, *my King*," I say, touching his cheek.

With that, Crymzon has a new King, and Khaos doesn't hesitate to address the crowd with a voice that carries both authority and gratitude. "Let the celebrations begin! We feast in the courtyard tonight, and all are welcome to join us in the revelry!" he proclaims, his words met with cheers and applause from the assembled crowd.

"But before we go," I add, pulling on his hand, "there is something I need to get off my chest."

The room falls silent.

"Today, I stand before you with a heart overflowing with gratitude for your unwavering loyalty. Your sacrifices have not gone unnoticed, and I am humbled by your strength and dedication in aiding our kingdom," I continue, directed at the soldiers sprinkled through the cathedral before my eyes move to the other Crymzonians. "To those who, beneath the prison in the tunnels, tirelessly worked to keep our citizens alive, your selfless efforts have been the foundation of our resilience. You are the unsung heroes, and I extend my deepest appreciation for your commitment to the well-being of our people."

I pause.

This is the part I've been dreading. Mentioning Myra's and Queen Synadena's names is still too painful, so I do the best I can.

"In the annals of our history, there are moments that define us," I begin, swallowing hard. "Today, I want to share news of two remarkable women who, with unparalleled bravery, sacrificed themselves to ensure the safety of our kingdoms. With their selfless act, they not only ensured the survival of Crymzon, but their courage united our land. Because of them, we're here today."

Khaos gives me a reassuring squeeze as I take a moment to let my words settle in.

"As we mourn the fallen soldiers who fought valiantly, let us also celebrate the enduring spirit of those who gave everything for the greater good. We owe a debt of gratitude to these courageous women and our fallen soldiers. Their sacrifices pave the way for a brighter future, and their legacy shall live on in the hearts of every citizen."

Another squeeze.

"In honor of their memory, a sculpture now stands tall in the desert, a testament to the indomitable spirit that unites us all. As we move forward, let us remember the lessons of unity, bravery, and sacrifice that define our kingdoms. Together, we shall continue to build a land worthy of its enduring legacy."

"May the flame of their sacrifice forever burn brightly in our hearts," Khaos adds, raising our intertwined hands into the air, and the room erupts into cheers.

The cathedral's doors swing open, revealing the streets with vibrant banners. The scent of exotic spices fills my nostrils as we pour into the kingdom to partake in the festivities.

Long tables covered with an array of delectable dishes await the hungry revelers, stretching from the cathedral to the courtyard. Musicians play lively tunes, and the courtyard becomes a kaleidoscope of laughter, music, and the clinking of goblets.

"My Queen," Khaos says, holding my hand as he leads the procession into the courtyard.

"My King," I muse back, biting my lip. "Your new name suits you."

Khaos chuckles as he strengthens his grip on me.

As the feast unfolds, dancers twirl to the rhythm of joyous melodies, and laughter ricochets beneath the starlit sky. The courtyard, illuminated by the flickering glow of torches, looks exactly as I remember during my parents' celebrations.

"Thank you again for keeping your promise," Queen Cleolia says to Devana, and I circle closer to observe their interaction.

"No, I have to thank *you*. Without your help and your creature—"

"Kraken," the Queen corrects.

"Without your Kraken, we wouldn't be standing here."

Interesting. That beast that tried to pull the Underworld into the abyss has a name. Still, I wonder what promise Devana kept.

I lean in even closer.

"Do you want to hold him?" Queen Cleolia asks as she turns to me.

"I don't want it," I say, pressing my lips together as my eyes land on the tiny baby swaddled in seaweed in her arms.

"It's just a baby," Devana chuckles as the Queen presses her new bundle of joy into my arms.

It's so fragile, so small. She can't just hand me her most precious thing, thinking I know how to support it properly.

"I'm not really confident in holding it," I mumble, trying to press it back into Cleolia's hands, but she takes a step back.

"I've heard babies are contagious," Khaos whispers into my ear, and I almost drop it.

"Take it back," I say, holding it far away from me, but the Queen takes another step away. "I said, take it back."

I try to look at her, but my gaze is glued to the big, round eyes that smile back at me.

"His name is Reef, after his grandfather," she says, marveling at him.

Why? Why do people do that? Giving their babies a name makes it so much harder not to connect with them.

"He's adorable," I whisper, staring at him for a few heartbeats before returning him. "But you shouldn't trust other people with Reef. Protect him," I say, turning to Khaos to shove him. "You happy now?"

"I don't know what you mean," he replies, playing with the white strand of my hair.

"I know you put her up to this," I snarl, scrunching my nose.

He clicks his tongue. "Can you prove it?"

"Not yet," I grin, closing the distance between us. "But I will."

The courtyard erupts into another round of cheers, a crescendo of happiness that carries through the night.

Underneath the moon, Khaos and I share a quiet moment, his eyes still reflecting the luminous glow of the Heiligbaum as his smile falters. He leans in, capturing my lips in a tender kiss that speaks of promises kept and a future yet to unfold.

"Promise me you will always wake up beside me," he whispers into my mouth.

"I promise," I whisper back, pulling him even closer.

ACKNOWLEDGEMENTS

Thank you so much, dear reader, for reading the Crymzon Chronicles and being a part of my journey.

When I wrote Monsteress, it started as a tiny voice telling me to stop trying to fit into a mold most females have to squeeze into. There was a particular moment when I had to be nice, but instead, I wanted to scream; when I had to stop talking just for people like me.

That's when I realized fitting in sucks.

Just like you—I presume—I love morally gray male characters. When I searched for similar female characters, I couldn't find much.

That was the beginning of Monsteress.

Instead of writing the usual damsel in distress, who gets saved by a knight in shining armor—or rather a high fae or shadow daddy—the idea of a morally gray female character intrigued me.

I wanted to create a woman who doesn't care what other people think of her; a woman who unapologetically reaches for her dreams while laughing into the faces of nay-sayers. Yet, I also wanted her to be vulnerable and relatable.

I hope you can see the *real* Soulin beneath the Monsteress and that you love her as much as I do.

As I wrote Devana, I thought of my oldest childhood friend. I've watched her battle an illness without ever letting her smile crumble. Her love for life and her strength amazes me every day, and because of her, I turned my life around because there's always a light at the end of the tunnel—you just have to believe in that!

In my opinion, she's the real badass of this story, and I hope she finds an ending just as beautiful as the one I have written for her.

Which brings me to Avira.

If you're like me, I have a lot of love and trust to give. Well, I did until my trust was broken and the betrayals piled up.

If you ever find yourself in a similar situation, be like Avira—and no, I don't mean unaliving people and tearing down kingdoms. Burn bridges, speak up, and find your voice because you're too amazing to be trampled by others.

The Crymzon Chronicles would have never seen daylight if it wasn't for my friends and family members who kept encouraging me to keep writing, and my Conqueress Unleashed group chat and Crymzon Baddies Discord group for supporting me.

Putting your heart and soul onto paper is intimidating and yet so freeing.

My biggest shootout goes to my husband. He's my cinnamon roll male character in real life. He loved me when I was unlovable, repaired my heart after it was stabbed too many times, and showers me with his support in everything I set my mind to. He's there on my good days and doubles down on my worst. Without him, I couldn't have written the love you felt between the characters, and I hope you enjoyed it.

If you ever feel like the world is too big and you're too small, think about Soulin, Devana, and Avira. I know you have a little of all three inside you, and I hope you use that strength to your advantage!

xoxo
C.K. Franziska

ABOUT THE AUTHOR

C.K. Franziska is the author of the finished A *Speck of Darkness* series, and her second series, The Crymzon Chronicles. She is the wife of a traveler, as well as the mother of two mini versions of herself and way too many pets. In her spare time, she is also a photographer, traveler, full-time entertainer, and animal lover. She does her best writing at night, at the beach listening to the waves, or while camping. C.K. loves to play make-believe, transporting readers to a place where the heroes have to step out of the seemingly endless cycle of family curses, where the magic is as beautiful and untamable as we think, and where every person deserves to be celebrated.